WITCHES WILD

Bewitching Bedlam Series, Book 4

YASMINE GALENORN

A Nightqueen Enterprises LLC Publication

Published by Yasmine Galenorn

PO Box 2037, Kirkland WA 98083-2037

WITCHES WILD

A Bewitching Bedlam Novel

Copyright © 2017 by Yasmine Galenorn

First Electronic Printing: 2017 Nightqueen Enterprises LLC

First Print Edition: 2017 Nightqueen Enterprises, LLC

Cover Art & Design: Ravven

Editor: Elizabeth Flynn

ALL RIGHTS RESERVED No part of this book may be reproduced or distributed in any format, be it print or electronic or audio, without permission. Please prevent piracy by purchasing only authorized versions of this book.

This is a work of fiction. Any resemblance to actual persons, living or dead, businesses, or places is entirely coincidental and not to be construed as representative or an endorsement of any living/ existing group, person, place, or business.

A Nightqueen Enterprises LLC Publication

Published in the United States of America

ACKNOWLEDGMENTS

Thanks to my beloved husband, Samwise, who is more supportive than any husband out there. (Hey, I'm biased!). He believes in me, even at times when I'm having trouble believing in myself. Thank you to my wonderful assistants—Andria Holley and Jennifer Arnold. And to my friends—namely Carol, Jo, Vicki, Shawntelle, and Mandy. Also, to the whole UF Group gang I'm in. They've held my hand more than once this past year as I've made the jump from traditional to indie publishing. It's been a scary, exciting, fast-track ride and I'm loving it.

Love and scritches to my four furbles—Caly, Brighid (the cat, not the goddess), Morgana, and li'l boy Apple, who make every day a delight. And reverence, honor, and love to my spiritual guardians—Mielikki, Tapio, Ukko, Rauni, and Brighid (the goddess, not the cat).

And to you, readers, for taking Maddy and Aegis and Bubba into your heart. Be cautious when you rub a kitty's belly—you never know when you might end up petting a cjinn! I hope you enjoy this book. If you want to know more about me and my work, check out my bibliography in the back of the book, be sure to sign up for my newsletter, and you can find me on the web at Galenorn.com.

Brightest Blessings,
~The Painted Panther~
~Yasmine Galenorn~

WELCOME TO WITCHES WILD

Can you ever really trust ghosts from your past?

As the mist rolls off the ocean and into Bedlam, October brings with it all manner of haunts and spooks. But the mist doesn't arrive alone. Fata Morgana returns from the depths of the ocean, bringing with her a message: One of the ancient vampires has risen. He's coming for Maddy, and he'll eliminate anybody who stands in his way. Now, the witches wild must band together one more time, if they can keep from destroying each other first.

CHAPTER ONE

The club was alive, filled to capacity with a bizarre mix of goth kids and pagan metal heads. Aegis's band attracted an oddly diverse audience, from the *hampires*—humans who desperately wanted to join the fangster set—to the audiophiles who loved the mix of Celtic folk and darkwave metal. They came together in a startling meetup, dancing and drinking from the first song to the last encore. It didn't hurt that Aegis's voice was heady, deep and rich and reminiscent of a certain "Lizard King's" voice. Or that he was more than easy on the eyes.

Up on stage in his black leather pants and jacket, his open-to-the-navel silk shirt, and shit-stomper boots, Aegis was the living embodiment of sex on legs. His jet black hair hung down his back in smooth waves and his natural glamour gave him a dangerous, intoxicating allure.

I was sitting at a table to the left side of the stage,

nursing a drink, watching as the Boys of Bedlam rocked the house.

The Vulture Underground was a new club in Seattle. With a capacity of five hundred people, it was one of the largest clubs around. The guys had managed to pack it, making the manager happy. Word about their music was starting to spread, and they were getting more and more calls from events wanting to book them for gigs.

Ferris Parks, their rep from DreamGen Productions, was sitting beside me, watching them with a critical eye. She jotted down notes as they played. Part of me wanted to sneak a peek over her shoulder to see what she was writing. It was bound to be something nasty. I didn't like Ferris, and she didn't like me, but we did our best to coexist because I sure as hell wasn't going away, and unfortunately, neither was she.

A woman ran up toward the stage. Before security could catch her, she had scrambled onto the raised dais and was yanking off her underwear. The bouncers managed to catch her but not before she had tossed her panties in Aegis's face. I let out a groan and rubbed my head.

Lovely. Just lovely.

Aegis swatted them away, managing to finish the song without a glitch. Then, grabbing the mic, he raised his hand for attention. "We're grateful how many of you came out to cheer us on tonight. Thank you, Seattle, for an awesome reception! Remember, rock on! You can find the Boys of Bedlam merchandise tables out in the hallway. Good night!"

Amid cheers and whistles, and cries for another

encore, the guys exited the stage as security escorted the panty-less woman through the exit.

Ferris glanced at me. "That was a good set. I have a page of notes for the guys, but overall, not bad."

I stared at her. "*Not bad*? I thought they were brilliant. They set the room on fire. Couldn't you feel the energy of the audience? They were begging for more."

Ferris arched her petite, exquisitely groomed brows. "I wouldn't expect *you* to see the imperfections. It's a professional thing. Just nuances, places where they could have made the audience cream themselves had they taken advantage of it."

I gave her a long look. The heat they had set off in the club hadn't touched her at all. She was still dewy fresh and polished. Then again, Ferris never looked ruffled. That was only one of a number of things that bothered me about her. She could have passed for one of the Winter Fae, she played the ice queen so well.

"True enough. Focusing on minor imperfections seems to be *your* job, doesn't it?" Without skipping a beat, I was out of my chair and headed backstage.

THE CLUB WAS MORE THAN JUST A HOLE IN THE WALL. THE Vulture Underground actually had a dressing room, as well as a green room. Aegis had already changed into dark jeans and a V-neck sweater. The other band members were in the middle of shedding their stage clothes as well, but I didn't blink an eye. Nakedness wasn't an issue, at least not for me.

"Great job, guys. You brought the house down." I slid

into Aegis's outstretched arm, nestling against him. His body was cool, even though he had been playing nonstop for two hours under stage lights. He never sweated. Vampires were always crispy cool, like cucumbers.

I had gotten used to it, though now and then I missed snuggling with somebody who generated actual body heat. But I produced enough for the both of us, given my proclivity with fire. If I got too cold, I just raised the temperature of the air around me by a couple of degrees. I couldn't hold it for too long, but it was enough to keep me from freezing. If I happened to get lost in the snowy woods for days without the fuel to start a fire, I'd slip into hypothermia, but otherwise, I could take the edge off the chill enough to make myself comfortable.

"You think so?" Aegis gave me a quick kiss.

"I *know* so, regardless of what her majesty's going to tell you."

He sighed. My ongoing feud with Ferris both annoyed him and yet seemed to comfort him, most likely because I always took the band's side against her.

"She had some issues with the gig?"

"Apparently, you didn't make the audience cream themselves enough." I zipped my lip as she walked through the door.

Ferris's gaze bounced briefly onto Aegis, then flickered over Keth and Jorge, but lingered on Sid. I squinted, staring at her for a moment. There was a subtle shift in energy as she watched the bass player. That cold exterior slipped ever so slightly, to one of a tiger waiting to pounce. Could Miss Prissy Pants have a thing for Sid? If so, bad news, since he was married with five kids and Sylvia, a wife who adored him.

Aegis seemed to sense the shift too. He frowned and gave me an ever so subtle nudge, pressing against my side with his fingers. I gave him a curt nod. We had worked out our own form of silent communication, and it seemed to be growing stronger every day.

"I have some notes for you." Ferris glanced at me, as though she expected me to interrupt.

Ignoring her, I yawned and wandered over to Aegis's stage wear, folding the leather pants and tucking them into the duffle bag, along with the slinky shirt.

"Aegis, you're stroking the audience but damn it, man, when a woman throws you her panties, acknowledge the offering. As long as they don't belong to a blimp, or aren't grandma panties, whirl them around your head or take a sniff. Just do *something* to show you appreciate the gift from her pussy."

I froze. For one thing, none of the band members *ever* looked at their audience as meat. For another, her crudity made me wince.

Aegis cleared his throat. "The only underpants I'll ever be likely to smell belong to Maddy. I'm not in the habit of flirting with my fans."

"It's *all* about flirting with your fans, and you'd better get used to it," Ferris said, her mouth folding into a frown. "At least acknowledge the gift." She turned to Jorge, the weretiger in the group. "You ever thought of shifting into your tiger shape on stage?"

He stared at her like she was crazy. "For one thing, I'd have to strip and I'm not showing my bits to the audience. For another… Just no. No, no."

"You don't have to get snotty. A simple, 'No, Ferris, but thank you for the suggestion' would do. I thought it might be fun. You could shift and go around the room, let people pet you—" She stopped as he let out a low growl. "All right, it seems my suggestions aren't going over well tonight. Keth, you're next. The horns—will they ever grow out? You ever thought of getting them extended?"

Keth was half-satyr. Satyrs were always male. When a satyr mated with a human, their sons were half-satyr, their daughters, full human. When satyrs mated with wood nymphs, their sons were full satyr and the daughters were full wood nymph. Keth's mother had been human. As a result, the residual horns on his head would never grow longer. He was heavily tattooed with a Mohawk and had a trippy, freakster vibe to him. All the men in the band were gorgeous, though.

Keth finished pulling on his sweater. "Woman, you have a lot of balls asking that. Are your boobs ever going to grow? Have you thought of having implants?" Sweeping up his pea coat, he glanced at Aegis. "I'm going to warm up the bus. Come on, Jorge. Help me? The guys should have broken down our equipment and loaded it by now."

The Boys of Bedlam had bought a used school bus, and they were now using it to haul the equipment to their gigs. They had found an artist who had done a film noir-ish painting of the band on the side.

Ferris let out an exasperated sigh. "Don't get your balls tied in a knot. DreamGen is doing its best to get behind you. We just need you to cooperate. You're a great band, and we wouldn't be backing you if we didn't believe in you. But you have to meet us halfway. If you *ever* hope to be on the cover of *Rolling Stone*, you have to get with the program."

She shook her head. "Go ahead. Hey, Sid? Can you stick around for a moment? I want to talk to you. I have some detailed notes for you. The rest of you can leave."

Sid looked uncomfortable. "All right, but we should hit the road soon or we won't be home till dawn. Aegis has to get home."

"You'll make it in time." She hustled the rest of us out of the green room.

I conveniently left my purse on the chair next to me as I exited the room. Jorge and Keth had already headed for the bus. I pulled Aegis off to one side, watching until they left.

"What the hell is going on with her and Sid?" I was friends with Sylvia. They had five kids and with the exception of a few glitches along the way, they were happy, in love, and all about their family.

"I don't know," Aegis said, glancing back at the door. "Sid hasn't said much, but he wasn't very enthusiastic about the gig tonight. That much, I do know. I wish I had an excuse to go back in there."

"I don't need one." I strode over to the door before Aegis could stop me. As I opened it, I said loudly, "Forgot my purse."

Sid was leaning back on the sofa, with Ferris looming over him. She had one knee on the cushion to his left, and looked about ready to straddle his lap. Her clipboard was on the table, and she had taken her hair down from the chignon she wore it in. He was holding up his hand as though he were trying to ward her off.

"I can't—" Sid was in the middle of saying.

"Looks like I crashed an impromptu party," I said. "I

forgot my purse. Sid, we're waiting in the bus, if you're done here."

He flashed me an incredibly grateful look. I was surprised. It wasn't at all the look of someone angry I had interrupted. Sid shifted around Ferris so that he could stand up. Ferris, on the other hand, looked like she wanted to kill me.

"Here's your purse, Maddy." Sid grabbed my bag off the chair. "I'm ready. I'll walk you out." He glanced back at Ferris and his voice dropped into a mumble. "Thanks for the…notes."

As I hustled him out the door, I whispered, "What the hell is going on?"

"Wait till we're on the bus," he whispered back. "But thank gods you came in when you did."

Aegis was staring at the two of us, a perplexed look on his face. But he turned and followed us as we made a beeline for the bus. Jorge was driving—he was good with big vehicles—and we buckled ourselves into the cushioned seats the boys had retrofitted the bus with. Without another word, we pulled onto the street and Jorge pointed the bus north as we headed home to Bedlam.

I waited until we were underway, then swiveled around to look at Sid. "You have something you want to tell the band?"

"What's going on?" Aegis asked.

"I think Jorge better find a parking lot because this is something you all need to address. Isn't it, Sid?" I knew what was going on.

He blushed, but nodded. "Maddy's right. Jorge, find us a place to park, please."

Five minutes later, we turned into the parking lot of a Target store and parked near the end of a row. Nobody was out at this time in the morning, save for the homeless, the night owls, and whatever vampires might be roaming the streets. October in Seattle was blustery enough, but we were into a strong La Niña season, and the weather had shifted to extremely cold and wet. The sky was dark, not a star to be seen, and the clouds hanging thick and heavy, ready to burst at any moment.

I glanced out the window at the street running past the store. I didn't miss living here. In fact, while Seattle was one of the best big cities I had lived in, I was far happier living in Bedlam. Too much congestion, too much traffic, too many sirens blaring along the dark, concrete streets.

"All right. Tell us what's going on," Aegis said.

Jorge joined us, but only after making certain the bus doors were locked. "Yeah, I want to get home before it's morning and I know Aegis wants the same. So what's up?"

The guys were all good friends, but after a gig, they were all a little wound up and snippy. But beneath all the snark and jostling around, they had forged a bond that was all but unbreakable. I just hoped Sid's news wouldn't shake it.

Sid blushed, staring at the floor. Finally, I decided to take the reins.

"I found Sid on the sofa. Ferris was coming onto him so hard I thought she was going to rip his clothes off. Sexual harassment, plain and simple. Isn't that right, Sid?"

He blinked, then nodded, looking miserable. "I've tried

to ignore it but she's been getting more and more blatant. Tonight, well, that's the farthest she's gone. I don't know what would have happened if you hadn't come back for your purse, Maddy."

"What would have happened is you would have told her to go fuck herself with a dildo if she's so hard up." I was angry. Sex was a wonderful thing, but not when it was coerced.

"Is this true?" Aegis asked Sid, the bewilderment on his face turning to understanding.

Sid nodded, still looking miserable. "Yeah, Ferris has been trying to…*seduce* isn't even the right word. She's been pushing me to fuck her for weeks now. Ever since we signed with DreamGen. I was hoping that she was a temporary rep and that they'd replace her, but when she told us last week that she'd be traveling with us on tour, I knew things were going to get ugly. She knows I love Sylvia, but she just keeps badgering me."

"Why the hell didn't you say anything, man?" Keth looked pissed. "She's been a thorn in our sides ever since she started working with us. I can't stand the bitch, to be honest."

I knew why Sid hadn't said anything. "Guys, he didn't say anything because he saw this as your big chance and he didn't want to muck up the works. Am I right?"

Sid nodded, staring at his feet. "We might never get another chance. Opportunities like this don't come around very often. I didn't want to screw things up by complaining."

Aegis closed his eyes for a moment, looking pained. "You thought that you had to put up with her crap just for the band? Listen, nothing's worth harassment like that. *Nothing*. Not the band. Not a gig. Not a record deal."

Jorge cleared his throat. "Well, as long as we're all being honest, I've missed just…being *us*. I mean, we were going to put out our own album, our own way, weren't we? Now, we have to change our act to please DreamGen. We're not a bunch of drunken idiots, but that's what Ferris and DreamGen want us to be. I don't know about you, but I liked the way we were. I'm not having fun anymore."

"What exactly are you trying to say?" Aegis slumped back, his gaze flickering up to the guys. "Do you want to kill the contract? I think we can, but if we want to go back to being an indie group, we'd better do it now before they can claim we owe them a fuckton of money."

Sid slowly raised his hand. "I think, if my marriage is to survive, I have to quit the band or quit working with DreamGen. If we complain to them about Ferris, you know they'll laugh off my concerns."

Keth shrugged, tossing his drumsticks on the floor. "We were doing fine before we signed with them. We'll do just fine without them. I'm up for going back to being a garage band."

Aegis straightened his shoulders. "All right, then. We'll break the contract with DreamGen. But if we do, we do things *our* way from now on, because a bigger company would be even worse. I guess it's hard to find a producer who isn't out to screw over the band in one way or another, isn't it?"

"Or, in Ferris's case, just screw the band," I said. "Seriously, guys, you have a sound that's hard to match. You start slanting it the way she's pushing you to, and you're going to sound like a canned act. You've got a solid audience and you can build your way up doing things the way you want. And that doesn't include encouraging groupies to throw their panties on stage or fucking your handler because she can make life miserable if you don't."

Sid paused. "Do you think they'll try to sue us?"

Aegis grinned and shrugged. "There's only one way to find out, now, isn't there? We'll look over the contract and figure out how to break it at our next meeting."

And with that, Jorge returned to the driver's seat, and we headed back to Bedlam.

AEGIS AND I HOPPED OUT OF THE BUS AND WAVED AS KETH drove off toward his place. He lived with his mother and father on ten acres just outside of town. There was plenty of space to park the bus there.

I glanced at the sky. It was four-thirty and we still had almost three hours till sunrise. Aegis stretched, bringing his arm down to wrap around my shoulders. As we headed toward the kitchen slider, it occurred to me just how lucky we were.

The town of Bedlam was located on the island by the same name. Located off the northern edge of the San Juan Islands, Bedlam was overlooked by most humans. We didn't exactly cloak the town, but rather, used some of the magical energy that permeated the area to keep ourselves from being noticed. The town had been founded by my kind—witches—and had a population of around six thousand permanent residents. A quirky, old-fashioned charm surrounded the area, and truly, it was beautiful here. The foliage was much like the rest of the west coast of Washington—with tall firs and wide, drooping cedar trees, and juniper and other evergreens that kept their needles year-round. Intermingled with the conifers were oak and maple trees of all varieties. Birch, black chestnut, and alder dappled the heavy forests, and the ever-present scent of moisture filled the air.

Bedlam experienced about sixty-five cloud-free days a year. The rest of the time the sky was partially or fully overcast, with a silvery sheen that soothed the heart and emotions. Rain was ever present, whether in drizzles or in downpours. We received more precipitation in terms of rain and snow than the rest of the San Juan Islands because the magical energy of the island and its inhabitants acted like a magnet for storms, drawing them in. So here, rain shadows were few, and we could always expect snow during winter and the gales of autumn to blow through.

A ferry ran from Bellingham over to Bedlam, docking once per hour most of the night. On weekends, it ran later, which was good for us or we would have had to find a vampire-safe hotel over on the mainland.

The Bewitching Bedlam—my bed-and-breakfast—was an old house. It had been built over two hundred years ago. We knew that because our house ghost, Franny, had been born here in 1791. She had died in 1815. I wasn't sure how much older it was, but the foundation was solid, even though the weathering stone walls showed their age. The house had been abandoned when I found it, falling apart on the surface but with good bones. I had restored it to its original beauty on the outside, and had fully modernized the inside.

The Bewitching Bedlam had room for four guests, if I counted our private guestroom. The house had fifteen rooms, not counting the bathrooms, and was two stories, not including the basement and the attic.

As we unlocked the slider leading to the kitchen, I made sure Bubba and Luna weren't poised to run out. Sometimes they would lie in wait, then pounce when I opened the door. Bubba was my massive red boy of a cjinn, and Luna was his girlfriend, a lovely calico who didn't seem to mind that she was "dating" a magical creature.

But Bubba and Luna were nowhere to be seen. I flipped on the light, and Aegis immediately headed toward the fridge.

"You must be hungry. They didn't have any food at the club. At least, nothing substantial."

In addition to being one hunka hunka burning vamp, my boyfriend was also an excellent cook and baker. He loved mysteries and jigsaw puzzles, and had an intense fondness for kittens. When he found out I had taken in Luna, he had been delighted.

My stomach rumbled. "Actually, I am. I was going to just go to bed. It's been one hell of a long day, but I don't know if I can sleep if I don't eat first. Leftovers are fine."

He poked around. "There's some chicken left from lunch yesterday. And some macaroni and cheese. That work?"

"Yeah." I yawned again, my eyes heavy. "I'm so tired. Just nuke them."

The chicken was from my favorite chicken joint— Chicken Chicken. It kept crisp after being reheated, and the breading was so good, just thinking about it made my mouth water. As Aegis fixed a plate for me and popped it in the microwave, I let out another yawn.

"So, what did you make of the way Ferris was acting toward Sid?"

"It pisses me off," Aegis said. "Nobody harasses the people I care about. I don't care whether you're male or female, you don't get a free pass to force yourself on anybody else."

"Sylvia would freak if she knew. They've been working out some relationship issues and this wouldn't help at all. I think we should keep quiet about it unless Sid decides to tell her. After all, you guys have decided to stop working with DreamGen." I paused. "How do you really feel about it? I know you had a lot of hopes pinned on this."

Aegis shrugged as he set my plate in front of me and handed me a fork. He slid into the chair next to me, a beer in his hands. Vampires could eat and drink all they wanted without ever being affected by the food, but blood was still their actual sustenance.

"Disappointed, I won't lie about that. But I refuse to work with someone who pressures one of my boys to go against his wishes. Sid doesn't even *like* Ferris. After the initial rush of signing the contract, he told me that she made him uncomfortable."

"Ten to one, she was working on him even then." I bit into the chicken and scooped up a forkful of mac 'n cheese. The creamy, salty taste melted in my mouth and I let out an audible sigh, relaxing as the food slid down my throat. I hadn't realized just how hungry I had been.

"You're probably right. Well, I'll talk to DreamGen after the guys and I go over the contract. Even if I have to pay a penalty to break it, that's fine. I won't ask the guys to chip in. I know none of them can afford it." He watched me eat for a moment, then reached across the table. "I want to thank you. I wouldn't have gone in there, and Sid would have been screwed over, in more ways than one. Thanks for recognizing a problem that I hadn't put my finger on yet."

I smiled and patted his hand, still eating. Once I finished, I carried my plate to the sink to rinse it off to put it in the dishwasher. Once I got to the counter, however, I paused. There was a sack sitting there. It hadn't been there when we left in the morning. I opened it and froze. Inside, was an urn, with an envelope beside it. I opened the letter and read it, then set the paper down and backed up a step.

"What is it?" Aegis asked.

I couldn't answer. I hadn't thought this would affect me so much, but now that the time had actually come, my heart rose into my throat. Pressing my lips together, I turned toward Aegis, feeling a thousand years old.

"Maddy, what's wrong?" Aegis took a step toward me.

I tried to answer, tried to form the words, but they didn't want to come out. It was as though my lips were frozen and, no matter how much I wanted to say something, they wouldn't move.

"What the…" Aegis paused by the counter and stared down at the urn. He slowly picked up the note. "May I?"

I gave him a faint nod. He picked up the paper and began to read aloud.

"Dear Ms. Gallowglass:
We wish to express our condolences in your time of

sorrow. We have enclosed the urn with your mother's ashes in it, as you requested, and you will also find a copy of her death certificate. We are the legal team representing your mother's posthumous wishes. She asked that her remains be returned to you for dispersal, and that all her personal magical effects and family photographs and documents be sent to you. In accordance with her will, we will be packaging her magical supplies, photographs, and papers, and mailing them to you shortly. Everything else will be sold and the proceeds will be remitted to you after payment of any outstanding debts, according to her instructions. If there's anything else we can do, please ask.

Sincerely,
Jessie Midas
Midas, Timmons, & Smith, Solicitors"

I stared at the stone urn as though it was going to jump up and bite me. Zara, my mother, had died a few weeks ago, and now she was home with me. I had spent a lifetime despising her, and only in the last months of her life had I come to understand—if not exactly love—her. We had parted as friends, as mother and daughter rather than antagonistic relatives. But seeing her remains on the counter brought home, once again, the realization that we had been robbed of nearly four centuries together, thanks to my grandmother and my father. My mother had been forced into living a lie most of her life. For that, I would never forgive them.

I reached out and slowly took the urn out of the sack as Aegis watched me, a cautious look on his face. Finally, I slid my fingers down the cool stone and over the name they had etched on it: Zara Malina Gallowglass. She had kept her mother's family name, as had I even though I had been married for a time.

Trying to navigate the minefield of emotions that were waging war in my heart, I closed my eyes and whispered, "Welcome home, Mother." And then, slowly, the tears began to fall.

CHAPTER TWO

I slept a good share of the day, exhausted from the trip, but also from the emotional upheaval that had hit when I saw my mother's ashes sitting there. Sandy, my best friend, texted me while I was asleep. I woke up around noon to her text. Unable to decide whether to call her, I finally passed on it. I wasn't ready to talk about how I felt. Instead, I headed outside, leaving Kelson—our most illustrious housekeeper who kept the Bewitching Bedlam running like clockwork—to handle anything that came up. We were sparse on guests right now, with just Mr. Mosswood to cater to. He had taken permanent root in our inn, it seemed. But things would pick up with the coming holidays, and I decided we should use the downtime to plan out a series of events that might attract guests.

As I folded my arms across my chest, facing the wind, the tall firs shivered and shook as clouds rolled by overhead. Shivering as a blast of chill air hit me, I thought about what an odd and winding road I had taken to come to this place in my life.

My name is Maudlin Gallowglass—Maddy for short. I was once known as Mad Maudlin, and with good reason. I'm a witch, and I'm also the High Priestess of the Moonrise Coven here on Bedlam. I was born on October 28, 1629, in a little cottage that nestled in the countryside in Ireland.

Long story short, I'm *the* Mad Maudlin mentioned in the folk song "Mad Tom of Bedlam." He—Tom—was my lover, until he was turned by vampires and corrupted. Let's just say that I went a little crazy when that happened, and together with my best friends Cassandra—Sandy—and Fata Morgana, I took vampire hunting to a new level. I became the scourge of vampires throughout Great Britain and Europe. I rained down fire and death on them, and together, the three of us managed to destroy hundreds of the creatures over a period of about a dozen years.

But the intense focus burned me out. By the end, when we stood above a village of vampires, watching as it burned to the ground—with the vampires caught in it—my passion for vampire hunting vanished with the ashes and smoke. Sandy, Fata, and I went into party mode, spending the better part of ten years in an old-school sex, drugs, and rock 'n roll phase—sans the rock 'n roll. We were hanging with a group of satyrs and wood nymphs. Then Fata and I had a falling out, and she—wild water spirit that she was—rode out to sea on the waves, furious.

I had pushed the argument away, not wanting to remember it, and so Sandy and I made new plans.

We decided to travel, to cloak ourselves up and so, taking Bubba with us, we journeyed from country to country, and finally came to the United States. And here we stayed, making new lives for ourselves. And when the Pretcom came out in the open, we came out, too.

There's so much I haven't mentioned, but it could take a lifetime to tell my story. For now, a few paragraphs will have to do.

I WAS BRAINSTORMING A WINTER CARNIVAL EVENT FOR THE Bewitching Bedlam when Aegis woke up. We both loved autumn and winter because he had more time to spend awake, as the sun rose late and set early. My stomach rumbled, but the sun was setting shortly before six-thirty, so I decided to wait on dinner until he woke up. As I was wrapping up my work for the day—specifically, I was going through my Rolodex, looking for an ice witch who could conjure up an ice elemental for a party—I heard Aegis in the kitchen, as the basement door opened and then shut. It had a distinctive squeak that I recognized every time. We kept meaning to oil it, but that was about as far as we had gotten.

"Maddy?" His voice echoed down the hall.

"I'm in the office," I called back.

"Come into the kitchen, please! I have something you need to see."

Frowning—usually Aegis came in to give me a kiss—I put down my pen and stretched, wincing as my back cracked. I should visit the chiropractor. Or maybe start adding yoga to my workouts. I was a haphazard gym bunny. Wilson, my trainer, wasn't thrilled with my progress but he constantly said some exercise was better than none, and he had given up trying to transform me into Ms. Fitness USA.

I yawned and headed for the kitchen. Kelson was standing by the sink, smirking. Aegis was sitting at the table, his hand on the handle of a large wicker basket. It was covered, and the trim poking out around the edges was gingham.

"What's this?" I asked, moving in for a kiss.

He wrapped his arm around me, pulling me onto his lap as he planted a kiss on my lips. "Don't you know what today is?"

"Um…October fourteenth? Saturday?" I wasn't sure where he was going with this.

He looked disappointed. "Really? You can't have forgotten."

I blinked, trying frantically to remember if we'd agreed to make tonight a date night or what. And then, I saw the roses on the table behind him, and it clicked. I felt like an ass.

"Happy anniversary!" I smiled, almost shy. The last time I had said those words to a man, all I had gotten was a torrent of verbal abuse.

But Aegis cuddled me, kissing my cheek. "I knew you wouldn't forget! Happy anniversary, my love," he murmured, sniffing my hair.

I let out a contented sigh, then glanced up at his face. "I'm so sorry. I guess I didn't think you would remember, and then I just put it out of my mind and forgot about it."

"*Of course* I remember. We've been together a year." He teased my nose with his lips, then kissed me again. "I'm not Craig. I'm not any other man you've ever been with."

"That's for sure," I whispered. And he was right. I had never dated a vampire before. I reached for the basket, but he swatted away my hand. "Hey, I was just looking."

"It's a surprise."

"All right, so, picnic in the parlor? You can't be thinking of picnicking out in the park. It's pretty cold."

"No worries, my frozen little dumpling. We're not going to the park."

I snorted. He was more romantic than I was, but even that was a hair too cloying for an anniversary.

"The basket is filled with your favorite foods. And the roses are for the flower of my heart."

I pressed my lips together. *I will not laugh. I will not laugh.*

It wasn't that I didn't appreciate the gesture, but the juxtaposition of a top-of-the-chain predator offering to take me on a romantic picnic conjured up all sorts of ironies in my mind. I still wasn't used to dating a vampire, even a year into our relationship. But maybe that wasn't a bad thing. It kept me on my toes and alert.

"I think I love this idea. But where are we going?"

"Just bundle up. I know you can generate body heat for yourself. We're going on a secret little evening getaway."

I blinked. "Should I bring Bubba? Luna?"

Aegis let out a quick, "No! They wouldn't like this, trust me. No, this is just for us. You and me and a basket full of chicken and chips and pastries."

My stomach rumbled again and I decided to STFU

and just let the man woo me. "In that case, let me go change. You said bundle up?"

He nodded. "I guarantee, you'll want the warmth."

Wondering just where we were going, I headed upstairs and changed out of my trousers and tank top and into a pair of jeans and a thick cable-knit sweater with a cowl neck. I slid on a heavy jacket and a pair of ankle boots and pocketed a pair of gloves, then dashed back down to where Aegis was loading the basket in his Corvette. Without another question, I grabbed my purse, hopped in the passenger side and we were off, to whatever surprise he had prepared for us.

Much to my surprise, we headed directly for East Cove Marina. As we eased into the parking lot, I glanced at Aegis.

"We aren't, by any chance, visiting Gillymack?"

"Oh good gods no. I wouldn't subject you to that on our anniversary. Now, come on and don't question me. Just follow."

He led me over to Pier 17, where a small motorboat was waiting. As I gingerly took his hand and he helped me into the boat, I pulled my jacket tighter. The winds were whipping through the marina, playing the masts on the boats like a melancholy symphony. It was called "wind chiming" and it produced an eerie concert that reminded me of long-forgotten ghosts high on the slopes of Everest. I had half a mind to ask Aegis if we shouldn't wait till later, but that would spoil his gesture. And to be honest, the wind didn't scare me. At least, not much.

The boat looked familiar, and then I saw the name, "The Dust Witch," and recognized it as the one Garret James owned. A snakeshifter who was a Dirt Witch, Garret and I had taken this boat out to Patos Island a few months ago in search of an herb from a siren's garden.

"You borrowed Garret's boat?" I sat down on one of the side benches, smiling.

"Yeah. Actually, I was asking Garret where I should rent one, and he suggested borrowing his. How could I turn down such a generous offer?" Aegis blew a kiss at me as he started up the motor. Vampires could cross flowing water, or ride on it or swim in it, but they couldn't change form till they hit land again. Aegis loved being out on a boat, as long as it wasn't near sunrise.

As for me, I loved the feeling of motion, be it boat, car, or plane. Or broom, I thought with a snicker. I stretched out, leaning my legs into the boat as I rested against a custom headrest that Garret had installed.

"So, one year, huh?" But the wind overshadowed my voice, so I gingerly picked my way over to where Aegis was steering the boat and sat shotgun. I repeated myself.

Aegis broke into a wide smile. "One year. And you thought I'd forget? Ha! Admit it. *You're* the one who forgot."

"I didn't forget," I said, trying to dodge the truth. "I just never got to celebrate much with Craig and so things like anniversaries went by the wayside. On the other hand, Sandy was always good for celebrating birthdays and other holidays with."

"Craig was an asshole. I still think I should pay him a visit someday." Aegis cast a speculative look my way. "Why did you?"

"Why did I what?"

"Marry him? You can have just about any man you want, Maudlin Gallowglass. Why would you pick someone like Craig?"

I blinked. I hadn't expected to dip into the ex-files. "Why did I marry someone like *his majesty* Craig Vincent Astor? I don't know. A fit of madness?"

"Seriously, why? What could he have possibly had that attracted you?"

I realized Aegis wasn't going to let this go. I could always tell when the pit bull side of him was in full force. I let out a long breath. I had deliberately avoided talking about my decade-long marriage to Craig the asshole.

Finally, I shrugged. "I was going through a bleak period. Sandy was married to Bart and we all thought it was a wonderful marriage. Except, I guess, Bart, considering he was gay and in the closet. I was bored, to be honest. I had hung around Seattle, trying to figure out what I wanted to do. The Otherkin were all out of the closet, so I could have done just about anything and not worried about being found out. I guess the sudden decrease in the need for secrecy was a radical change. Once I didn't have to pretend, I didn't know what to do."

Aegis gave me a puzzled look. "I don't think I understand. What did you do before then?"

"You'll never guess," I said, laughing.

"Secretary?"

"Nope, can't stand fetching and carrying for other people." I wasn't a go-fer type person.

"I can't imagine you as a doctor or nurse."

I decided to give him a break. "Nope. I owned a wine shop. That's how Craig and I met. He came in weekly to check out my wine selection. I would point him to the highest-priced wines and he wouldn't blink, even if they weren't that good. Craig was pretentious. He was a snob, and he had a thing for busty brunettes. Since I owned the shop and wasn't just the manager, he deigned to talk to me. I was lonely and it had been awhile since I'd been in a relationship. I had started to feel invisible to men, though I'm pretty sure I had other customers flirting with me. I guess…really…I started to feel invisible to myself."

I paused. That was the real reason. I felt boring and bored, and that wasn't a good state for me. I had Bubba, but I wasn't inclined to ask him to help me meet someone. I hung my head.

"When Craig started paying attention to me, it felt good. I felt like I might still have a spark of who I used to be. So I went out with him. And even though I fell in love, I knew all along there was something wrong. I decided to look the other way, I guess, because I didn't want to go back to my old life."

"Did he know you were a witch?"

A swell rocked the boat and I caught my breath as we rose up, then dipped as the wave rolled under us. The night sky was so dark you couldn't see a star in the sky, and the winds had risen substantially since we had come out on the water.

"Yeah, he knew. He didn't like it, but we were already engaged, and the invitations had gone out and the notice was in the paper. He changed, though. He started by telling me to sell my shop and when I refused, he threatened to leave me. So I sold it, because we had been together about two years and I didn't want to make waves."

Aegis said nothing, just waited for me to continue.

"I can't believe I actually did that, but you know how it goes. You get used to something and you start thinking it's normal. Then he started cheating on me. He hid it though, as much as he could because he knew I could hex his ass. Instead, he opted for trying to convince me I was crazy and imagining things."

"Common move by scumbags."

"Common, and unfortunately, effective. I took another job, this time in a hotel as a general manager, but Craig got me fired by calling to check up on me four to five times a day, every day. He was the one cheating, but *he* didn't trust *me*. Finally, Sandy made me do a Divining spell and the truth came out. Not only had he gone through a string of girlfriends during the ten years we were together, but he had spread lies about me. In general, he turned into a giant prick."

"Not turned into. Just showed you his true colors." Aegis cut the motor. "I think this is a good place for our picnic. We're out in the open water now." He swiveled his chair around to face me. "So, what did you do?"

"Left his ass. Sued him for what I could get. I got the condo, which I sold to buy the Bewitching Bedlam. But it took me awhile to snap out of it. I had been so uncertain about what I wanted when I met him that I lost myself along the way." I paused, then leaned forward to take his hands. "I want to thank you. You didn't rescue me, but you helped me rediscover myself and my needs. You and Sandy both. Gods know she tried for years."

Aegis pulled me onto his lap and the boat rocked in the current as we kissed. I was about to undo his shirt buttons but he shook his head, holding up one finger. "First, we eat dinner, and I give you my present."

"I thought this was the present. A midnight picnic." I slid off his lap, wistfully eyeing him. He was aroused—either that or he was packing one hell of a banana in his pants. But I'd play it his way. I was curious to see what he had planned next.

Aegis pulled the picnic basket to his side and opened it, handing me a cloth to spread out on the bottom of the boat. Then he brought out a container of fried chicken, a container of macaroni salad, a bag of biscuits, and a cherry pie. I laughed as I arranged the food.

"I bet this is all homemade, isn't it?"

"Nope," he admitted. "I actually had Kelson order everything. I left her a note this morning and she had everything ready and packed by the time I woke up." He reached back into the basket for plates and forks, and then pulled out a long, slender box. "This, however, I picked out myself." He handed it to me.

I slowly took the smooth velvet box, and flipped the lid up. There, under the lights of the boat, in the dim night, a pendant sparkled like stars. It had to be a diamond. I knew cubic zirconium, and this was *not* CZ. I slowly lifted the pendant out of the box and held it up. It was on a chain that looked like silver but that I already knew was white gold. Aegis couldn't touch silver, but he liked the look.

The pendant itself was in the shape of a key, the diamond at the bottom. I glanced over at him, clutching the necklace. It tingled in my hands. "This...is beautiful."

"Let me see it," he said, and I handed it to him. He reached over and fastened it around my neck. "I give you the key to my heart," he whispered. As my reserve melted, he leaned closer and kissed me, laying me back on the boat, under the windswept night.

We cuddled for a good half an hour before my hunger drove us to our midnight supper. The thought of having sex in the boat was appealing, but although Aegis couldn't get cold, I could, and even though I could raise the air around me enough to keep warm, being so vulnerable in a tempestuous ocean didn't seem worth it. So we settled for snuggling until my stomach rumbled loud and clear.

"Let's get some food into you," he said, laughing. He pulled me up and we scooted over to the blanket with the food on it. As I opened the container of chicken, Aegis scooped potato salad onto plates.

"Does it bother you that food doesn't fill you up?" I had refrained from asking a number of questions over the past year that seemed too personal, but seeing how I just told him about Craig and how I had stayed throughout emotional abuse and infidelity, I felt that it was his turn.

"Not really. I like being able to eat what I want without worrying if it's healthy for me. But having to drink blood still worries my conscience. The truth is, blood from a blood bank or from animals never tastes as good as blood from a person. It's the warmth in my mouth, the flavor on my tongue. I think sometimes it's the act itself of sinking my fangs into somebody's neck that makes it feel so good." He paused at my look. "I'm being honest, Maddy. You don't want me to lie to you, do you?"

I shook my head, though part of me wanted to say, "Yeah, about stuff like that? I don't want to know." But the truth was, I wanted honesty, even when it made me uncomfortable. Craig had lied to me over and over again and I grew to hate him for it, especially since I could always tell. I touched my throat, sliding my hands along the skin, wondering what it would feel like to let Aegis drink from me. Would it hurt? I knew it could be good—so incredibly good. In a way, I realized I was jealous of all the people he singled out to drink from. They got to experience a side of him that I had held at bay. And yet…

He must have read the struggle in my face. "I will never ask that of you. I will never demand to drink from you, nor will I drink from you without your consent. I love you too much for that. It's a violation of will, and I don't take joy in it, though it does feel good. But Maddy, you're special. You're my girlfriend, my lover, my mate. How could I ever hurt you?"

I wanted to say, "Drink from me. Now. Here." But I couldn't. I was a witch and my blood held power. I had been taught never, ever to allow anyone else to use it. And all of my years hunting vampires had never once resulted in me getting bit. It had been a badge of honor to all three of us—me, Fata, and Sandy.

Aegis seemed to sense where my thoughts were drifting. He shook his head, holding his finger to my lips. "Hush," he whispered, "Don't say a word." He brought a chicken leg to my mouth. "Eat."

Silently, I took the drumstick and bit into the crunchy breading. It was like heaven in my mouth. I relaxed and with my other hand, fingered the pendant that lay around my neck.

"Thank you. I love it," I said. "This is so perfect."

"It's the way I look at you. You stole the key to my heart, love." He kissed my forehead, then picked up a chicken thigh and bit into it. "I don't want your blood, I just want your love." After a pause, he swallowed and added, "Not that I'm rejecting drinking from you, but…"

"I know what you're saying." I handed him a roll. "Here."

The tension lifted, and I took a deep breath of the chill air. Aegis had thought to bring an extra blanket and I wrapped myself in it. It was fleece, toasty and soft. We ate in comfortable silence, the only sounds the rushing of the wind and the lapping of waves. The rain hadn't broken yet—for which I was incredibly grateful—but the air felt laden with moisture. We finished the meal, including most of the cherry pie, and Aegis cuddled up to me again, wrapping his arm around me.

"So, what are your plans for the Bewitching Bedlam this coming year?"

I shrugged. "I don't know. I guess finish the landscaping and the outside camping area I wanted to put in on the back three acres. Why?"

"Just wondering if we should draw up a timeline for what we want to do and when we want to do it." He leaned back, pulling me to snuggle against his side. We watched the rumbling sky. Even though it was the dark of the night, the clouds were boiling overhead and I suddenly felt very much alone out in the middle of the water, as though we were the only two people alive.

A few minutes later, Aegis sprang to a sitting position, tumbling me to the side. Dazed, I sat up, about to ask him what the hell, but he motioned for me to be silent. He was scanning out to the water, as though he were looking for something. Vampires had incredible hearing and I realized he must have heard something that alarmed him.

I crouched, one knee on the bottom of the boat, one hand on the side. The rocking of the waves felt more intense, and then, as Aegis started to stand, looking alarmed, a brilliant flash split the sky, zigzagging from cloud to cloud, and almost immediately, a deep rumble rolled through the air, shaking the boat with its power.

"Crap, lightning!" I tugged at Aegis. "Down! Get down! It's right overhead!" All I could think about was that he would end up a giant lightning rod. Fire could fry a vampire—and lightning was fire on steroids.

"Stop, Maddy! It's not just lightning—" He was drowned out by a loud roar and before I could turn to see what it was, the boat began to spin and dip, sweeping up on a massive wave that rolled beneath us. I gasped, stumbling forward to land flat against the bottom of the boat. Aegis immediately had hold of me, dragging me up. "Where's your life vest?"

I shook my head. I had taken it off the minute we were under way.

"Find it *now*!" Aegis began searching for it, but I caught sight of the brilliant orange vest as the lights of the boat rocked back and forth with the wave that had caught us up. I crawled forward, trying to grab it, but it slid out of my grasp. The next moment, Aegis leaped over my head, landing five feet in front of me, next to the vest. He grabbed it and tossed it to me.

I slid the vest over my head, then snapped the buckle and pulled the cord to inflate it. Thank gods it worked, because we heard a crashing at the bow of the boat and then, the fiberglass and wood and metal began to screech as the wave picked up the boat and twisted it like a housekeeper wringing out a sponge.

The boat couldn't hold, and as it began to break apart, Aegis took hold of my arm and pulled me overboard with him. I wanted to yell, "My purse!" but then stopped. The last thing I needed to worry about was my purse. Right now, I just needed to stay alive.

"Can you swim?" Aegis yelled over the cacophony raging around us.

"Yes!" I nodded vigorously. We were in a rough current. A whirlpool seemed to be sucking the boat down. I struggled to keep from being caught in it, but then Aegis took hold of my waist and began driving his way through the water with powerful kicks. He steered with one arm, while he held me with his other, and slowly, we pulled away from the giant vortex that was forming in the water behind us. It swallowed the boat, and all I could do was whisper prayers to Arianrhod that she see us safely through the storm. I really didn't want to die like this. I really didn't want to *die*, in fact, but especially not sucked into the depths.

We were starting to make some headway when another flash split the sky and opened it wide. Rain began to beat down on the churning waves, and I struggled to keep my face above the water. The life vest was helping, but it wasn't necessarily a promise of salvation.

We were nowhere near the shore. In fact, I couldn't even *see* the shore. Aegis wouldn't necessarily tire, but could he find our way back to land before a wave swamped us and drove us under? Or before the sun rose?

We had a good seven hours to go before sunrise, but right now, I had no idea how far out we were.

Another wave spun us around and I realized I had no clue which direction we were headed at this point. I tried to help by turning on my back so I would float easier, but the waves were slamming us around so much that I was afraid of being dragged down. I closed my eyes, trying to calm myself as I ran through the spells that might be useful.

None of my fiery spells would do much good. Nor would any divining or information-seeking spells. I could do minor tricks, and I had a few odd spells that didn't seem to fit anywhere, but nowhere in my repertoire did I have a *build-a-boat spell* or *please-don't-drown-me* spell. I wasn't even sure any of those types of spells existed.

Aegis continued to propel us through the water, though I had no clue if he knew where we were going. I didn't want to ask, either, because I didn't want to interrupt his focus. Vampires were extraordinarily strong, but that didn't mean they were invincible, and if a shark came along and decided to make a meal out of us, it could. And then, there was the ocean. The ocean was stronger than any other force on the planet. The element of water was relentless and it crept in through cracks and overwhelmed even the tallest of mountains.

We slowly pulled away from where the vortex had sucked down the boat, but the thunderstorm continued unabated and I was still worried the lightning might strike us. I wasn't sure how much of a target we were, but the thought of a billion volts of electricity running through my body did not strike me as an experience I wanted any part of.

After a while, Aegis stopped. He was treading water, while my vest was keeping me afloat. "Love, I hate to tell you this, but I don't know which way the shore is."

I was crying, but it was impossible for him to tell because of the incessant rain splashing down my face. I forced a smile into my voice. "Well, this is one anniversary we're never going to forget."

He wrapped his arms around me and, without a word, started off again. I closed my eyes, willing him on, trying to feed him my energy via osmosis. But another moment and there was a roar behind us as the water swelled. Another wave crashed forward. Surely, this one would swamp us and drag us down to the bottom. I bit my lip, wondering why now, why was this going to be my end? And who would know? Kelson would realize we weren't back in the morning, and so would Garret, but by then? It would be too late.

I decided to face my death with the courage I faced hunting vampires. I sucked in a deep breath and turned to face the rolling water that thundered toward us. As the wave towered over us, there was another wave forming below us. It lifted us into the air and as I caught a dizzying breath, the wave rushed forward, carrying us with it, and everything went black.

CHAPTER THREE

"Maddy? Maddy? Can you hear me?" The voice seemed to be coming from a distance, but it sounded familiar. "Maddy, wake up. Maddy?"

My eyes flickered and the next moment, I was staring at Sandy. I realized I was in a bed, warm and dry, and there was an IV needle in my arm. What had happened? Why was I in the hospital? I closed my eyes and a vision of swirling waves lashed around me, and all I could see everywhere I looked was dark, rolling water. The taste of brine lay heavy on my tongue. Another moment and it all swept back to me. The boat. The storm. The waves trying to drag us—

"Aegis? Where is he? Is he all right?"

"It's okay, hon. Yes, he's all right. He's asleep for the day, safely tucked away from the light. You're lucky, though. Garret thought the storm might be too much so he called you and Aegis, but neither one of you answered. So he went down to the marina and found both of you on the shore. Aegis was struggling to carry you up, but he was weak—something sapped some of his energy."

"Vampires aren't exactly like the Energizer Bunny. They can over-exert themselves and he was doing his best to get us both to shore. But I don't know how he swam all the way in." I was starting to remember the details.

"He told Garret that some massive wave came rumbling beneath you and carried you to shore, tossing you on the beach before retreating. Garret called an ambulance for you, then he contacted me. Once they determined you'd live, I made Aegis go home." She brushed my hair out of my eyes. "Maddy, we almost lost you," she said softly. "You were hypothermic. Aegis said you passed out when the wave picked you up, and that you had been in the water far too long."

"Every time I close my eyes I see spinning whirlpools and waves. It's making me dizzy." I leaned back against the stark white pillows, shivering. I felt incredibly cold. "I'm chilled to the bone."

"Your temperature's normal," Jordan Farrows said as he walked through the door. He was a doctor who specialized in magical ailments but I had started going to him because he was good at his job and I trusted him. "But you'll likely feel that intense chill for a while. You don't have the energy to spare to try to raise your heat level, so don't even think about it, but I'll have the nurse bring an extra blanket."

"How am I doing?" I shifted, trying to stop the feeling of motion. "It feels like everything spins when I move."

"You ended up with a lot of water in your ears. We drained them, but you're going to have one hell of an earache by tomorrow and you will probably have some pretty strong vertigo for a few days." He looked over my chart. "You should be fine, but you were knocked around a lot and you're going to have a lot of bruises. If you were human, you would have frozen to death. It looks like your sense of survival kicked in and you instinctively raised the temperature around your body enough to keep you alive, but it depleted you magically. You'll need to rest up for a while before you try any heavy-duty spells. Got it?"

"Yeah, I get it. When can I go home?" I wanted to hide out in my own bed, safe under the comforter.

"I'll discharge you around noon, if you feel up to leaving. But no driving for a few days. Agreed?" He tapped the chart with his pencil.

I nodded. "Agreed." Another flash of memory hit me and I reached for my neck, hoping that Aegis's present was still there. "My necklace—and my pentacle. Please don't tell me they were ripped away in the water."

"I'll have the nurse check. We have everything you came in with up front." And with that, Jordan started toward the door. He glanced over his shoulder. "You were very lucky, Maddy."

"I know," I said softly. "Can you disconnect the IVs now? I want to get up."

Jordan laughed. "Only you would ask that. Yes, I think you're fine now. We had to get some nutrients into you and you were—don't laugh—dehydrated." He motioned to the nurse, who began to disconnect the IVs from my arm. I winced as she withdrew the needle and put pressure on my arm for a moment, then taped a cotton ball over it.

I couldn't stand without the room spinning, so the nurse brought me a shower chair and I sat beneath the warm water, leery as it splashed down on me. Even though it felt good, the fact that it was showering my face made me feel claustrophobic and I was grateful when I was done.

Sandy helped me dress. She had brought me a change of clothes, and grateful, I slid into the warm, flowing dress. It was a soft knit, and I felt like I was snuggled in a soft blanket. I slipped on the socks and boots she had thought to bring, and she guided me over to the banquette by the window that overlooked the parking lot. The realization of how close I had come to dying hit home, and the fear from the night before rushed back. My stomach tightened into a knot.

"I almost bit the big one, Sandy. Is this how you felt when that car hit you?" I realized I was shaking. A few months back, in late June, a couple of discontented thugs had tried to take out my best friend. We had managed to catch them, but that had been far too close of a call.

"Yeah, pretty much. At least after I woke up in the hospital. During the attack, it was all too quick for me to really think much of anything."

I nodded. "Last night, all I can remember is the waves crashing over us and the chill of the water and Aegis trying his best to swim us to shore. If that wave hadn't pushed us in, I don't think I would have made it. Aegis would have, but not me."

Just then a nurse came in with an envelope. "I've brought your possessions that were on you when you came in."

I knew my purse wasn't there—which meant I'd have to replace all of my ID, as well as my phone and my keys. I opened the envelope and shook it out in my lap. There was my pentacle, and the necklace from Aegis. I slipped them around my neck before realizing there was something else in the envelope. As the last item landed in my hand, I gasped.

"Sandy…" I held it up.

The second pentacle was exactly like mine, only it was bronze. I looked over Sandy. She stared at it, then touched her chest, where her gold pentacle rested—again, exactly like mine.

"Fata," she whispered.

Fata, Sandy, and I had commissioned matching pentacles from a jeweler. He had made them, and mine was silver, Sandy's gold, and Fata's had been bronze. I turned the pentacle over and sure enough, on the back was an engraved "F."

"Is she really here? Did she bring me in? Aegis would have mentioned her, surely." I desperately wanted to talk to him, but he was asleep.

"He didn't say a word." Sandy slowly reached out and touched the pentacle sitting in my hand. "Fata. I wonder if she's on the island."

"The storm—it was her doing, I know it in my gut. She brought me to safety with her waves. That has to be it. But why didn't she stay?" I wasn't sure how I felt. Nearly drowning was rough enough, but wondering what Fata was up to added a whole 'nother level of stress.

"I think we'll have to wait until she decides to show herself. Maddy, it's been a long time. We don't know who we'll be dealing with. Fata Morgana was always on the wild side. I know you don't like talking about it, but when she left—s"

I cut her off. I really didn't feel like talking about that

last night, especially right now. "Yeah, she had slipped over the edge."

"Exactly. We don't know if she's still there, dancing on the wild side, or if she's had time to let the past go."

And with that, we fell silent. I wondered what Sandy was really thinking, but given I didn't know what I was thinking myself, I decided to change the subject until the doctor discharged me.

An hour later, I was ready to go. Sandy made me sit in a wheelchair until we reached the parking lot. When we were at her van, I stood and immediately was grateful for how pushy she had been. I almost faceplanted onto the asphalt. As she helped me into the passenger side, her phone rang.

"Can you get that while I run back to grab a bottle of water from the vending machine?" She motioned to her purse. "It's probably Max."

I pulled her phone out of her purse and frowned. The number was unfamiliar. "Cassandra Clauson's phone. May I take a message?"

"Is Ms. Clauson available?" The voice was deep and very, very business-like. "It's important. This is Mills Wayfair, her lawyer."

"She'll be back in a few moments. May I help you?" I wasn't sure if I could do anything, but he sounded insistent.

"Please have her call me back immediately." He hung up abruptly. I wasn't sure whether to be offended, but decided he was probably busy. If the news was as important as it seemed to be, he'd be focused on whatever it was and not up to playing Mr. Congeniality.

Sandy returned a few minutes later, water in hand.

"Phone your lawyer. He called and said he needs to talk to you and that it's important."

"It can wait till I get you home," Sandy said, buckling her seat belt and starting the van. She eased out of the parking lot and fifteen minutes later, we were sitting in my driveway. "Once I get you inside, I'll call Mills."

"Is he human?" A number of lawyers were human— they seemed to excel at the profession.

"No, actually." Sandy opened my door and helped me get out. She brushed off my insistence that I could make it into the house without a problem and guided me across the back yard from the driveway.

Kelson saw us coming and opened the door, running out to help. She, too, refused to listen to my protests and took my other arm. I felt like a little old lady they were helping to cross the street, but I bit back my irritation. The doctor had said I would be unsteady for a few days, and he was right— if Sandy and Kelson let go, I'd probably end up on my ass.

I eased into a kitchen chair and leaned back, sighing. "Sometimes, home looks mighty fine," I said.

"You hungry?"

"Oh gods, yes. Hospital food sucks. Well, actually, I didn't have hospital food. Just nutrients in an IV solution. So bring on the bacon." I flashed Kelson a wide smile, grateful for her presence.

Sandy pulled out her phone and moved off to one side to return Mills's call.

Kelson brought out a dozen eggs, a loaf of bread, and a

bowl of fruit salad. She began heating a skillet, then cracked three of the eggs into a bowl, pausing to gesture at Sandy. Sandy shook her head, so Kelson left it at that and whipped the eggs into a frothy blend, then poured them into the crackling skillet. She popped two pieces of bread into the toaster, then put away the carton of eggs and the rest of the loaf. After spooning fruit salad into a bowl, she began to scramble the eggs.

Sandy let out a soft cry. "You can't be serious?" She didn't sound excited, just shocked. "They couldn't be mistaken, could they?" A pause, then, "All right. Yes, I understand, No, I'm fine with that, but… Oh, Mills. How am I ever going to tell her?" She sounded heartbroken, now.

I straightened up, watching her carefully. Kelson quietly set my plate of toast and eggs in front of me, along with the bowl of fruit. I nodded her my thanks and absently sprinkled salt on the eggs and bit into them, my gaze glued to Sandy.

She was wiping away a tear, and she looked so bereft that I knew something had gone horribly wrong. A few more murmured words into her phone and she slowly dropped into the chair opposite me, setting her phone on the table. She stared at it like it might bite her.

"What's going on?" I asked.

She raised her gaze to meet mine. "Derry's dead. My lawyer called to tell me that Jenna's mother died, and she left specifications in the will that I am now Jenna's legal guardian."

I blinked. Derry Knight was a gadabout woman who probably never should have had children. She was fun loving and free-spirited, but not the best mother. Jenna had turned out remarkably well for a child whose main parent wasn't invested in their existence. Derry had taken off on a two-year world tour, leaving Jenna in Sandy's care, and Jenna was blossoming out. She lived at the Neverfall Academy for Gifted Students, but she stayed with Sandy every other weekend and knew she could always call us if she needed.

"Derry's *dead*? What happened?"

"Apparently, Derry was hiking in Kakadu National Park in Australia. They told her not to go out alone at night, because that's when a number of the venomous snakes come out." Sandy rubbed her forehead, pinching her brow between her fingers.

"I can see this one coming. Derry ignored their warnings." The little I remembered of Derry had mostly been her refusal to play by the rules.

"Yeah. She hiked out to Jim Jim Falls late one night. She slipped out of camp before their guide could notice. By the next morning, they discovered her disappearance. The guides went out to look for her and found her near the falls, dead. She had been bitten by a coastal taipan and she was dead when they found her." Sandy gave me a mute look. Finally, she said, "How the hell do I tell Jenna? It's up to me. I'm her legal guardian now."

"Do you want help? I can go with you." With food in my stomach, I felt like curling up under a fuzzy blanket and taking a nap, but if Sandy needed me, I was here.

She shook her head. "No, this is my responsibility. I'll ask Max if he can help. He's scheduled to leave on a business trip over to Bellingham for a day or so, but I think he'll have the time to drive up to Neverfall with me before he catches the ferry." She quietly accepted the mocha that Kelson pressed into her hands.

Kelson brought me a triple-shot mocha. Not as strong as I wanted it, but it would do for now. I sipped the frothy chocolate and peppermint and closed my eyes, trying not to picture Derry, lying there alone, dying. It was just too harsh.

Finally, I rested my elbows on the table. "Derry lived life on her own terms. She knew the dangers. She was warned and yet, she decided the risk was worth it. Sometimes you can play the odds and win, and other times, you lose. This time, her number came up. There's nothing you could have done to stop it. The best you can do now is to be strong for Jenna. I know Derry was your friend, but that little girl is going to need you. She adores you."

Sandy finished her drink, and pushed back from the table. "I know. Derry was selfish, when it comes down to it. She never cared as much about Jenna as she did herself. I'll head out now."

"Let me know how it goes," I said, waving as she left.

Kelson carried my empty dishes back to the sink. I let out a long sigh, staring at the table. "Well, it's been one hell of a twenty-four hours. Last night was Aegis's and my first anniversary. I guess the party got a little wild, didn't it?"

She settled in at the table with me. "You know, sometimes life just likes to put the hammer down on celebrations. But you're both safe, and I imagine after you've had a few days to relax, you'll be fine."

I thought of the bronze pentacle in my pocket. "Fine" wasn't exactly the word I would use to describe my life at this moment. I wasn't sure whether to tell her about Fata

Morgana. Kelson lived in the Bewitching Bedlam. She would find out sooner or later, but right now, I needed to process everything that had happened.

I was saved from making a decision when the house phone rang. Kelson went to answer it, and that reminded me that I needed a new cell phone as soon as possible. And identification, and I had to call the bank about my credit cards, all of which were lying at the bottom of the Salish Sea.

"It's Delia," Kelson said, bringing me the cordless unit.

"Hey, what's shaking?" I wasn't sure if Delia had heard what happened to me. She had to have tried my cell phone.

"You lose your phone? I've been trying to get you all day." She sounded worried and irritated, rolled up into one.

I let out a soft breath. "I spent part of last night and this morning in the hospital, and right now my phone, along with my identification and credit cards, is down under the water, feeding the fishies. What's going on?"

That stopped her, but only for a moment. "What happened?"

"Aegis and I went out for a midnight boat ride to celebrate our first anniversary and unfortunately, the storm broke the boat and sent us into the water. If it hadn't been for Aegis I would have died. He did his best to swim to shore with me, but I passed out. A giant wave came in, swirling us into the shore. I'm not sure of what happened after that. I don't even remember being on the beach. I woke up in the hospital, with Sandy by my side.

"She said that Aegis had managed to save me. Garret had come down to check on us, since we were in his boat.

He was worried about the storm and with good reason. He found us there on the shore. I'm not sure what would've happened if he hadn't come to check. Aegis would probably have managed to get me to safety and then himself into the dark, but there's no telling."

For a moment, Delia was silent. Then she said, "Maddy, I'm so glad you're all right. I had no idea. We didn't get any notice at the station—and even if we did—I was home for the evening with a stomachache. Is there anything you need?"

"Well, I can't drive for a few days. Apparently I have a serious case of vertigo. I need to get a new copy of my driver's license, and I need to buy a new phone. I can do the latter online, but I think to replace my driver's license they're going to want to see me in person. Could you drive me there? Sandy had some bad news this afternoon and she had to leave."

I could have asked Kelson to take me out to get my license, but I didn't like to leave the Bewitching Bedlam empty. Granted, we only had Mr. Mosswood as a guest, but you never knew who was going to drop in. I also had a feeling Delia wanted to talk to me and right now, I didn't feel like talking on the phone.

"Do you mind if I drop over? I'd be happy to take you down to the DMV, and there's something else I want to talk to you about. I might as well do it in person. I can be there in fifteen minutes."

"That's fine. I'll have to ask you to help me out to your car because I'm a little unsteady on my feet." I hated asking for help, and it was hard for me to admit when I needed assistance. I was the first one there when my friends needed help, and I was always willing to lend a hand. But when it came to my own needs, like a good share of the women in this country—be they human or witches—I always put myself last.

"You can always ask me for help, Maddy. You know that. I'll see you in a little bit." The line went silent and I handed the phone back to Kelson.

DELIA DIDN'T BOTHER COMING TO THE FRONT DOOR WHEN she arrived. She just came around back and knocked on the slider. I motioned for her to come in. The worried look on her face concerned me, and I had the feeling it wasn't for my benefit. Which meant something was wrong.

Gingerly, I stood, holding the table for balance. The room swayed like a pendulum. Yeah, I wasn't ready to walk on my own.

"Whoa, I feel like I was partying all night instead of flailing around in the water." I grasped the back of the nearest chair as my knees folded and my butt abruptly met the chair seat. "Okay, so much for that attempt."

"Are you sure you should go downtown?" Kelson hurried over, frowning. She glanced at Delia. "Maddy just got home from the hospital. I'm not sure if it's a good idea that she goes out."

"Thank you, mother hen, but I'm all right." Even though I didn't feel okay, I wasn't about to admit it.

Delia stared at me for a moment. "I think your driver's license can wait for a day. Come on, let me help you into the living room so you can rest."

"You too? I'm fine, really." With both of them hovering over me, I knew I'd never get anything done.

Delia backed up about five feet away from me, away from the chairs. "All right, I challenge you. You walk to me without falling down or weaving, and we can go. No using the chairs for balance, and one misstep sends your ass into the parlor, to rest on the sofa."

"Challenge accepted." I motioned for her to step back. As I cautiously stood, another wave of dizziness rushed through my head. I tried to steady myself, taking a deep breath and letting it out slowly as I set one foot in front of the other. The first two steps I managed. But on the third, everything went rushing around me in a widening circle. The room was starting to spin. Before Delia could jump to help me, I landed on the ground on my knees and elbows.

"Maddy, are you all right?" Kelson ran forward and knelt beside me. I lifted my head, having a hard time focusing on her face.

"Uhhh…" I couldn't speak, I was so queasy.

"I thought so." Delia motioned to Kelson. "Help me get her up and into the parlor."

Together, they carried me into the parlor, where they unceremoniously dumped me on the sofa, with a bunch of pillows behind my back. I moaned. I had bruised my knees when I hit the floor. We had beautiful tile in the kitchen, but it was a hard surface to fall on and it wasn't smooth. Instead, it was slate slabs that jutted up enough in some areas. Kelson took one look at my knees and elbows and vanished, calling back over her shoulder that she was going for first-aid supplies.

"I don't need first aid. I'm all right. And I *don't* want to spend my day stuck on the sofa." I was starting to feel cranky. The past twenty-four hours had been one big clusterfuck and I was right at the center of it.

"You stay put. You're in no shape to be going anywhere. What did your doctor tell you?"

I started to huff, but then gave it up. I didn't even have the energy to be indignant. "Jordan told me to go home and stay off my feet for four days. I guess you're right. I'm in no more shape to go shopping than I am to run a marathon."

"Then that's what you need to do. I can talk to you right here, and when you're feeling better I will happily drive you down to the DMV to get your license. It's not like anybody swiped it and is going to try to steal your identity. And you can make a call to the credit card company from the sofa." Delia pulled a chair over next to the sofa and sat down, leaning back as though she had had a rough day.

"You were going to talk to me about something. What happened?"

Kelson came through the door right then with bandages and antibiotic ointment. Delia waited until she had finished doctoring my knees and my elbows. Then, without a word, Kelson vanished back through the kitchen door.

"We have a problem on our hands," she said. "We found a dead body this morning about ten minutes from Neverfall."

"Not a student?" I asked, instantly worried about Jenna.

"No, this was a woman. I'm not sure of her age but she looked to be in her thirties. I believe that she's a shifter, but I'm not certain. We couldn't find any identification on her, but I think she's from Bedlam. She looks familiar, but I can't place her." Delia pressed the tips of her fingers together as she stared at the floor.

"What happened to her? You wouldn't be telling me this unless there was something suspicious going on."

She gave me a long look, then nodded slowly. "The reason I'm telling you this is because it was a vampire kill. She was drained of blood. Exsanguinated. I don't think there was a drop left in her body." Delia closed her eyes and shook her head. "It was ugly, Maddy. A brutal death. The fang marks were deep and thick, and it looked like whoever the vampire was, they meant it to hurt."

I caught my breath. Vampire kills in Bedlam were rare, especially since the vampires who lived here remained on notice of good behavior. The town council allowed them to stay as long as they behaved themselves. And I was on the town council.

"Have there been any other attacks that you know of?"

"No. That doesn't mean there haven't been any, but none have come to our attention. Maddy, have you talked to Essie lately?"

I happened to know the Queen of the Pacific Northwest Vampire Nation. Actually, I had an uneasy truce with Essie Vanderbilt. We shared several secrets that neither of us wanted the rest of the island to know. Delia knew about them, and a few others, but if the knowledge we shared managed to get out to the general populace, there would be widespread panic and that was the last thing either of us wanted.

"I haven't talked to Essie for a while, actually. It looks like it might be time to pay her a visit."

"Not until you're in good-enough shape that you can run. Though time may be of the essence. I hate to ask this, but can you call her and ask her to come over to your place?"

I shook my head. "No way am I letting Essie Vanderbilt in my house. However, Aegis could drive me over there after he wakes up, and stick around to make sure that I'm safe. I can ask Essie to meet us in front of her house. That may be the best way to go about this. I don't trust her in my house. Even though I could rescind the invitation, you never know what spells she's dug up." Realizing what I had just said, I shut my mouth before Delia could ask what I meant. There were some secrets I hadn't told her, for her own safety.

"I suppose that will have to do. Thank you, Maddy. You know I wouldn't ask if it weren't important. We haven't had a vampire kill on Bedlam in fifty years. At least not vampire against one of the Otherkin. And definitely not a vampire against the humans. The only ones that the vampires have killed in those fifty years are other vampires."

"Don't forget about Rose. In the end, she was a vampire casualty, even though she was killed with a knife."

"You're right." Delia rose, straightening the top of her uniform. She stared at me for a moment, then added, "Be careful. Remember, you're a target and you know why. Never forget that, because the moment you do, they'll come out of the woodwork after you. And that's the last thing you want."

I hesitated, wondering if I should tell her about Fata Morgana, then decided she had enough on her mind already. After all, anticipating a visit from an old friend who was fucknuts cuckoo was quite a different thing than worrying about a rogue vampire running around town killing people.

As Kelson showed Delia to the door, I yawned and leaned back against the pillows, grateful that they had made me stay home. Before I knew what was happening, Bubba and Luna were curled up on my legs and I fell asleep to the soft hush of the wind blowing outside.

CHAPTER FOUR

I woke up around five o'clock. Kelson happened to be leaning over the back of the sofa, staring at me. I jumped as I opened my eyes and saw her eyeing me.

"What? Have I grown an extra head?"

"I just wanted to make sure you were still breathing." She smiled as she said it, so it didn't seem quite so creepy.

"I seem to be breathing just fine, thank you." I struggled to sit up. I was still dizzy, though I didn't feel quite as wiped out. "Can you help me into the bathroom? You don't need to stay with me when I'm in there."

Kelson leaned down so I could slide one of my arms around her shoulders. I eased myself to my feet. So far, so good. I took a step with her help, and realized it wasn't nearly as rough as it had been earlier in the day. It took a few moments, but she got me to the downstairs powder room. I had made it as spacious as possible when I had had it renovated, and one of the things that I had thought to put in were handrails along the side of the wall. That way if I ever had a disabled guest, they would be able to use the facilities without a problem.

Of course, they wouldn't be able to get to the rooms upstairs. A little lightbulb went off over my head as I thought about adding on an extra bedroom to the house on the main floor. Then I could advertise it as available for disabled accommodations. I'd also add a side ramp by the front porch steps so they wouldn't have to go around to the kitchen slider to get in.

I managed to use the toilet and wash my hands and face without a problem. I tapped on the door and Kelson opened it, helping me to the kitchen. As she set me down at the table, the room began to spin again, but I held onto the table and it stopped after a moment.

"Are you hungry?" She moved over to the stove where I smelled something bubbling. "Since it's only Mr. Mosswood and us tonight, I decided to make a pot of chicken soup and a pan of biscuits. Henry asked for a tray for his room. He's been eating in there the past few nights. I hope he's all right."

"I hope he's all right, too. He's usually more conversational. Maybe he's just had a rough week. Writing a book can't be all that easy, can it?"

A cloud of steam wafted over from the stove, bringing with it the incredible smell of mouthwatering soup. Chicken soup was one of my favorites; it was a comfort food. It took me back to Ireland, when Granny used to make a pot of soup on cold winter nights. Zara had never been one for cooking, and Granny was so particular with her demands that my mother had just let her take over the kitchen.

"I didn't think I was hungry, but the smell of that soup

is making me salivate. I would love a bowl, and a couple biscuits."

"One thing I've learned from Aegis is to make enough for unexpected company." Kelson went to call Henry to the table while I picked up the cordless phone and, after a moment of trying to remember Sandy's number, punched it in.

"Clauson residence, Alex speaking. May I help you?"

"Hey Alex, it's Maddy. Is Sandy there?"

"She's with Jenna right now. Is this really important, because we've had some bad news here today. I don't know if you heard, but Jenna's mother was killed in Australia."

"I was with Sandy when she got the news so yes, I know. This isn't an emergency, so just ask her to call me back as soon as she can. Is Max there?"

"No, he caught the ferry for Bellingham. I'll tell her you called."

"Thanks, Alex. Be sure to remind her that I lost my phone, so she'll have to call the house."

Alex paused, then said, "That's right. You were almost killed last night. How are you doing?"

"I'm alive, although I won't be clubbing for a few days. Sometimes that's the best we can hope for, right?"

As I hung up, I felt the weight of the world settle on my shoulders. My mood had plummeted with the news about the vampire kill. That, combined with a night spent in the ocean, and the knowledge that Fata Morgana was out there somewhere aimed for Bedlam's shore, and my world had suddenly turned upside down. I wanted to stand up without the room spinning. I wanted to not have to worry about a rogue vampire on the loose. And deep in my heart, I realized I wasn't sure I wanted to ever see Fata Morgana again.

We were partway through dinner when Aegis appeared at the top of the stairs. I started to stand but once again the room swirled, just enough to send me back onto my chair again.

He said nothing, but strode over to the table and cautiously pulled me into his embrace, holding me so tight that I almost couldn't breathe. I started to speak but he silenced me with a kiss, running his hand through my hair. After a moment, he pulled away, slipping onto his knees on the floor in front of me, clutching my hands.

"Oh Maddy, you don't know how worried I was. I couldn't go to the hospital with you because it was too close to morning, and even though Sandy and the EMTs promised me that you would be all right, I kept having visions of you slipping away into the water and not being able to reach you. I can't believe I put you in such danger." He was crying, crimson tears trailing down from his eyes. Vampires cried blood. He laid his head on my knees. "Please forgive me. I'll never put you in danger again."

"Aegis, *I don't blame you*. It was a lovely gesture. In retrospect, we were both idiots to go out on that boat—you just don't go boating in a storm like that. But hindsight is twenty-twenty. You *saved* me. If I had been out there alone, I would have died." I stroked his hair back from his face and touched one of his tears, bringing my finger to my lips.

He jerked his head up. "Don't taste my blood, Maddy. It's not safe."

"What would happen if I did?"

"Just don't. We'll talk about that later." He took my finger and licked it clean.

I urged him to get up, and he slid into the chair next to me, leaning close to gaze in my eyes. "The fact is, you never would have gone out there if it hadn't been for me. Can you honestly tell me you would have gone boating in the middle of the night if you had been on your own?"

"My love, I can't answer that. Hell, I've done a lot of dangerous things in my lifetime. Forget about blame. I'm all right. Yes, I have some vertigo, and I'm not supposed to drive for four days according to Jordan. I'm a little unstable on my feet, but I'm all right. *Please* don't blame yourself." I motioned to the table. "Kelson made soup, and biscuits. Come and eat. It may not fill your stomach, but it's warm and comforting."

We spent the rest of the evening talking about what had happened. I showed him the pentacle and told him it belonged to Fata Morgana. Aegis stared at it silently for a moment.

"So you really think she is coming back?"

"I think she's already back. It's a matter of when she shows herself. And I also think she was the one who pushed us to shore with that wave. What I don't know is what she wants, and neither does Sandy. And that makes her dangerous. As much as I loved Fata, she's wild and unpredictable. There's another thing that I need to discuss with you—actually two."

Telling him about Jenna's mother was going to be difficult, Aegis had taken a liking to the girl and always asked how she was doing. But telling him about the vampire kill was going to be even harder. Aegis prided himself on his restraint and his ethics. Vampires who went around ripping people's throats out pissed him off to no end. Not only that, but when he found out I needed to visit Essie, he wasn't going to be happy.

Aegis wasn't comfortable with my association with the vampire queen. And quite honestly, I didn't enjoy hanging out with her, especially since she had kidnapped me and used me to cover her tracks. Granted, she had good reasons for what she had done, but I still didn't like finding myself a pawn in a game of vampire politics.

"You look worried," he said. "Did I do something wrong? Other than almost get both of us killed?"

"Oh, don't go all Angel on me." I still rewatched episodes of *Buffy*. "I can't handle an emo-vampire boyfriend. Just…it happened, it was a freak accident, it's over."

He shook his head and, for the first time since he had woken up, smiled. "All right. I won't play the angsty boy toy."

"You're not my boy toy. You're my lover. Okay, well, this afternoon, Sandy received a call from her lawyer when she was driving me home. Derry did what Derry always does and broke the rules. Only this time, it was a fatal mistake. She rambled off on her own after the guide told her not to, and she got herself killed by a coastal taipan snake. The woman always did have numbnuts for brains. I hate to say that. She and Sandy were good friends. But truthfully? I think Jenna is better off with Sandy."

Aegis stared at me. "Jenna's mother died from

snakebite?" He paused, thinking. "Does that mean her father's going to come take over?"

"Nobody knows who he is. Derry never told anybody who Jenna's father was. I think she did it to protect both herself and Jenna from him. She hung out with some scary-ass dudes. Anyway, she stipulated in her will that Sandy's to become Jenna's legal guardian."

"This is going to change Sandy's life. I mean, it's one thing to be somebody's temporary guardian, but this basically means that Sandy is Jenna's mother now. How do you think she's going to react?" Sometimes, Aegis could ask incredibly astute questions.

"You want my honest opinion?"

He nodded.

"I think Sandy has come to love that little girl a whole lot more than she would admit. I never pegged her as the nurturing type, but sometimes people can surprise you." I shivered. The Bewitching Bedlam had been fully insulated when we renovated it, but still, it was a big old house and big old houses had drafts. I shrugged into a sweater that was hanging over the back of my chair.

"What about you? Your mother asked me when she was here, what about children? I mean, it's obvious that you and I can't have any. Do *you* want to be a mother?"

I could see the fear in Aegis's eyes, and I could hear the hesitation in his voice. He was afraid that I would leave him someday, in favor of someone who could give me children. I thought carefully how to answer his question, because I wasn't sure myself.

"I'm not sure whether I ever want children. I'm not particularly geared toward being anybody's mother. I love being an auntie—although granted, I don't think I'll ever be able to become one of the Aunties. But if you're asking if I'm going to leave you because you can't get me pregnant, then stop worrying. There are so many other ways of becoming a parent. There's adoption, and fostering, and even surrogacy if it came down to it. When we were in the water and I thought I was going to drown, the only thing I could think of was how much I would miss you. I love you, Aegis. I hope you realize just how much you hold my heart in your hands." I held up the necklace that he had given me the night before. "I may have the key to your heart, but you have my heart in your hands. Now, carry me into the parlor and let's light a fire in the fireplace."

He did, setting me on the sofa before he lit the kindling that was arranged in the fireplace. One of Kelson's duties was to make sure the fireplaces were laid and ready to light.

I pulled a fleece throw over me as we watched the fire crackle. Bubba came bouncing through the room, chased by Luna. They tussled, rolling over into a wrestling match, before Luna sat on top of Bubba and began to groom his face. I laughed, relieved to find something that didn't leave me with an "oh-shit" feeling.

Aegis relaxed. He sat on the end of the sofa and pulled my feet onto his lap, rubbing them gently. I leaned my head back, enjoying the massage, desperately wanting to watch some sort of mindless sitcom or cartoon, but I still had the other piece of news to tell him, and I decided to do so before we relaxed any further.

"There's one other piece of bad news."

Aegis paused, his knuckle pressing into a knot on the midpoint of my arch. "Oh?"

"Yeah. This one's a doozy. Delia dropped by today, and she had some news. There's been a vampire kill on the island. She wants me to talk to Essie tonight, to see if she knows anything. Apparently it was brutal, Aegis. Brutal and vicious. Whoever attacked the woman completely drained her."

Aegis slowly let go of my feet, his shoulders stiffening. "And she's absolutely sure it's a vampire? I'm not questioning her skill, but she needs to be very, very sure of this."

I let out my breath, huddling under the fleece throw a little bit more. The wind was whipping outside, scraping the roof. It sounded like animals skittering across the shingles. The storm had started again—or maybe it was a new one—and out the parlor window, rain pounded down so hard that it looked like snow.

"Delia knows a vampire kill when she sees it. I'm not sure what's going on, but we can't let it continue."

"No, of course not. Have there been any other attacks?"

"Not that she knows of, but that doesn't mean there haven't been any not come to light yet. Aegis, Essie keeps rigid control over the vampires who live in her nest. She wouldn't let this happen on her watch. I don't trust her, and I doubt I ever will, but she needs to know about this too, because she's going to want to know if any rogue vamps are in the area. I need you to take me over to talk to her, since I'm not supposed to drive and I don't want her coming here."

He nodded. "Right. I don't like the idea, but I suppose this can't be helped. When do you want to go? Surely, you need to rest tonight?"

"I need to call her. Meanwhile, please run out and buy me a new phone. I can activate it online and back it up from the cloud. Once I have it, I'll give her a call."

"I'll be back in an hour. Meanwhile, I'm telling Kelson to lock up. Don't let anybody in unless you know who they are." And with that, Aegis grabbed his leather jacket and headed out the door.

While Aegis was gone, I decided to tackle a task I had been putting off for several weeks. I had made a promise to my mother, and now it was time to fulfill it. I called for Kelson and asked her to bring me my office chair, which was on wheels. Using that, I was able to roll myself into my office. I sat down at the computer and pulled up my email. There, in an email I hadn't opened yet, was the name and contact information for my half-brother—Gregory Oakstone.

Zara had made me promise to contact him when she died. I had tried to encourage her to reach out before then, to give him a chance to know who she was. But she refused to believe that he would forgive her for giving him up.

I clicked on the email. My mother's solicitors had done their work. Gregory Oakstone was alive and well, and living in London. They even had his email address for me. I tried to decide whether the shock would be less via email or through a phone call. I finally decided an email would give him more time to process the information. I opened a new message and typed in his email address, and then sat staring at the screen, trying to figure out exactly what to say.

Dear Gregory: You don't know me, but we have something in common. My mother's solicitors indicate that you know you are adopted. What you probably don't know is who your birth mother was, or that you have a half-sister. I never knew you existed until a couple months ago, and my mother made me promise not to contact you until after her death. My name is Maudlin Gallowglass. I want to tell you the story of our mother, and why she was forced to give you up when you were a baby.

The hardest part of the letter over, I leaned back and stared at the words. Then, with a sigh, I went into explaining my mother's story. Finally, half an hour later, I took a deep breath and hit send. Now, all I could do was wait.

By the time Aegis returned, I had managed to roll myself to the bathroom, and then back into the kitchen where I was sitting in my makeshift wheelchair, eating cookies. I had managed to eat a dozen of them, and was contemplating another handful. I considered my restraint a triumph, given the emotions raging within me. At least sending Gregory the email had taken my mind off of Fata Morgana.

Aegis glanced at the tray and a smile crinkled the edges of his lips. "I suppose I'd better make some more cookies while I'm at it. Let me help you to the computer so you can activate your new phone. I got you the latest model, and they said as long as your information is on the cloud, you can do everything over the phone and online."

I grabbed another handful of cookies before he rolled me back to the office. I told him that I had emailed my brother.

"Clever idea with your office chair."

"It's amazing what you can think of when you have to."

I glanced at my email. No answer yet. Not that I had expected one this soon, but I was knew that I'd be checking my email several times a day until I heard back from him.

Suddenly, a thought hit me. What if he *didn't* write back? What if he didn't want to talk to me? There wouldn't be much I could do about it, but the thought of never hearing back from him made my stomach clench. I didn't even know him and yet, I knew that I wanted some form of contact, especially now that Zara was dead and I knew her full story.

Trying to push the thought from my mind, I opened the box and pulled out the sleek new phone. There was something about gadgets that I loved, and technology never ceased to amaze me. I had seen the days when the newest gadget had been the latest torture device to use against witches. That kind of advancement I could do without.

As I immersed myself in playing with my new phone, Aegis went back in the kitchen to make cookies. He left me a loud bell to ring if I needed him. I logged into my account at the phone company's website, and as I began to download the information I needed, Franny appeared.

"You really got yourself in a tangle last night, didn't you? I'm so glad that you didn't drown. Do you know I've never been in the water? My mother didn't believe in girls learning how to swim." She settled into a chair nearby and remarkably, didn't sink halfway through it, but looked like she was actually sitting on it.

Grateful to see her, I leaned back and turned around. "What *did* your mother believe in girls doing? It seems like she kept you from a whole lot of things."

"My mother believed that women were decorative until they got married, at which point their job was to direct servants, spend money, and generally make everybody miserable. I swear to you, she lived for making other people jump."

"Why do you think that was?"

Franny mused. "I think she was unhappy. I've been thinking about what we found out about my aunt and my father, and I think that Mother somehow knew about the affair, even though she never said a word." She paused for a moment, then said, "I wonder where she and my father went after they died. Same with my aunt. I have no clue where any of my family went after death. I never thought about it before, but now it seems so strange. None of them came back to see me, and yet it seems that at least my aunt and my father knew that I was around here."

That did seem strange, now that she mentioned it. "Would you want to see them? Do you feel like you're a different person than you were in life? Do you think they would be different?"

Franny shrugged. "I suppose I'm different, yes. I know

more, and if I could just be free of this curse there would be so much to explore. You know, I've never met another ghost, actually. Except for the ones in the online support group I found a few weeks back. That seems strange to me, doesn't it to you?"

I nodded. It did. "Tell me more about this group. What's the name of it?"

"STOE—short for 'Spirits Trapped on Earth.' It's a group for spirits who are trapped in this plane in one way or another, and who've managed to find a connection in cyberspace. We all know we're dead, so that lets out the ones who are trapped and don't know what's going on. And we keep out the hostiles. The ones who hate the living."

"What do you talk about?"

"Oh, esoteric things, I suppose. All of us lived in different times and have managed to keep up with the world. A few of the others actually seem to exist *inside* cyberspace—it's as though they became part of the computer." A pensive look crossed her face. "For some reason, that also seems dangerous to me."

I managed to hook up my phone to my computer and began downloading information from the cloud. As I thought about what Franny had said, it occurred to me how incredibly multifaceted the world was. There were so many things in it that we didn't understand, even those of us who had been around for several hundred years.

"I suppose it could be, if they could get hold of information that is private. Or if they could somehow affect information in cyberspace. After all, if you had the right equipment and the right contacts, you could probably set off a world war."

Franny's hand fluttered to her mouth. "Oh my, I hadn't even thought about that possibility."

As I finished the last cookie, Franny went on to lighter subjects. She told me all about the book she was reading, and then segued into her latest Netflix addiction. She had discovered the world of *Friends*, and was binge watching it.

"I'm in season three," she said. "Do you think Ross and Rachel will ever get married?"

I forced myself not to smile. "I am not giving you spoilers. You'll just have to watch and see for yourself."

The doorbell rang. Before I thought about it, I started to stand but I had made it two steps before Aegis went racing by in a flash. I fell back into my chair.

"You sit your pretty ass down," he called out.

Shaking my head, I obeyed. A few minutes later, he peeked around the door.

"It's Ralph. Do you want to see him? He's in the living room and I don't really feel comfortable bringing him in the office." Aegis was extremely protective of me around Ralph. The satyr had seemingly reformed, but ever since he showed up in my bathroom while I was in the shower, Aegis had given him the side-eye. He didn't trust Ralph and I had the feeling he never would. Come to think of it, *I* didn't trust Ralph. Even though I accepted his apologies for the mess as he had made in my life, I had the feeling that one good round of partying would set him off again.

"Yeah, help me into the living room. Might as well make my day even more miserable."

Aegis slipped into the office and before I could say a word, he swept me up in his arms.

"I said help me into the living room, not carry me." But I took the opportunity to give him a quick kiss.

"Oh, hush. Let me carry you around, considering I'm the one who almost drowned you. I don't care it was an accident, I don't care that you keep saying *no blame.* I *do* blame myself. I put you in danger in a way that I never want to happen again." And with that he carried me into the living room and gently deposited me on the sofa. Ralph was sitting in one of the wing chairs, staring at us as we entered the room.

"I heard you almost bit the big one last night," he said.

"You heard right. Aegis and I had an accident out on the water when the storm came up. It was a rough night. What can I do for you?"

Ralph hemmed and hawed, crossing and then uncrossing his hooves. "I know I have no right, and this is probably not the best time, but I have a favor to ask."

I grabbed Aegis's wrist as he tensed. "And what might that be?"

Ralph blushed. "I feel like a fool asking you, Maddy. But Ivy's birthday is coming up, and I want to buy her something nice, but I don't know what to get her. Can you help me figure out a present for her? I was going to get her a negligee from Frederick's of Hollywood, but then I stopped and asked myself, would that be something Maddy would buy? And somehow I didn't think so."

Oh my gods, I thought. *Ralph is playing WWMD, now?*

I blinked. "Why would you ask yourself if I would buy a negligee from Frederick's of Hollywood?" That seemed a little intimate to me.

"I mean, I thought about whether you would buy something like that for Aegis. Somehow, I just can't see it."

I was having a hard time keeping a straight face. Beside me, Aegis let out a snort.

"I hope she wouldn't buy me something like that. I don't look good in marabou."

Ralph grew even more flustered. "I didn't mean that *you* would wear a negligee. I mean she wouldn't buy you a cock ring or something like that, would she?" The moment the words came out of his mouth he gasped. "I mean, she might, but for your birthday?"

I was tempted to let him run on for a while and stuff both of his feet into his mouth, but finally I took pity.

"Stop, Ralph. Just stop. I get what you mean. How long have you been dating her, and are you even sleeping with her? Or is that a stupid question?"

Ralph shrugged, looking about as miserable as I had ever seen him look.

"Actually, yes, we are sleeping together. But it was her decision. We've been dating for a few months. Remember, I told you a couple months ago I had met her at a solstice party? And we're exclusive, believe it or not. But this is her birthday, it's not an anniversary or anything. And I want something nice for her."

I thought for a moment. Wood nymphs—and Ivy Vine was a wood nymph—liked expensive presents. They were high-maintenance partners, and easy to offend. I had the feeling that Ralph wasn't the one in charge of this relationship.

"What kind of perfume does she wear?"

"I'm not sure. Should I ask her?"

"I swear, sometimes you're clueless." Most of the time, actually, I thought. "No, I don't think you should *ask* her. Wood nymphs tend to have a temper, and if she thinks that you haven't been paying attention to what perfume she wears, she's probably going to bean you one. You know what I suggest? Plant her favorite tree on your property."

Ralph gave me a startled look. "But then she'd move in. I'm not ready for that yet."

"I give up. Buy her a beautiful emerald necklace. Wood nymphs tend to like emeralds. And make sure the setting and chain are 18-karat gold. Don't stint on the bling. That would be the easiest way to make certain that she ends up your *ex*-girlfriend." I paused, wondering whether his parsimonious nature would outweigh his libido. Wood nymphs were the ideal partners for satyrs, given their incredible sexual appetites. They make good matches, but yeah, the wood nymph usually ran the relationship.

Ralph let out a long sigh. "All right. I'll buy her a necklace. Thanks, Maddy. I hope you feel better." And with that, Aegis escorted him to the door, and I went back to configuring my new phone.

CHAPTER FIVE

By the time Ralph left, it was around nine o'clock, and my phone had finished configuring. Luckily for me, I backed everything up in the cloud, even though I didn't trust it very much.

"I suppose I'd better call Essie," I said. I wasn't exactly looking forward to it. The Queen of the Pacific Northwest Vampire Nation was intimidating, and I always felt on guard around her. But given the circumstances, I felt it was my civic duty. Vampire kills were serious business in Bedlam. Actually, they were serious business anywhere you went, but here in Bedlam they were few and far between because of our rules. When a rogue vampire broke those rules, we didn't look the other way.

"I still don't like it," Aegis said. "I think Essie's trouble, and I don't like the fact that she pulled you into her business. By doing so, she's made you more of a target. And *that* pisses me off." He glowered at me, twisting his mouth as though he had just eaten something rotten.

"I know you don't like Essie. I don't like her either, but

you *can't* go off on her. Do you realize what would happen if you staked her? It would bring far too much attention from the rest of the vampires to Bedlam, and we already have problems with the fangster set. I don't want to engage them anymore than I have to."

Aegis slumped back in his chair. "I'll be good. I promise. I don't like you hanging out over there, though. I don't trust Essie and I don't trust any of her cronies."

"Your protests are duly noted," I said with a smile. "Now why don't you run off into the kitchen and finish baking while I give her a call? Then we'll drive over for a visit."

As he took off into the kitchen, saying something to Kelson that I couldn't catch, I put in a call to Essie. I didn't expect to actually reach her, given she had an assistant named Shar-Shar, a pit bull of a secretary who ran interference between the outer world and the vampire Queen. Sharlene was aware of her position, and considered herself about five notches above the general populace. She was extremely proud that she had never been fed on, and that she wasn't a bloodwhore. She was also pretentious as hell. The phone rang three times before Shar-Shar picked it up.

"Essie Vanderbilt's residence, Sharlene speaking. To whom do I have the pleasure of addressing?"

"Maudlin Gallowglass. And I need to talk to Essie, pronto. It's important. I suggest you put her on the phone immediately." I had my own prestige in town and my own weight that I could throw around.

Sharlene cleared her throat. "Ms. Vanderbilt is otherwise occupied right now. May I take a message?"

"You can tell her that she better call Maddy right away, or there's going to be trouble." And with that, I hung up.

It wasn't more than five minutes before Essie called me back.

"Maddy, what's going on? Sharlene is fit to be tied. She tells me you were rude to her."

"Sharlene should be used to that by now. Listen, Essie. There's trouble in town and I need to talk to you about it. It's something I'd rather not discuss over the phone, so can I come over tonight? Aegis will have to drive me, given I'm not allowed behind the wheel of a car for the next few days."

There was a pause. I didn't hear Essie breathing, of course, because she didn't breathe. But I could hear the wheels turning in her head.

"It's that important?"

"You haven't heard yet, or you'd know why I want to talk to you. Delia asked me to pay you a visit. There's been a *murder* in town." And that was all I wanted to say. Even on a new phone, I didn't trust that nobody was listening in. There were some very tech-savvy people in town, and everybody seemed to have hidden agendas.

Essie grew very quiet. Then, after a moment, she said, "Come over in an hour. I'll make sure we have privacy."

"Actually, about that, can you meet me out at the car? I had an unfortunate run-in with the rogue wave last night out in the straits. I have a horrible case of vertigo, and I can barely walk." All of a sudden, the dizziness seemed to pay off. Anytime I could avoid dropping into Essie's house, the better.

Essie laughed. "That's the oddest thing I've heard in a long time. You'll have to tell me all about your adventure.

All right, call me when you arrive and I'll meet you out at the car. And tell Aegis I look forward to seeing him."

She hung up, the latter comment feeling more of a threat than a greeting. Essie didn't like Aegis because he had refused to join her vampire nest, and because he didn't take her seriously. But he was a lot older than she was, and a lot more powerful, except for the Voudou that she had learned when she was alive.

Essie Vanderbilt was born in New Orleans, in 1844. She had studied with Marie Laveau, who had been the Queen of New Orleans Voodoo and then, later on, with Marie's daughter. Over the years Essie grew in power until she was one of the most respected Voudou priestesses there was. By the time she was thirty, people were coming from all around to ask for her help. Unfortunately, a few years later—when she was thirty-three—Essie ran into the bad side of a vampire in a dark alley. No human would ever dare hurt her, but Philippe, a Parisian vampire, didn't pay much attention to human spellcasters. He was an old vampire, although I wasn't sure whether or not he had been part of the Arcānus Nocturni. He was also considered the Vampire King of the Southern States at the time, before the vampire nation had divided off into official regions.

Philippe had attempted to seduce Essie for some time, thinking to align his power with hers over both humans and vampires. She wasn't interested, but like so many "nice men," Philippe refused to take no for an answer. He killed her and turned her, expecting her to knuckle under. He had been in for a surprise.

As a vampire, Essie managed to retain some of her powers as a Voudou priestess, although she was ousted from her House, and she started a blood feud against Philippe. It ended in front of his court, with a stake through his heart and Essie standing triumphant over his ashes.

Shaking thoughts of the vampire queen out of my head, I called out to Aegis.

"We're due at Essie's in about fifty minutes. So if you're in the middle of baking anything, you'd better get it in the oven now and put a timer on for Kelson. Can you help me to the bathroom?"

Kelson darted in. "Aegis is beating the egg whites for a meringue and asked me if I could help you. He'll be done in twenty minutes. I'll watch as the goodies bake. He made me promise not to eat them. At least all of them." She grinned. We all loved Aegis's baking and I couldn't imagine not having a ready-made source of bakery-quality treats on a regular basis.

After she helped me to the bathroom, where I took care of business and then fixed my makeup and hair, I asked her to help me to the kitchen. I was listing like a drunken sailor. The room wasn't swirling as much, but my knees were rubbery and felt like they could give way at any moment.

Aegis finished his baking, and handed me a cupcake, a black forest cupcake with chocolate cherry icing, no less. He caught me up in his arms and carried me out to the car. I wasn't looking forward to the upcoming visit, but I texted Delia to tell her we were on the way to see Essie.

THERE WAS NO MISTAKING ESSIE VANDERBILT'S HOUSE. IT

was the only one in Bedlam that seemed to have been modeled after the Addams family mansion, although the interior was far less daunting as far as cobwebs and dirt went. The Moonrise Coven had taken on the role of monitoring how many vampires Essie had under her thumb.

While she might be queen over the entire Pacific Northwest region, Bedlam only allowed her a certain number of vampires in her nest at any given time. Most mainland cities didn't pay much attention to the vamps amongst their midst. In fact, most mainland cities just didn't want to admit they had vampires living among them. But here on Bedlam, we knew all too well how powerful the bloodsuckers were. And while we tried to integrate them into our community, we also kept them under strict observation. Because when push came to shove, most vamps played true to their nature. As it was, we had suspicions that Essie had plans to infiltrate Bedlam in a way that we really weren't prepared for.

Of course, once we got there, Essie made us wait. She had to prove her regality in some way. Aegis had eased into the driveway, which already held a dark van, with which I was all too acquainted, and several sedans. Essie liked to live in comfort, that was for certain. The mansion had a foreboding air about it, although I kept thinking it was far too emo for my taste.

About ten minutes after he turned off the ignition, the plantation-style door opened and Essie stepped out onto her porch. She was flanked by two men in dark suits, bodyguards no doubt, and both vampire. Essie was wearing a long satin dress, crimson in color and ornately embellished with black lace and gold sequins. At least she wasn't wearing a hoop skirt this time, but the dress skimmed the ground, and just looking at it was enough to conjure up the swishing noise of taffeta. Her hair was red, and usually she wore it in an elaborate coif, but tonight it flowed down her shoulders, a cascade of ringlets falling down her back. She wore a diadem of sparkling diamonds and rubies. I knew they were real jewels. There would be no costume jewelry in Essie's collection.

Followed by her bodyguards, Essie slowly descended the porch steps, making her way over to my CR-V. Aegis had wanted to bring the Corvette, but I had thought the better of it, especially when I was asking Essie to sit in the back seat. She peeked through his window, giving him a cool smile, her fangs pearlescent in the evening. Then, before he could say a word, she made her way around the front of the car, tracing the hood with her fingers until she stood by my side. I opened my window, but not the door.

"Pardon me, but my vertigo's really strong right now. That's what I get for spending the evening in the water." I motioned to the back seat. "Why don't you get in the car so we can talk in private. I'd rather keep what I have to say between us for the moment." I stared at her bodyguards, then my gaze flickered back to Essie. "*If you know what I mean.*"

Essie frowned, but she nodded to her guards and they stepped away as she hoisted herself into the back seat. She smoothed her skirt.

"I don't think I care for your taste in cars."

"Well then, it's a good thing you don't own one. I love my CR-V." I paused. I hadn't come here to debate automobiles. "Essie, Delia asked me to speak to you. Let me get right to the point. Last night, there was a vampire kill in town."

Essie said nothing for a moment, then in a strained voice, she said, "Does she think someone from my nest is responsible?"

"Boy, you come right to the point, don't you?"

"No faster than you." Essie snorted. "If Delia sent you here to talk to me about a vampire kill, she'll want to know the whereabouts of everyone in my nest. I had a feeling it would be something like this, so while I waited for you to arrive, I gathered the information. I'll email it to her and she can fact-check it as she likes. But tell me, where did it happen?"

"Ten minutes away from Neverfall. That's another reason why this is so important. We can't have a vampire targeting schoolchildren. Not that we want them targeting anybody else, either."

While we all knew that vampires—including Aegis—fed on the townsfolk, most of them followed the rules. Essie had her own stable of bloodwhores who volunteered for duty. She and her nest usually didn't feed around town.

"Does Delia have any clue of who did this? I keep strict tabs on my nest. I can guarantee that no one in my service is at fault for this." Essie shifted to make herself more comfortable. "I would never allow my vampires to feed on children. This isn't the Middle Ages, and I certainly don't want *Mad Maudlin* to come knocking at my door." The latter was said in a sarcastic tone, but with enough of an edge that I realized that *I* intimidated *her*.

I glanced over at Aegis who looked one minute away from blowing up.

"Trust me, Essie. I don't want a reason to come knocking at your door. Especially carrying my silver stake. So do you have any idea of what's going on?"

I glanced in the rearview mirror but the back seat looked empty. It still unnerved me, but I was getting used to it. Several times I had taken a picture of Aegis without thinking about it, forgetting that he wouldn't show. I turned around, holding Essie's gaze as she stared back at me.

"If you know something, you need to tell us. You know the rules. I didn't make them, I just help enforce them." And that was true as well. The witches who founded Bedlam early on had agreed on a policy about vampires. Perhaps back then, it was needed more. Or perhaps, we were still wise in enforcing it today. Either way, the town charter contained specific codes on what vampires were allowed to do.

"This is the first that I've heard of it. I give you my word. I'll put out feelers and see what I can find out. Rogue vampires aren't good for my kingdom, either."

"Then I'll tell Delia to expect your email. She may have more questions, but that's a good start." And with that, I nodded to her, indicating the interview was over. "Thank you for your help. And I'm sure Delia thanks you as well."

"A word to the wise, Maddy. It's not a good idea to accuse members of the vampire nobility of murder. Just a little thought that you can take back to Delia." She slipped out of the car, shutting the door quietly behind her. Her bodyguards swung in behind as she headed back to the house. She didn't look back.

The skies opened up, and a torrential rain began to pound down. Essie didn't seem to notice it as she ascended her porch steps. I glanced at Aegis. He started the ignition and then in silence, we edged out of her driveway and back down the road.

When we arrived back home, Kelson had finished the baking. The day was wearing on me, and even though it was only ten P.M., I couldn't help but yawn. I tried to hide it from Aegis. I wanted to spend more time talking to him, but the truth was I was having a hard time keeping my eyes open.

He noticed, of course, and over my loud protestations, he carried me toward the stairs.

Kelson came running behind him. "Stop! You can't take her upstairs. She's probably still going to be dizzy in the morning and I don't know how she could make it down the stairs without help. I'm strong, but I don't think I could carry her."

Aegis froze. "I don't know why I didn't think about that," he said. He glanced down at me, a puzzled look on his face. I had my arm around his neck and the truth was, I didn't really care where he took me as long as I was able to lay down. The vertigo was getting worse as the evening wore on and I felt queasy and tired.

"Where do you want to sleep, Maddy?"

"I suppose the sofa will have to do." It occurred to me that my idea of creating a handicap-accessible room on the ground floor was definitely going to happen. It didn't matter if it was for a guest or for one of us, if we needed an accessible bedroom, we were going to have one.

"You can sleep in my bed if you want," Kelson said. "I can sleep in one of the empty guest rooms upstairs."

"I hate to put you out of your room. But you do have a private bathroom. It would make it easier for me to get up when I need to." Kelson's room was compact but tidy, and I could probably make it to the bathroom without help. If I had to crawl, it wouldn't be far.

"That's not a problem," she said. "I'd rather know you were safe down here than trying to careen around upstairs. You would probably be fine in your own bedroom, except for morning."

"There's another option," Aegis said. "You can sleep in your bed and I'll come up right before sunrise and carry you downstairs. Then you can snooze on the sofa for the last hour or so. Since the sun is rising later and later, it won't be too early. And there's a rolling chair in one of the guest rooms that you can use to get to the bathroom."

I thought about it. I kept track of sunrise and sunset now, ever since getting together with Aegis. It was vital that we knew the danger zones. We considered any time during the last thirty minutes before sunrise to be a danger zone—and we always tried to make sure he was in the basement by then. Sunrise tomorrow morning wouldn't be till 7:29 A.M. And that was my usual waking time anyway.

"That sounds good. If you come up at seven o'clock, I can be ready to go downstairs. I'd prefer to sleep in my own room because I know my way around better. Hopefully, by morning, the vertigo will have calmed down. The doctor said four days on the outside, so I imagine after another night's sleep, I should be all right."

"Then it's settled. I'll carry you upstairs and then I'll come up and get you at seven. I can sit with you if you like, to make sure if you wake up you can get through to the bathroom and back to the bed."

Inwardly, I groaned. Here it came—the hovering. Aegis

felt so guilty over what happened that his natural protectiveness had gone full speed ahead. I appreciated his concern, but I didn't like people hovering over me.

"Okay, but you have to promise me to go about your usual routine tonight. Go ahead and check on me a couple times but please, if you sit by the bed I'm not going to get any sleep. Knowing somebody's watching you while you're asleep seems kind of creepy. All stalkerish, you know. And dude, you don't sparkle."

He carried me up the stairs, stopping in front of my door to open it. Bubba and Luna came bouncing along behind us.

"Did you remember to feed them tonight? Or did Kelson?"

"Oh, the little beggars got fed. Trust me, their stomachs aren't empty." He opened the door to my room and carried me in, sitting me on the bed. "What do you want to wear? If anything?"

I thought about it. I preferred to sleep in the nude usually, but considering I might need help at some point during the night, I decided to opt for a loose nightgown. "The short lilac gown, please. It's in the top right-hand drawer of my dresser. Also, the matching panties."

Aegis carried my lingerie over to the bed, grinning. "I remember the last time you wore these," he said, leering.

"So do I, but don't get your hopes up. I'm so tired it's hard to keep my eyes open, and I'm so dizzy that I have a feeling any foreplay, afterplay, or anything in between would make it worse." The thought of sex sounded pretty good, but I knew my body and I knew how I felt. I had to listen to reason, even though my hormones were urging me otherwise.

"Spoil all of my fun, why don't you?" But he winked at me. "Would you like a bath before bed? I can draw a bubble bath for you. Or if you'd like a shower, I can take one with you and make sure that you don't fall. I promise no funny business." He paused for a moment, then added, "Or if you'd like a sponge bath, I can help you with that. I can rub lotion on your back too."

"Stop! Give me a chance to think." A bath sounded heavenly, especially a bubble bath. Part of me just wanted to fall asleep right then and there, but I knew that a little time in a hot tub would serve me well. "I would love a bubble bath."

Aegis went to draw the bath while I pulled off my clothes. When he returned, I tried to stand, but he was over by my side in a flash. Vampires could move incredibly fast at times, so fast that it often seemed like teleportation. He had startled me more than once with his speed. He carried me into the bathroom and I realized I was starting to feel like some teacup dog.

The tub was filling with toasty warm water, and he had added lavender bath gel.

"I wasn't sure what scent you'd like, but I thought lavender would be soothing."

I actually preferred vanilla, but I wasn't going to tell him that, not after how much he was doing to help me. And the lavender was faint enough to be calming. As he lowered me into the tub, I leaned back against the cool porcelain and rested my head on the bath pillow. I closed my eyes as the bubbles rose around me.

At first, the soothing scent began to relax me, and I was just starting to drift as a sudden whirl jerked me out of my reverie. All I could see were the rolling waves around me and the icy cold water that threatened to drag me down. Crying out, I shot straight up, clutching the sides of the bathtub as I frantically looked around.

"What's the matter, love?" Aegis was on his knees immediately, leaning over me.

"Everything began to spin and I felt like I was back out in the water, drowning. On second thought, I don't think a bath is such a hot idea. Let me rinse off and then you can carry me back to the bed. I know I'm not going to be able to stand up on my own now."

In truth, the entire room was spinning. I accepted a washcloth and scrubbed myself quickly, trying to soothe the vertigo with the feel of the cloth against my skin. When I was done, Aegis let the water out of the tub. I wanted to rinse off the soap, so he took off his shoes and then, holding me in his arms, stepped into the shower fully dressed, and turned it on.

I pressed against his chest, trying to keep the feeling of motion from overwhelming me. "You silly man, I love you so much. You're getting soaked, though."

"I don't care. Clothes will wash. But you, my love, are worth more to me than anything in this world." He stepped out of the tub and grabbed a towel, then carried me back to the bed. He tossed the towel on the comforter and lowered me onto it. Then, he brought me back a thick bath sheet, and vanished back into the bathroom while I dried off. When he returned this time, he was naked, wearing a towel around his nether regions, much to my chagrin.

"Well, this has been one hell of an evening, hasn't it?" I thought again about Sandy, and thought about calling her, but I knew that Alex would have given her my message. She'd call me as soon as she was ready.

"You can say that again. It's been one hell of a weekend, actually. The Boys of Bedlam broke up with Dream-Gen, Jenna lost her mother, and I almost accidentally drowned you." He shook his head. "I hate to say it, but what's next?"

"Don't ask. I don't want to know. And don't forget—there was a vampire kill this weekend and Fata Morgana is hanging around." I slid under the covers, breathing a sigh of relief as the dizziness started to wane. "This helps. Lying down."

"I'm glad, love. I'm going to take my clothes down to the laundry, and then I'll be back with a bottle of water and a snack in case you get hungry. I promise I won't hover, but I am going to check on you every hour or so. Do you need anything else right now?"

I shook my head, my eyes heavy. As Aegis left the room, Bubba and Luna bounced up on the bed and snuggled next to me, one on each side. I turned on my side so that Luna was snuggled against my back and Bubba was curled in my arms, and before Aegis could return with my water and snack, I fell into a deep, restful slumber.

CHAPTER SIX

I would have overslept my alarm, but Aegis woke me up promptly at seven. I dressed in a black and green plaid skirt, and a hunter green V-neck sweater. I asked Aegis to find my big tote bag in my closet, because it would be easier to carry everything I needed around in it. The dizziness seemed to be under control until I stood up, but even though I could stand on my own, one step told me that I was still incredibly unstable on my feet. He carried me down the stairs and into the kitchen, set me down, and I leaned on his arm as I made my way to the table from the door.

"An email came in for you about four A.M. this morning. I was updating our accounts, and I saw the notification. I think it's from Gregory." He fixed me a steaming mocha, piled high with whipped cream, with cocoa powder dusted on top. "There are five shots of espresso in there to get you started."

"You know how to make a girl's heart sing," I said, smiling. "I want to see what he said." I started to stand, but Aegis shook his head and motioned for me to sit down.

"Wait right here. I have a surprise for you. This one, I think you'll like."

He hurried out of the room, and I noticed he was wearing sneakers. I blinked. An unusual fashion choice for Aegis. I preferred the motorcycle boots, but he had the right to choose his own footwear. He returned carrying a laptop.

"I bought this for you so you can take your work around the house, instead of staying in the office. The password is 'ENCHANT,' but you can change it to anything you want."

I blinked. I'd been meaning to buy a laptop soon, but hadn't got around to it.

"Thank you," I said, stroking the smooth black surface. As I opened it and turned it on, I saw that the laptop was loaded with just about every program I could want. And then I realized it was top of the line, probably costing about five thousand dollars.

"I can't believe you bought this for me. When did you get it?"

"It was a secondary anniversary present. I was going to give it to you when we got home the other night, but I didn't foresee us ending up as fish food. I almost forgot about it with all the aftermath, but then I remembered after I put you to bed last night. I transferred all of your email and documents over to it as well last night. The wireless is strong, so you can take it anywhere out in the backyard, up to the edge of the trees."

He glanced at the clock. "I should get to bed, love."

As he leaned down, gazing at me with those deep,

brown eyes of his, they pierced into my heart and once again I felt a surge of love and gratitude that he was in my life.

"Do you know how much I love you?"

He stroked my cheek. "I have an idea, but I like to hear you say it."

"You are unlike any man I've ever known." I leaned up and pressed my lips to his, kissing him long and deep. A wave of hunger rushed over me, but we didn't have any time this morning. "Tonight, I need you."

"Tonight, I'm all yours." And with that he kissed me again, this time on the nose and, waving good night to Kelson, who was entering the room at that moment, he headed downstairs to sleep before the first rays of sun touched the sky.

"He's a keeper," Kelson said. "He's really quite extraordinary."

I waited, but she didn't finish it the way I expected her to. "Thank you."

"For what?"

"For not finishing your sentence with 'for a vampire.'"

"Those who qualify their compliments don't usually mean them." Kelson winked at me. "What do you want for breakfast? Eggs, bacon? I'm in a cooking mood, so just ask."

"I want English muffins, sausage, and a cheese omelet."

As she got to work, I brought up my email. The laptop ran extremely fast. Aegis hadn't skimped on the memory or the CPU speed. And there it was, an email from Gregory Oakstone. With shaking hands, I tapped the touchpad and opened the letter.

Dear Maudlin: I can't believe I'm writing this. I'm still in shock over your email, but first let me say how grateful I am that you wrote to me. I always knew I was adopted, but my parents would never tell me where I came from, or who my real parents were. They just told me that I was given to them with love, and to let sleeping dogs lie. I would love to talk to you after I have processed all of this information. As you can probably guess, I never expected to discover who my birth parents were, not after all this time. I will be in the United States next year for a conference. Perhaps we can meet then, as I will be passing through Seattle on my way home. Meanwhile, I'll be taking some time to think about what you said, and I will email when I know how I feel. Ever grateful for your note, Gregory O.

I stared at the screen, not sure about what to think. I was glad he had actually written back, but I had expected one of two responses: either he would freak and tell me to fuck off, or he would immediately swamp me with questions.

"Are you all right?" Kelson asked.

I nodded. "Yeah, just a little disheartened."

It was then that I realized I had been hoping for an exuberant email instead of a noncommittal thank-you. I closed my email after scanning the rest. It seemed obvious that Gregory didn't want to hear from me until he had processed through the information I had left him with, and I wasn't the type to bother someone when they made it clear they didn't want to be approached.

"Your breakfast will be ready in a moment. I just need to butter the toast," she said as the bread popped out of the toaster.

I stared at the laptop. I had no clue that Aegis had been planning such an elaborate anniversary. And here, I had almost forgotten it. I frowned.

"Kelson?" I asked as she set my plate in front of me.

"Yes?"

"Can you help me plan a romantic evening for Aegis and me? He tried, but luck was stacked against us." Luck and the weather. And possibly Fata Morgana, if she had driven the storm into Bedlam on purpose. "He has rehearsal tonight, but I think he's free tomorrow night, so let's shoot for then."

"Should you plan it for next week, when your vertigo should be gone?"

I let out a sigh. "I suppose you're right. I don't want to be staggering all over the place."

"All right." She grabbed a pen and notebook and sat down. "What do you want?"

"For one thing, we need a romantic dinner. Since we couldn't have a picnic at sea, and I'm not about to try a do-over on that one, see if you can get us reservations at the Surf Side."

The Surf Side was a new restaurant, beautifully decked out, with a menu that had made my mouth water when Sandy told me about it. Max had taken her there two or three months ago. I had laughingly pointed out that if she went there again, she would be competing with her own seafood bar, now that it was newly built in a safe location. But she pointed out that the Oyster Bar was fast food. The Surf Side was haute cuisine.

"I'll call them as soon as we're done." She paused. "Should I see if they have an no-vampires-allowed policy, before making the reservations?"

I blinked. I hadn't even thought of that, but it made perfect sense. "Yeah, good idea. It wouldn't have occurred to me to ask, and that would be a quick way to ruin the evening." I thought over what I wanted to do. The Surf Side had dancing, too, so I'd buy a new dress. "See if they have a dress code? I may need to surprise Aegis with a suit jacket and tie. I don't think I've ever seen him all decked out in fancy clothes."

"I'll get right on this after I serve breakfast to Henry. Did you want to buy Aegis a gift?"

I thought about it. What could I give him that would mean as much as the key pendant he had given me? The laptop was a lovely gift, and I was going to enjoy using it, but the key—now, that packed a punch. Then it occurred to me. "I need to go down in the basement today, or send you down there. I need to know what his ring size is."

She frowned. "How do we do that?"

"You—because I don't think I can make it down the stairs—measure his right ring finger with a string and mark it. Then we take it to the jewelry store." I was going to buy him a gift he'd never expect.

"Oh, so much joy on that one." Kelson grimaced. "It's all too much like measuring a corpse, you know? I don't mean any disrespect, but—" She paused.

I snorted. "That's because you are, in a way. I don't mind you being blunt. He's a vampire. He's no longer alive —at least not in the normal sense. But let's leave it at 'He's a vampire' and drop it, okay?"

Kelson laughed. "All too happy to. I suppose we should

get right on this, given you want to surprise him next week."

I beamed. "You got it. I'm going to eat breakfast, then we can get moving. I'll need you to drive me to the jeweler's as soon as you've finished the other errands. Meanwhile, I'll take a look online to find out which one I want to go to." Cranking up the laptop, I got busy.

Delia called shortly after I had decided on which jewelry store I wanted to visit. I still hadn't heard from Sandy and was starting to get worried.

"Hey, I just got Essie's email with the attachment listing the whereabouts of her nest members. Thank you for talking to her."

"It wasn't pleasant, but at least it's done."

Delia paused. "But do you trust her? Really? If you tell me you think she's telling us the truth, I'll accept what you say."

"I wish you wouldn't put it on my shoulders like that."

"I'm not, but I do trust your opinion and it's probably more accurate than mine."

I thought about Essie and how she had acted. "She was almost…*afraid*. I think she really *doesn't* know who the rogue vampire is, but the news about the vampire kill spooked her. She was her usual high-and-mighty self, but there was an edge of fear behind the pretense."

I paused, gazing outside where the wind started whipping the trees with stiff blows. One of the younger birch trees in my yard was bending back, and for a moment, I was afraid it might snap. "Hell, are you getting the wind I am here? I checked the weather last night and it said blustery, but this is a gale-force gust."

"Yeah, same here. Hold on." She put me on hold for a moment, then returned. "There's a major wind advisory coming through. We're in the path of an incoming storm that's likely to rival any Bedlam has had in the past ten years."

"Typical November weather, but in October. We'd better batten down the hatches, then." I thought about Essie. "I wonder if Essie thinks another vampire is targeting her territory. We know how vamps ascend to the throne."

"You could be right. Well, we'll keep our eyes peeled for any more attacks. Meanwhile, take it easy and recover." She paused. "Maddy, that was a dangerous thing to do, going out onto the water. Next time, listen to your head instead of your heart. I know that Aegis meant well, but sometimes when you're damned near immortal, you can forget other people aren't. And I don't care how long of a lifespan you have, you aren't anywhere near as invulnerable as he is."

With that, she signed off.

I put in another call to Sandy while I was waiting for Kelson to finish cleaning the sink. She was meticulous about never leaving a dirty dish on the counter and I didn't complain. I enjoyed having a clean freak in the house.

This time, Sandy answered. "Maddy?" She sounded like she had been crying.

"Are you all right? How's Jenna doing?" I knew I shouldn't bombard her with questions but I couldn't help myself.

"Me? About as good as can be expected. But Jenna, I'm not so sure about. She's locked herself in her bedroom and won't come out. I'm worried. She won't talk to me. She won't talk to Alex, and she won't even talk to Max. I'm at my wit's end." Sandy sounded exhausted. I didn't even want to think about how tired she must be.

"Want me to come over and see if I can get her to open up?" I wasn't much of an expert on teenagers, but Jenna and I liked each other and she seemed to enjoy talking to me.

Sandy let out a sigh. "No. I'll call you in a little while if it seems like we're still getting nowhere. How about you? Are you healing up?"

"Yeah. Still have vertigo and not about to drive myself, but I'm better than I was yesterday. I had to talk to Essie last night, and you *know* just how much I enjoy that." I didn't want to burden Sandy with anything more than she was dealing with, but she had to know. "Listen, and this is hush-hush until Delia gives us permission to speak about it openly, but there was a vampire kill in Bedlam. Delia found the body yesterday morning. She dropped by yesterday, asking me to pump Essie for any information she might have."

Sandy barked out a laugh. "I can just imagine how much fun pumping Essie was. At least you're not a guy and you didn't have to pump her the old-fashioned way."

I choked. "I don't think it matters to Essie whether I'm male or female, and...*ewww*. I love Aegis. He's a vamp. But the thought of doing the vampire queen? Oh, hell no. Bite your tongue."

"Better than biting hers," she said, again letting out a stifled laugh. "All right, I'd better get off the phone and see if Jenna is ready to talk yet." Sandy sounded like that was the last thing she wanted to do. "I guess I need to learn and learn fast on how to be a mother. My only fear is that now that I *am* her mother, or at least her guardian, she's going to start resenting me like she did Derry."

"I don't think Jenna will ever resent you," I said. I had no clue whether that was true or not, but I felt the need to reassure her. I set my phone down and looked over to Kelson. She had just finished putting the last of the dishes in the dishwasher. "Are you ready to go?"

"Five minutes, while I get my purse and make sure the front door is locked." She glanced outside at the rising storm. "Wear a jacket. Even though we're mostly going to be in the car and in stores, it looks nasty out there."

"Delia told me that a storm front is coming in. It's supposed to be the worst storm Bedlam has seen in ten years, so once we get home we need to make certain that everything outside is either tied down or put away. I'm afraid I'm not going to be much help there."

"That's what I'm here for. Come on. While we're out, I'll stop and get some more milk and eggs and a few other things we're running low on." She hustled through into the living room, and returned with our jackets and her purse. "Here, put your arm around my shoulder and I'll walk you out to the car."

I stood, taking a deep breath to steady myself. "I think if you just hold me by the elbow and maybe put a hand on my back to steady me, I will be fine. As long as we go slow, that is."

Kelson placed her left hand on the small of my back, and angled toward me so that she could take hold of my right hand. Slowly, we made our way to the sliding glass door, and then out into the backyard. It was quicker to the driveway than going through the front door.

As we crossed the grassy side yard, a sudden gust almost blew us off balance. The wind had to be blowing at around forty miles an hour. Kelson stopped, holding me steady as the gust blasted past. A branch from one of the tall firs went sailing past to land in the yard. A good three feet long, it was splintered on the end that had broken off from the tree.

"Are you sure you want to go to the store today?"

I nodded. "Yes, we have blustery weather all the time. I'm not going to let a little storm stop me. It's not like I'm heading out onto the water again." In retrospect, Delia was right. Aegis's plan had seemed foolhardy. But hindsight was always best, and it had seemed like an incredibly romantic idea at the time.

The fresh air seemed to strengthen me, and by the time we reached the gate I could walk a few steps on my own. Kelson shut the door after I slid into the passenger side. I buckled my seatbelt. The skies cracked wide, then, and a heavy rain began to pound down around us. Kelson raced around to her side of the car and dove in, laughing.

"Well, we're in no danger of a drought, are we?" She started the ignition, and the car purred smoothly. Kelson had traded in her sedan for a Subaru Outback. As we eased out of the driveway, I glanced at my CR-V longingly. I liked to drive, and I didn't like having to be dependent on anybody else.

"I have a feeling we're a long ways from a drought." Another branch went flying by, landing too close to Aegis's Corvette for comfort. "This is shaping up to be a tidy little storm, isn't it?"

Bedlam was a magical little town. Literally. There was so much magic in our town that it changed the very weather of the island. With about six thousand permanent inhabitants, I suppose we were actually a village, which was more apt, given the nature of Bedlam. Oh, we had a few chain stores, but most of our shops were boutiques, privately owned and inherently unique.

The town was spread out across the island, but with a fountain in the square and a large park where we held community events, downtown Bedlam had a quirky charm all of its own. The lampposts and shops were decorated for Samhain. Brightly colored streamers were draped from lamppost to lamppost, and orange and purple lights wound around the poles. The park had a massive display of jack o' lanterns—all carved by townsfolk. A few of the witches who worked for the city had enchanted them so that they wouldn't rot until Samhain was over, and at night, they lit up, a sparkling display of the haunting reminder that it was the season of death and the time of the ancestors. The Fae who lived on the island had enchanted them with faerie fire, so they glowed with the twinkling lights that darted in and around the display.

"We should stop at Calou Bakery for some bread. I know Aegis likes to make dinner rolls, but I've been hankering for croissants and French bread lately." I loved the bakery. Run by a hearth witch named Glenna, Calou Bakery was intensely comforting. She kneaded magic into every bite.

"All right, but I'm going in. You're going to stay in the

car." Kelson found a parking spot right in front of the bakery.

I grinned. "You call on the parking goddess again?"

Kelson had a knack for finding open spots right when she needed them.

She laughed. "So, what should I get?"

"French bread—several loaves. A couple croissants. Maybe some of her cinnamon rolls? And if she has it, a fresh apple pie." I could have gone on—there was a long list of things that Glenna made that I loved—but I decided to opt for a little self-control. Not to mention, I had noticed that Aegis was starting to get mildly offended when I brought outside baked goods into the house. The more he baked, the more he enjoyed it. I didn't want to stomp on his ego.

Kelson returned, her arms full of fragrant packages. My mouth began to water, even though I was still full from breakfast. I promised myself that when I got home, I could have a cinnamon roll with a peppermint mocha. Until then, I'd be good and keep my hands to myself.

I had decided on Diamond Promises for the ring. We turned left on Brandy Street, and sure enough, there was a spot right in front of the store. I glanced at Kelson.

"I'd like to know what kind of magic you use for that," I said with a laugh.

"I'd like to know too. You know I don't do magic—I'm a werewolf. But I do seem to have an innate ability to track down a spot wherever I go. Ready?"

I unbuckled my seatbelt and slipped on my jacket. The sky was awash in an army of gray clouds, and fat droplets bounced on the sidewalk. The air crackled with static electricity. It smelled like thunderstorm weather. Kelson dashed around to my side of the car and opened the door for me, helping me out. The vertigo was still strong, but it was definitely on the wane. She guided me to the door of the shop, and we slipped inside out of the storm.

Diamond Promises was more of an artisan's studio. One large main room was divided into two sections—three display cases with benches in front of them for the clients to sit on. And then, across the back of the room, looked to be a jeweler's studio, with workbenches, and a Chinese apothecary cabinet, which I assumed held various jewelry clasps and the like. One door led to a back room area. Vines from a large potted plant to one side trailed up a wooden stake that touched the ceiling, weaving through a rope trellis suspended across the room. The storefront windows glimmered with a faint light. Magical protection, no doubt.

A woman was dusting the jewelry in one of the front cases, and a man was seated at the bench in the work area, intent on his work. They both looked up as we entered.

"May I help you?" The woman stepped around the case. She was Fae, I could tell that from her energy. She wore a knee-length black dress, with a discreet nametag that read "Nera." She motioned to one of the seats by the front counter. "Have a seat."

"I'm Maddy Gallowglass. I'm looking for a ring for my boyfriend." I sat down.

Nera fluttered around us, overly excited for my mood. "Oh, are you going to propose? We have some lovely men's wedding rings or we can make a custom one—"

"Hold that thought," I said, holding up my hand. "Nobody's proposing to anybody. I just want... Think of it as a promise ring. A love token. I'd like something with

Celtic knotwork on it, if possible, and here's the width of his finger." I handed her the string and flashed her a smile. "Trust me, when—if—we ever shop for wedding rings, it will be together."

That punctured some of her balloon, but she got right to business. "What kind of metal?"

"Has to be gold. No silver. He's a vampire."

That brought a double take, then a nervous laugh. "Of course. I don't want to be responsible for hurting him." She looked through the inventory in the right-hand case. "What about a claddagh band? We have one in gold with Celtic knotwork running around the band." She took the string and measured it. Then she brought out the ring and set it on a cushion in front of me. The gold band was highly polished, with two hands holding the traditional claddagh heart with a crown over it. A *fede* ring, it stood for all that was loyal: vows and oaths, promises, hope, and faith.

I picked up the ring. It made sense, truly. I wanted a ring to promise my love to Aegis, to reassure him of my trust and loyalty. Just like the key to his heart that hung around my neck.

"This is lovely. Is it the correct size?"

"Actually, yes, and you're lucky—we'd have to order in another if he needed a bigger size. This ring can't be sized due to the design."

The knotwork was beautiful, intricately interwoven. I glanced at the man in the work area, who was wearing an eyepiece while he looked over a ring. "Did he make this?"

"No, Mr. Diamond didn't make that ring, but he ordered it straight from the smith in Ireland who did. The jeweler who makes these comes from the Winter Court."

She motioned to the case. "I have a few others if you'd like to see them. Some have birthstones, others are simple knotwork, but very beautiful."

I nodded, still staring at the ring. Something about it called to me and I knew it was the right choice. "I really like this one. How much?"

Nera looked surprised, but relieved. She probably received a commission on sales and no doubt, I was her easiest one of the day. "Twelve hundred, marked down from one thousand, five hundred. We're having a special this week, though, with twenty percent off any purchase over five hundred dollars."

"Can you gift wrap it for me?" I suddenly froze. "Oh hell, I forgot. My purse is at the bottom of the lake."

Nera's smile vanished and her eyes narrowed. "Oh?"

"Can you hold this for me for an hour? I'll go to the bank and get cash—" Again, I froze. Even though they knew me at the credit union, I didn't have any identification.

Kelson came to my rescue. "I'll put it on my card and you can write me a check when we get home." She pulled out her wallet.

"I can't ask you to do that—"

"It's not like I don't submit a bill each week for groceries and household goods. I'm fine with it. Go ahead and ring up the purchase." She handed Nera her credit card.

We were out the door, jewelry box in hand, and back in the car within a few minutes. "We need to replace your identification. You can do it online, but that may take awhile."

"You want to drive me to the DMV?" Luckily, Bedlam's

department of motor vehicles was small, given the population, and wait times were generally short. I had my Pretcom identification card, but needed a state one as well.

We spent the next forty minutes going through the hoops of getting me a new license. I had already filed reports on my lost credit cards and replacements were on the way. I never carried my social security card, so that was still safe, as was my passport.

Complete with a temporary license and feeling much more secure, I wove my way out of the DMV, holding on to Kelson's arm. The wind had picked up even more, and was now blowing a steady forty miles an hour. The gusts were worse.

"We should get home so I can anchor down anything that might take a mind to go sailing," Kelson said. She glanced up at the clouds. The rain had abated, but looked like it could return at any moment. The sky was an ominous mixture of gray and silver, coming out of the northwest, down from the Discovery Islands that dotted the Strait of Georgia and the Johnstone Strait in British Columbia. "My instincts say this is going to be a bad storm, and a long one."

I could feel what she meant. There was a shift in the wind, and the bracing gusts bit with a bone-deep chill. The temperature had dropped at least five degrees since we had left the house.

"Let's stop and get some pizza on the way, but yeah, home we go."

As we paused at the stoplight by Turnwheel Park, an upsweep hit the car, rocking us as it whipped past. The streetlights swung wildly on their lines and I winced, hoping they would hold. All the birds had vanished, hiding in whatever safe places they could find to ride out the storm.

After a quick stop at The Pizza Stone for three large take-and-bake meat-lovers pizzas, we headed for home. We were rounding the bend where Elk Wood turned into Yew Tree Road—the street the Bewitching Bedlam was on—when a massive gust just about blew us off the road. Kelson clutched the steering wheel, turning hard so that we bumped onto the shoulder. We were next to Old Man Tee's farm, and the field next to us stretched for a good quarter-mile, filled with ripe orange pumpkins. He had probably sold half of them, but this weekend the rest would be gone. I caught my breath as we rode out the gust, waiting for it to subside.

"That was almost hurricane force." I shivered. This storm was shaping up to be no joke. Bedlam was in for a good blow, all right.

"We're almost home," Kelson said, easing back onto the road. She tapped the accelerator and we sped quickly along the last mile. We had just passed the Heart's Desire Inn—which was a ten-minute walk from the Bewitching Bedlam—when a massive crash behind us shook the road and everything on it.

I glanced out the side mirror. A huge oak stretched across the road, uprooted from the front yard of the Heart's Desire Inn.

"Crap. Ralph just lost that massive old tree in the front yard." And then it hit me that, had we been a few seconds slower, we would have been *under* that oak tree.

Kelson must have realized that too, because she whipped into our driveway. "Come on, let's get you inside first. Then I'll bring in the groceries. I forgot the milk, but we can drink juice."

I eased out of the car, shaking. She ran around to my side and slipped her arm around my waist. I clung to her as we quickly crossed the lawn to the kitchen. Once I was inside, through the slider, she ran back to the car to retrieve the baked goods.

Shaking, I was about to call Ralph to ask if everybody was okay when a flash of lightning broke through the clouds, so bright that it almost blinded me. Kelson made it back to the house, just in time to avoid the quarter-sized chunks of ice that began to fall. As the ice pellets bounced on the grass, coating it with a sheet of white, I stared out the window, thinking about the sudden onslaught of bad weather. Was Fata Morgana behind this? I wanted her to show herself, to quit hiding behind the storms. The bronze pentacle was sitting on the table where I had left it. I picked it up, fingering it gently. What was going to happen next? But even as I asked myself the question, I realized I wasn't sure I wanted to find out.

CHAPTER SEVEN

Before I could call Ralph, he called me. "Maddy, I need a favor."

"I saw the tree go down. Kelson and I barely managed to drive past it before it hit the ground. Is everybody all right? I was going to call you." I felt bad that I hadn't immediately called him to check. I got too caught up in my thoughts sometimes.

"We're all right, but can you take in two of my guests for the night? When the oak fell, it punched a hole in the roof right into their rooms." He sounded so forlorn that I couldn't help but feel sorry for him.

"I don't know. Let me ask Kelson. I think so, but I'll call you right back."

"Ask me what?" Kelson was putting away the bread. "You want some soup and toast?"

"Yeah, that sounds good. Ralph just called. When the tree fell, it punched a hole in his roof and he wants to know if we can take in a couple of his guests who were affected by it."

"Let me check. We were supposed to have two couples show up this afternoon." She put down the loaf of bread she was holding and hustled off to the office. Within a few minutes she returned. "We have the room. Because of the storm, both couples who were due to check in today left a message that they would have to reschedule. The ferry's grounded due to high winds, so they're going to check into a hotel in Bellingham instead. I assume you'll issue refunds to them, given the weather was unexpected?"

I nodded. "Yeah, totally not their fault. Okay, then I'll tell Ralph we have rooms for his guests. Though I hope they behave, given they signed up for the Heart's Desire. That place is a sleazy dive disguised as an inn." I hit callback on my phone and within seconds he answered. "Ralph? We can take your guests. But how are they going to get up here? I assume the oak is still blocking the road."

"We'll take the long way around. If we drive via Brambleroot Road, we can swing around and come down Yew Tree from the opposite direction. I'll bring them over. I doubt they want to walk in the pouring rain."

"I doubt it too." The hail had turned into a steady downpour. "Be careful on the roads."

Kelson was busy slicing thick slices of bread. The fragrance filled the kitchen with a heady, yeasty aroma. "The rooms are clean, so there's no worry there. I'll make up a big pot of soup unless you want to serve them some of the pizza. I doubt if they'll have had a chance to go out anywhere for lunch."

"No, freeze that for now. Slice up some cheese, toast the bread in the oven with a lot of butter, and along with the soup, that should be plenty for lunch. At least the rooms won't go unused, though Ralph better pay me for them, if his guests don't." I glanced out the window as another bolt of lightning cracked open the clouds with its brilliant fire. I counted, but only made it to two before the thunder rolled through behind the lightning. "It's close."

"Close enough to scare a cow," Kelson said. She shivered. "I'm glad we're not near the full moon. This would be bad weather to go running around in."

I usually didn't tread into areas that weren't really my business, but I was curious. "When you shift, what's it like? Being a wolf?"

She paused, staring out the window. "Painful in some ways. At least, the transformation is. After all, your body is changing shape and, natural or not, the bones and joints shift in drastic ways. The change only takes a short time, but there's always this moment that every shifter experiences. At least, every one I know. Halfway through, there's a brief moment where you get terrified that you might end up stuck between forms."

I blinked. "I never thought of that. But it has happened, hasn't it?"

"Oh, yes, it happens on rare occasion. Either something goes wrong with the process or there's a defective gene that suddenly decides to rear its ugly head. The poor suckers caught by it, well, it's kinder to put them out of their misery immediately. You can't live for more than a few minutes before dying from suffocation because the lungs are usually so twisted they can't keep the mishmash of bodies alive."

Shivering, I nodded. "That's something that isn't talked about very much, I gather."

"With good reason. Anyway, given you aren't one of the unlucky few, when you fully shift into your animal self, there's a freedom that comes from being able to run —or fly, or swim, whatever your shifter-self does. There's nothing to compare it to, not for the human form. I don't know if witches have anything comparable. It's easy to get caught up in animal nature, to want to stay like that instead of coming back. Now and then, Weres…shifters… whatever you choose to call us…don't return."

I processed her answer. It made sense. With all the complexities of daily life, it must be a relief to leave it behind. "Have you ever been tempted?"

She shrugged. "Now and then, but I don't have a lot of stress in my life to push me toward it. I have only myself to look after, and life as a wolf? Not always that easy, despite the way it might seem. You have to hunt, to find shelter, to keep on your guard against predators bigger and stronger than you."

Kelson buttered the bread and slipped it into the oven. Then she retrieved a container of homemade soup from the refrigerator and poured it into a big soup pot. She set it on the stove to heat up. "I'll turn on the oven when the soup's almost ready. By that time, Ralph should be here with the guests."

I put in a call to Sandy. She answered immediately.

"Hey, how's it going?"

"Rough. Jenna's still locked in her room. I know she has a stash of candy bars in there, and she has her own bathroom. She's making enough noise that I know she's alive. I was hoping the storm would chase her out but apparently, not so much yet. How are you doing?"

"Well, Ralph is bringing over two guests because he's got a big old hole in the roof thanks to a downed tree. We've had cancellations so we can actually take them in.

My vertigo is slowing down, and I now have a new temporary driver's license. I've ordered new credit cards, and I'm trying to remember what else I had in my purse. Keys, I have. I have a couple spares to my CR-V and to the house. So I'm okay there. I keep all the keys to the trunks that I have for storage on a ring at the house."

"You went out in this storm? You told the doctor you'd rest the next four days."

"Hey, I told him I wouldn't *drive* for four days. I haven't been." I glanced up as the doorbell rang. Kelson went to answer it. "I have to go. Ralph and his guests are here." I mumbled a quick good-bye as Kelson led Ralph and two elderly women into the kitchen. I stared at them. The women were at least eighty, and they looked human as all get out. What the hell were they doing staying at Ralph's inn?

"Hello. I'm Maudlin Gallowglass. Please forgive me for not standing but I have a bad case of vertigo." I graciously took their hands. "I hear you had a bad run-in with a tree."

"That's putting it mildly," one of the women said. "I was sitting on the bed, looking through a magazine when the oak came crashing through the roof. Mazy was in the bathroom."

"If I hadn't been, I would be flat as a pancake," the other one—apparently Mazy—said.

"May I introduce Henrietta and Mazy. They're sisters and they come to our inn every year for a bit of fun." Ralph winked at Mazy, who giggled.

"We just love these boys," Henrietta said, running her hand down Ralph's arm possessively. "We'd take them home with us, if we could." She let out a salty laugh.

I quickly reassessed my opinion of the sisters. They

might be old, but they definitely were Ralph's type. "Well, Henrietta, Mazy, I'm sorry you're going to miss out on Ralph's hospitality, but I hope you'll enjoy staying with us. We can't give you the same…*experience* that he would at the Heart's Desire, but I think you'll enjoy your stay with us."

Ralph snickered. "Oh, they'll come back over once we patch up that hole. You're going to extend your stay, aren't you? I'll pay Maddy for your room while we fix the roof, and then we'll offer you two days free at the inn for your inconvenience." He sat down and wrote me a check.

I stared at it. Ralph wasn't a leech, and I knew it was good, but I really had to hand it to him. He knew how to bring customers back, even without using his dick. "Kelson will show you to your room and then please come down for some lunch. Do you want to share a room or do you want separates? We have the space."

"We'll share. We always do." Henrietta and Mazy followed Kelson out into the living room.

"Their luggage is by the door," Ralph called. "I'll carry it up for you later if you like."

"Thanks, I can get it." Kelson didn't dislike Ralph, but she didn't like asking him for favors.

After they were gone, Ralph pulled out a chair and sat down beside me. I wasn't particularly fond of him, but neither was I about to be rude. If Ralph wanted to chat for a bit, I'd spare the time. It wasn't as though I was going anywhere, especially not in the storm. The winds were beating a tattoo against the side of the house, howling as they raged. The rain was falling so hard that it was raining sideways—a phenomenon anybody who lived in Western Washington was familiar with.

"So, you call somebody to come cut that tree up yet?"

He shook his head. "Might as well wait to see whether any more trees go down. I expect that my brother William will head out with a chainsaw before then. He likes chopping up stuff like that." He paused. "I'm going to buy Ivy the emerald necklace. Thank you for your advice." Then in a worried voice, he added, "Maddy, can I talk to you about something?"

"What is it?" Ralph was usually pretty happy-go-lucky, when he wasn't pissed off. But even the night before, he had seemed a little under the weather.

"I'm worried about my brother George. He's been acting strangely the past couple of days and I've never seen him like this. I tried to talk him into going to see a doctor, but he won't."

That, I hadn't expected. "What do you mean, 'strangely'?"

"He's lethargic. He's not interested in much of anything, even drinking. And George is always ready to party. But now, he seems tired and he won't do his share of the work. This came on suddenly, so I thought maybe he had a virus. But when I suggested visiting the doctor, he blew up at me and stomped off to take a nap."

I wasn't sure exactly what he wanted me to do about it. It wasn't like I had any clout with George. "Have you talked to William about this?"

"No, because he's oblivious to everything. You think I'm bad, he's ten times worse. I thought maybe you could come over, see George. He might listen to somebody else better than he listens to me."

"Now you're sounding desperate," I said with a laugh.

"You really think your brother would pay any attention to anything I had to say?"

"I don't know, at this point. His whole personality seems—different. I'm worried about him, Maddy." Ralph sounded so concerned that I finally caved.

"Sure, but you'll have to bring him over. I can't come over there right now."

Ralph had another surprise in store for me. "Thank you! I was hoping you'd say so. I'll go get him. I brought him with me when I drove the Fadero twins over. They are twins, by the way. Even though they aren't identical, trust me, they have the same birthmarks on their inner thighs."

I rubbed my head. I did not need to think about the Fadero twins and their thighs. "Thanks, but that's a little too much information. Go get George."

Ralph dashed out of the room. I decided to meet George in the parlor, and so cautiously standing, I began to lurch my way toward the door. Somehow, my rolling chair had gone AWOL.

I managed to make it halfway through the dining room before Ralph opened the front door again. He took one look at me as I staggered past the table and caught me up in his arms.

"Don't try to walk yet, Maddy. You were banged up pretty bad out there in the water."

He carried me in his arms—which I had to admit were strong and warm—into the living room. I shivered as he sat me down, thinking Aegis better not get wind that Ralph had been playing the white knight. George stood by the door until Ralph had deposited me on the sofa. I let out a long breath, a bit nonplussed by the musky scent that hung heavy around the satyrs as Ralph led George over to me.

George looked a lot like Ralph, though Ralph was definitely was more photogenic. George was usually a pedal-to-the-metal, back-in-black, bust-your-balls-if-you-cross-him type. But now, he mutely followed Ralph, holding his hand as though he were five years old. Ralph hadn't been joking. Something was definitely wrong. The Greyhoof boys were never meek and mild.

"George, why don't you sit by me. Do you mind?"

He shrugged. "Don't really care," he said. He was staring at the art on the walls. Franny's picture was there, a painting made by her long-unrequited love while she was still alive. "She's pretty."

"Yes, she was, wasn't she? She still is, although she's a ghost now. So, your brother tells me you aren't feeling well?"

Ralph prodded George. "Tell her what you told me."

"What?" he asked.

I spoke up. "Tell me how you feel, George."

"Oh." A long silence passed before he spoke again. "I'm tired. I just really want to take a nap." The satyr sounded distant, as though he were talking through a long tunnel. He kept his gaze on the painting of Franny, silent until Ralph smacked him lightly on the head.

"Dude, I said tell her what you told me."

George looked irked, but he shifted his shoulders and turned to me. "I don't have any energy. It feels like I'm running low on joy-juice and no matter how much I sleep, I don't feel better."

I frowned. Lethargy was highly unusual for a satyr. They were usually incredibly robust and virile. Their stamina, both in and out of bed, kept them running from dawn till dusk.

"I was wondering if he might be under a hex of some sort." Ralph glanced at me. "This isn't normal."

"If he won't go to the doctor, how about we bring the doctor to him? I can call Jordan Farrows. He specializes in magical afflictions."

"Would you mind?" Ralph's tone was so worried I relented, feeling sorry for him. He was obviously concerned about his brother.

"Let me give him a call. I don't know if he can make it over right away, but we'll see." I pulled out my phone and poked around till I found his number. The new phone had a lot of new features which, of course, made it harder to find what I wanted. The phone rang three times before Jordan picked up.

"Farrows here. What's up, Maddy?"

"Hey, I wondered if you could come over."

"Are you all right? Has the vertigo gotten worse?"

I reassured him I was fine. "No, it's still here but not worse. A friend of mine is having a hard time right now. His brother is lethargic and exhausted and there seems to be no reason for it. He's a satyr. One of the Greyhoof boys."

Jordan let out a laugh. "That's off kilter, all right. Let me see, it's three o'clock now. I'll be over in half an hour, if I can make it through the storm. The Greyhoofs at your house right now?"

"Yeah, they are. See you in a while." I hung up. "Jordan will be over in half an hour. Meanwhile, when Kelson comes back, I'll..." I paused as she entered the parlor, the twins behind her. "I think we could all use some soup and bread, Kelson."

She nodded. "Come on into the dining room, then."

Before she could help me up, Ralph picked me up and carried me to the table, returning to the living room to lead his brother in. Kelson arched her eyebrows and I could see the upturned lips as she suppressed a smile. The twins joined us, settling in.

Kelson motioned to Ralph. "Let me give you the dishes. Set the table, would you?"

They headed into the kitchen and Ralph returned with a stack of plates, setting them around the table. Watching Ralph do domestic work made me smile. He was so blustery normally, but another side of his nature was showing itself today. This side, I rather liked.

Kelson carried in my beautiful Woodland Spode soup tureen, filled with fragrant soup. Ralph helped her with the platter of rolls, butter, and honey. As we settled in to the hearty lunch, we ate in silence, savoring the rich broth and the hearty chicken and noodles.

I placed a slice of Gouda on a piece of toasted French bread and melted into the flavor as I bit into it. Yeasty and hot, crunchy but with a soft underside, the bread was so good it didn't need the cheese, but the pairing was exquisite.

"I think I've died and gone to heaven," I said, my mouth full.

"Yes, indeed," Henrietta said. "Don't you agree, Mazy?"

"Definitely, Henny. My compliments to the chef."

Mazy and Henrietta both had appetites to match their enthusiasm.

At that moment, Franny popped in, looking startled

when she saw us all gathered around the table. "I didn't know anybody would be here," she said, blushing.

"We're just having a late lunch." I waved my spoon at her.

"Franny? I found those photographs we were talking ab—" Mr. Mosswood strode into the room, stopping short when he saw us. He blushed. "I'm sorry, I didn't mean to interrupt."

I glanced from Henry to Franny, then back again. Something was up between the pair of them, that I could tell.

"Henry, I didn't know you were here or I would have called you to the table," Kelson said.

"Please join us for a late lunch." I motioned to the chair next to me. "Franny, feel free to stick around. These are our new guests."

Franny was staring at Ralph. "New guests?"

"Well, at least for lunch. The Fadero twins will be staying with us for a night or two until Ralph can have the roof of his inn fixed. Ralph and his brother are just staying for lunch. Mazy, Henrietta, George, this is Franny, our house ghost. And Mr. Mosswood is our other guest. He's been here, well, for some months now."

Mazy and Henrietta took Franny's presence with a blink and a smile while Ralph brought another place setting for Henry and Kelson served him a bowl of soup and some bread.

"I've always wanted to meet a ghost," Mazy said. "Tell me, are you housebound?"

"Yes," Franny said, looking like she wanted to dive into the wall and vanish.

"That must get utterly boring," Henrietta said.

"It wears on my nerves, for sure." Franny cleared her throat. "Well, I'll be running along. Mr. Mosswood, I'll talk to you later?" And with that, she vanished through the floor.

I wondered what the hell was up with her and Henry, but it wasn't my place to pry. Whatever secrets she had were hers as long as it didn't affect the running of the Bewitching Bedlam. I kept out of her affairs except for one. I had promised to try to free her from the curse that bound her to the inn. That promise, I intended on fulfilling.

Henry politely engaged the Fadero twins and kept them entertained with tidbits of Bedlam's history that he had managed to cull out of the locals. Ralph watched his brother as he ate—but George hadn't touched his plate except to nibble on the bread a bit.

Finally, the doorbell rang again and Kelson went to answer it. Relieved, I pushed back my plate. While the food was excellent, I hadn't been this uncomfortable in a long time. By the time Kelson returned with Jordan in tow, I was more than ready to end the awkward luncheon.

I asked Ralph to lead George into the parlor. It was obvious by now that George was in a bad state. He had barely eaten any lunch, a telltale sign right there. Satyrs had voracious appetites, and not just in the bedroom. He hadn't said a single word of his own volition. Kelson brought me the chair from my office and I rolled along behind them.

Jordan indicated for George to take a seat. "Please take off your shirt," he said.

George stared at him, unmoving. Ralph tapped his brother on the shoulder.

"Do as the doctor orders. Take off your shirt. Here let me help you."

George obediently held up his hands and Ralph pulled his T-shirt over his head. He set it to the side and stood back. I glanced at George. He was beefy, like his brothers, but he sure didn't have the abs that Ralph had. Then again, he was probably twice as strong. It was like comparing power lifters to bodybuilders—apples and oranges.

Jordan listened to George's heart, then tapped his back, listening to his lungs. "I don't hear a problem with his heart or his lungs, except his breathing is faint." He suddenly froze. "Wait a minute."

Ralph stiffened. "What are you talking about, doctor? Did you find something?"

Jordan nodded, crooking his finger for Ralph to come closer. I was sitting on my chair behind the sofa, so I could see what Jordan was doing. Jordan lifted George's hair off the nape of his neck and pointed to two rough scars. They were holes, fang marks.

"*Vampire*," I whispered.

"I do believe that's what we have here. George is in thrall. He's probably anemic as hell. I need to do a blood test on him right now. He probably needs an immediate transfusion." Jordan glanced out the window. The storm was blowing so hard it was hard to see beyond the rain. "I'm not sure if I can make it to the hospital. We need a heavier car than mine. I was blown all over the road when I came here."

"You can take my CR-V," I said. "Kelson can drive you."

"No," Kelson said. "I'm not leaving you here without a

way to get around. And I sure as hell wouldn't trust the twins to help you."

"We have to get George to the hospital. If a vampire has been drinking off of him, then there's a good chance that he's so anemic he could die. We have no way of knowing if the vampire made him feed, which means there is a possibility George could turn if he dies." I suddenly shut up, glancing at Ralph, who looked stricken. "I'm so sorry, Ralph. I didn't think before I spoke." I felt horrible.

Ralph looked like he was going to throw up. "No," he said. "I knew there was trouble. I knew George was in trouble. I can drive. When I brought the Fadero twins over here, I used the Jeep. We can take George to the hospital in that."

Jordan looked skeptical. "Are you sure you can drive without putting us in danger? I know you're worried, but I don't want to take a chance on *all* of our lives because of that."

"Kelson, drive them. You're good on the road and I'll be fine here until you get back. I can roll around in my office chair. If George needs a transfusion, we can't do it here. We don't even know what blood type he is, or if anybody here is a donor."

All the Otherkin, including witches, had their own special blood types. Most weren't interconnected, meaning that generally a witch couldn't donate blood for a satyr, and a satyr couldn't donate blood for a werewolf. There was one commonality—anybody could use blood from humans who were type O. Apparently, that had been an original bloodline for so many of us, and was present in all races.

"George is type S-7. William has the same blood type, but I'm S-8. And William is on the other side of the island today." Ralph looked at Kelson. "Do you have a blanket we can wrap him in? He's starting to shiver and I'm worried that he's cold."

That seemed to decide her, because Kelson headed for the door. "I'll get a blanket and the keys. Maddy, I want you to promise to call me if you need anything."

"I promise. Don't worry about me. I'm safe and secure inside, and it's warm in here. We may lose power, but I can always light a fire in the fireplace." I looked up at the clock. "You had better get a move on, though, before it gets much darker."

Outside, the storm had grown so hectic that the sky was almost black. It was the color of twilight, the color of dusk, and it wasn't even four o'clock yet.

"I wish Aegis was awake, but he won't be up for another couple hours." I fussed, wanting to help as Jordan led George to the door. Kelson came running back with a fleece blanket, which she wrapped around his shoulders. Ralph stopped beside me.

"Thanks, Maddy. I really appreciate your help. I can't believe this. Where on earth did he come into contact with a vampire? He'd never willingly let anybody feed off of him, so somebody had to do this against his will. I know that Essie has bloodwhores, and Aegis never puts anybody into thrall, does he?"

Ralph was searching for answers in a world without any. I reached out and patted his arm.

"No, Aegis never hurts his victims. Hopefully, we've discovered this in time for George. Jordan will do everything he can for him, and he'll probably be right as rain by tomorrow. I'll call Delia about this." I didn't want to tell him about the vampire killer, since that was a secret we were still keeping. But Delia needed to know that George had nearly been drained.

By the time Jordan and Ralph got George out to the CR-V, and Kelson joined them, I was rolling toward my office. Kelson dashed in one last time.

"Are you sure you're okay with me taking off like this?" she asked, looking worried.

"I'm fine. It won't be long before Aegis wakes up. Call and let me know how George is. You'll need to bring Ralph and his brother home. If Jordan wants to wait out the storm, he's welcome here, so he can take his car home."

Kelson gave me a long look. "Somehow, I think with as much blood as George has lost, he's going to end up staying in the hospital. Didn't you notice how pale he is, especially for a satyr?"

"True enough," I said, sighing. I had hoped a simple transfusion would do the trick, but Kelson was probably right. As she slipped into her coat, Kelson met my gaze.

"I hope George doesn't die. And I hope he didn't drink from the vampire. Because the last thing we need is a vampire-satyr on our hands." With that, she headed back out into the storm.

CHAPTER EIGHT

I put in a call to Delia. She answered on the second ring.

"I thought you needed to know this. George Greyhoof was bitten by a vampire. Jordan has taken him to the hospital for a transfusion. We're not sure if he's going to make it."

"Well, shit." Delia sounded as overjoyed as I felt. "Does he know when it happened or who bit him?"

"He's conscious but unresponsive. I think he's in thrall. Ralph was worried about him and came over to ask for my advice. Oh, and Ralph's roof got smashed by a tree, by the way. He brought George over, and after talking to him, I decided to call Jordan."

"He was able to get there in this storm? Impressive."

"He almost didn't. In order to take George to the hospital, Kelson had to drive them there in my CR-V. Jordan didn't want to chance going in his car. He said the winds were so bad that he was almost knocked off the road. I hope they make it through all right."

"Do you know if the vampire forced George to drink from him?"

Delia's mind was going where mine had.

"We don't know. I suppose, if George doesn't make it, we'll find out." The thought of the satyr ending up as a vampire hit me in the gut. I might not be the Greyhoof boys' biggest fan, but I didn't wish them any ill will like that.

"I wonder why the vampire didn't just kill George. If it's the same one that attacked the woman the other night."

"Maybe George managed to get away. Or maybe somebody interrupted him before he could kill George. If it is a *he*." The last vampire I had tangled with in Bedlam had been Aegis's ex-girlfriend. I had also ended up on the wrong side of a member of the Arcānus Nocturni while on vacation at the beginning of the year.

Delia hesitated for a moment. Finally, she asked, "Do you really believe that Essie is innocent? That she's telling the truth when she says she doesn't know who is doing this?"

"Honestly? I can't be sure, but in my opinion Essie doesn't want anybody messing up her gig here. If a vampire from her nest went rogue and was running around putting the fang on people, I think she'd stake them without a second thought. Remember, Essie took the throne via assassination. She has no compunction about staking other vamps when her ass is on the line, or when she stands to gain by it. I'll give her another call when the sun goes down. I'm not going over to her house tonight, not with the storm, but I'll talk to her."

"Thanks, Maddy."

"By the way," I asked, listening to the squall that was raging outside. "Just how bad is this storm supposed to get, do you know?" Another gust rattled the windows, and I glanced at the sliding glass door nervously.

"Winds are forecast to peak at a steady forty miles an hour, with gusts potentially reaching as high as sixty or seventy on Bedlam. The other islands aren't getting hit quite as bad. Bedlam always takes a harder hit. But it's not going to be fun anywhere out in the straits." She let out a slow breath. "We need to catch this vampire, Maddy, before he—she—it can do any more damage. I've managed to keep the news out of the paper so far, but we can't for long."

"I'll call Essie again, I promise." I knew Delia was leaning on my shoulders because of my background. She knew I had what it took to go out and hunt down vamps. She also knew that I still had my silver stake and dagger from three centuries back. But possessing them was a lot different than using them.

"Thanks. Call me if you need anything before Kelson makes it home. But then, Aegis should be waking up soon, shouldn't he?"

I glanced at the clock. It was five-fifteen. "Yeah, another hour or so. I'll let you know what Essie says." As I set down my phone, a bolt of lightning blazed through the sky, followed by a rumble of thunder. I rolled myself through the kitchen and down the hall to the bathroom.

By the time I got back to the kitchen, the twins were back at the table with Mr. Mosswood, playing pinochle. Crap—*dinner*! Kelson wasn't here to get it started. I rolled over to the refrigerator and peeked in. Nothing looked ready except for dessert. Then I remembered the take-and-bake pizzas.

"You guys mind pizza for dinner?"

Henry flashed me a giant smile. "That sounds wonderful."

The twins nodded, so I peeked in the side-by-side freezer. Bingo. I pulled them out and rolled over to the oven, turning it on to preheat. I slid them onto a baking sheet, then put them into the oven and set the timer for thirty minutes.

Feeling brave, I stood, leaning on the counter. I was still dizzy but I didn't think it was quite as bad. I decided to wash the dishes while I was up. I could lean on the counter and get used to having the blood flowing again.

The water was warm, and the soap smelled like lemon. I closed my eyes, my hands soaking in the water, and then slowly began to wash the plates that had been stacked on the counter. Kelson usually rinsed and put dishes into the dishwasher as soon as they were in the kitchen, but today had been an off day, all the way around.

As I finished up the last cup, I realized that I had been standing there for half an hour with no problem. I turned, but too quickly, and teetered, trying to catch my balance. My hands were soapy and as I grabbed the edge of the counter, my fingers slipped and I went careening to the floor. I narrowly missed hitting my head on the arm of the chair, and sprawled out across the tile. As I lay there, cursing, Bubba raced up and, more slowly, Luna. Bubba sniffed my face and I blinked, staring into his brilliant green eyes.

"What are you looking at?" I wrinkled my nose at him. "You could at least help me up."

He promptly flipped over on his back, spreading his legs. I stared at his massively fuzzy belly.

"Oh no. Nope. Nopety-nope. Not gonna happen."

"Are you all right?" Henry trotted over and knelt beside me. "Maddy, are you all right?"

I groaned as he helped me sit up. "I got a little too cocky and stood for too long. The vertigo got me. I'll be all right if I can get into that chair." I was jarred, and I knew I was developing a few bruises, but they would just add to the mess I had gotten during our night in the water.

Henry helped me roll over onto my hands and knees, and then, using the chair for balance, I was able to pull myself up and slide into it. The room was spinning, though not terribly, but mostly I just felt like an idiot.

"I overdid it. The vertigo is clearing up, but I got overconfident. It's going to take another day or so, I guess."

"You shouldn't have been doing dishes anyway. That's Kelson's job," Franny said, appearing halfway through the counter, which cut her off at the hips. She crossed her arms over her chest, staring down at me with a disapproving frown.

"Yikes, you look like you've been sawed in half."

"Never mind how I look. Maudlin, you know what you were told—" Franny leaned in to scold me. "What were you doing?"

"I wanted to stand up. I'm tired of sitting. My ass hurts." I snickered as she rolled her eyes. "Seriously, sitting down all day makes my tailbone ache."

Henry pressed a glass into my hand. It had ice and cold water. I thanked him quietly and sipped the icy liquid, though what I really wanted was a cup of hot cocoa or broth. I was saved from further scolding when the basement door opened and Aegis popped into the room.

"You're awake!" I started to stand but Henry laid a gentle hand on my shoulder.

Aegis looked at him, then at me, and then at Franny. "Did I miss something?"

"Only Maddy taking a tumble because she stood up too long and got dizzy." Franny floated out from the counter, into the center of the kitchen. She made a *tsk*ing sound.

Henry laughed softly, but said, "Franny, dear, now you shouldn't scold Maddy. She's a grown woman and she knows what she's capable of. She just took a little spill, that's all."

I froze. Franny *dear*? I glanced over at Henry, then at Franny, then at Henry again. Something was clearly going on here and I wasn't sure I wanted to know what.

"I was washing the dishes and stood up too long. I'm all right."

Aegis had apparently caught Henry's slip, too, because he was giving them both a close look as well. "Be careful," he said absently. Then, shaking his head, he gave me a kiss. "I mean it. Be careful. We don't want you hurting yourself. So, what happened today and—" He paused as another lightning fork split the sky, and the echo of thunder rolled after it. "Who decided we needed another light show?"

"Today's been—" I paused as my phone rang. I glanced at the Caller ID. Sandy. "Hold on, I should take this." I punched the talk button. "Hey, woman, how goes it?"

"I need your help." She sounded frantic.

"What's going on?" My stomach lurched.

"Jenna's conjured a giant snake. I'm in her room with her, and the snake has cornered us in the closet. I think it's venomous, Maddy, and I don't have any spells that will help. I'm using the force of the storm's wind to keep the door closed, but the snake is trying to bash it in."

"Where's Max?"

"On that business trip I told you he was taking."

"Hang on. We're on the way." I hung up and turned to Aegis. "We have to get over to Sandy's. I'll explain on the way. There isn't a lot of time, so help me out to your car."

"In this weather? We should take yours."

"Kelson has mine and I'll explain that, too. Now carry me out to the 'Vette and let's move."

I told Henry to take the pizzas out when the timer sounded and, with that, Aegis swept me up and headed for the door, not even stopping for a jacket.

AEGIS WAS A GOOD DRIVER, BUT EVEN HE WAS HAVING trouble in the storm. We wavered all over the road, the winds were roaring, and the Corvette wasn't that heavy a car. We were swept from side to side, but luckily there were few people on the road. We had to take an alternative route since Ralph's tree was still across the road. All the way over to Sandy's, we dodged flying boughs and downed wires.

A good share of the island had been plunged into darkness, but somehow we managed to find our way through and pulled into Sandy's driveway. She still had a couple guards from the goon squad that Max had hired from Rocco, a self-proclaimed weretiger vigilante who was intent on taking out the Pretcom mafia.

They recognized the car and came running over to help us out. Aegis strode around the back, tossed me over his shoulder, and raced to the door, where Alex quickly ushered us in.

"They're locked in Jenna's room," he said, as we hustled down the hallway. "I'd go in, but I'd just be in the way or get myself hurt. But whatever you need me to do, just ask."

"Do you know what the hell brought this on?"

"I can tell you right now that the snake is the same type that killed Jenna's mother. It's just about ten times bigger."

We stopped at the door of Jenna's room. Aegis carefully set me down.

"Do you have anything that can work against the snake?"

I ran through my repertoire of spells, then shook my head. "Nothing that won't set the room on fire."

"I can go in there without getting hurt. There's not much a snake can do to me, venomous or otherwise." Aegis stripped off his leather jacket. "I don't want it getting its fangs in my new jacket," he said.

"Well, you know your priorities," Alex said with a laugh. Then he sobered again. "I haven't heard anything for a little while. I hope to hell that snake hasn't managed to break through the closet door, where Sandy and Jenna are still hiding."

Aegis motioned for me to stand back, then turned Alex. "Get her a chair. She's unsteady on her feet." He waited until Alex ran into the other room and returned with one of the dining room chairs.

I sat down and nodded to Aegis. "All right, I'm going to prep a fire spell just in case. Hopefully, I won't have to use it."

"For luck," Aegis said, then planted a quick kiss on my lips.

"You've been watching *Star Wars* again, haven't you?" I patted him on the arm. "Go get the snake."

Aegis tried the doorknob. It wasn't locked, and he stood back as he flung open the door. From where I was sitting I could see a massive coastal taipan. It was a sleek, smooth snake, with reddish-brown scales, lighter on its sides than its belly. It was rearing up, coiling to strike with large, gleaming fangs. But I noticed something different about it.

There was a glow about it that wasn't natural. Obviously, Jenna had conjured it so it was a summoned creature, but there was more to it than that. It wasn't just a giant snake. I could feel the energy emanating off of it. It felt hot, prickly with frustration and irritation. And then, I *knew*.

I opened my eyes just in time to see Aegis throw himself on the giant snake, straddling it as best he could to hold it down. It swiped at him, but he managed to catch hold of its neck and, with his incredible strength, pressed its head to the floor, holding it down.

"That's a fire elemental." Cautiously, I stood. Alex was beside me, and he took hold of my elbow, steadying me. "You aren't going to be able to kill it. But since I work with fire, I can dispel it."

"Whatever you do, you'd better do it quick, because I

can't hold it for long. The creature's incredibly strong," Aegis said, struggling to hang onto it.

I held out my hands, turning to look at Alex. "I need you to steady me. This spell will pack a punch and I don't know if I can stand through it without help."

"Whatever you need," Alex said, swinging around behind me to hold my waist with firm hands. I noticed he smelled like gardenia and vanilla, an odd combination. But the thought quickly vanished from my mind as I focused on what I needed to do.

One of the first things a witch learns after she discovers her prime element is how to dispel that element. I focused on the snake, on the core of its fire, on its heart, which beat with a molten center. I reached out, whispering an incantation to ensnare the fire elemental.

> *Flare up, flare down, creature of fire,*
> *Bend to my will, to my own desire,*
> *Hear my call, hear my command,*
> *I bind your strength, I bind your brand.*
> *I speak your heart, I speak your name,*
> *I weave a net around your flame,*
> *I bind your will, I bind your soul,*
> *I bind you under my control.*

My voice grew louder, and as I shouted out the last, the fire snake slumped to the ground, waiting for me to command it. I turned to Alex.

"Help me get closer. It won't hurt you as long as I'm in control." I was shivering. The force exerted by the elemental was incredibly strong, and I felt it struggling against my will. I motioned for Aegis to get off of its back. He quickly stepped away.

As I neared its side, I knelt, laying both of my hands on the smooth, warm scales. It was beautiful, really. Incredibly powerful and strong, the fire snake hadn't asked to be here. I was just going to send it back to its home. Jenna may have conjured it here, but I was far stronger than she was, and it would bend to my will.

> *Creature of fire thou art,*
> *Summoned here by mistake,*
> *Begone back to your realm,*
> *You fiery snake.*
> *Now hie you hence, begone,*
> *Never more to return.*
> *By my will, so mote it be.*

With a soft breath, I blew on the scales and the snake shimmered, then vanished as if it had never been here. I slumped to the floor, shaking. The amount of energy it had taken to send the fire snake away had drained me of almost every reserve I had.

Aegis knelt beside me, softly lifting me up to set me on the bed, as Alex opened the closet. Sandy and Jenna slowly crept out, hugging each other. Sandy looked strained, but Jenna looked absolutely terrified. She surveyed the empty bedroom and burst into tears as she covered her face.

"I'm so sorry. I'm so sorry—I didn't mean it, really! Aunt Sandy, I could have killed you." Jenna was having a full-on meltdown, something I hadn't seen very often. The girl had a steady head on her shoulders and she was incredibly capable under a strain, but apparently this had been one step too far.

"Why did you conjure that thing up?" I leaned forward, balancing myself on the edge of the bed with one hand.

"She didn't mean to—" Sandy started to say, but I shook my head at her.

"Jenna has to learn responsibility for her magic at some point. You think this would go unnoticed at Neverfall, or that it would be excused away?"

I didn't want to come down hard on the girl, but as the High Priestess of the Moonrise Coven it was my job to step in when I saw situations like this. Literally, it was written in the Code of Honor that I had pledged to, that if I came across a gross misuse of magic, especially by someone who was attempting to work magic far beyond their means, I needed to step in. I didn't pay a lot of attention to others, and I didn't go poking my nose into other people's activities, but Jenna needed to learn and learn quickly that she couldn't just go around trying to summon up elementals she didn't have any control over. If Neverfall caught wind of this, she'd be expelled.

Jenna swallowed hard. She let out a soft sigh. "I know what I did was wrong. I didn't really mean to. It just kind of…happened."

"What do you mean, it just *happened*?"

"I was sitting on my bed, and I was thinking about my mother. She was always running off, leaving me with the servants, or with friends. I've always been angry at her for that. But ever since she left me in Aunt Sandy's care, I've felt a lot happier." She lowered her voice to a whisper. "Lately, I've caught myself wishing my mom would die, or never come back, so I could stay with Aunt Sandy."

I began to catch the drift of what she was thinking. "And now your mom *is* dead."

She nodded, a bubble of spit forming on her lip as she tried to sniff back the tears. "I should be punished. I wished she was dead, and now she is."

"So you've been feeling terribly guilty over what happened, and you somehow conjured the snake? As a punishment to yourself?"

She silently nodded.

I cleared my throat. "Jenna, honey, listen to me. You didn't cause your mother's death. If we could cause death with just a thought—with just our anger—there would be a lot fewer people in the world. It's normal to be angry at people we love when they hurt us. Your mother didn't hit you, I assume, but she left you on your own a lot, and that's a form of neglect. Derry was self-centered and she didn't know how to be a good mother. It's okay to be angry at her for that, and it's okay to be angry that she died."

I must have stung a nerve because Jenna started sobbing.

"She wouldn't have died if she had stayed home, if she hadn't wanted to get away from me." Her face was a mask of pain, and Sandy slowly edged over to her.

"Jenna, can I sit down?" She paused by the side of the bed.

Jenna nodded, furiously wiping her eyes.

"Your mother loved you very much, but she wasn't cut out to be a mother. Some women aren't, and they don't realize it before they have kids."

"I know that," Jenna said, but the look on her face told me she didn't fully understand. And she probably wouldn't, at least not for a while. Derry's death must have seemed like the final abandonment. And we couldn't exactly say it was an accident. Derry knew she shouldn't have been out where she was. She had ignored the rules and paid for it with her life.

"Your mother made a fatal mistake. But *you* didn't have anything to do with her death. Sometimes, things happen. Sometimes, life sucks and we have to just take it in stride." I knelt beside her and took one hand, while Sandy took her other. "Nobody's to blame, really. Even Derry. She made a fatal mistake, but she didn't do it on purpose. Trust me on that."

After a while, Jenna's sobs lessened and I handed her a tissue. She blew her nose and turned to Sandy. "I'm sorry. I almost got you killed," she whispered.

"No harm done. We're all safe and the snake is gone. You needed to express your anger. But next time, try talking about it, okay? You can *always* talk to me about whatever you need to." Sandy brushed a strand of hair back from Jenna's face and then stroked her cheek and booped her on the nose. "You must be awfully tired."

Jenna nodded. "I am. I feel all worn out."

"Jenna, did you know that you summoned a fire snake? A fire elemental?" I had to address it at some point and now seemed like the best time.

Jenna startled, whirling around to stare at me. "*What*? I kept thinking of the snake that killed Derry and I got madder and madder at her. I was so angry, it felt like I was vibrating. And then, just as Sandy walked in the room, the snake appeared."

"Your anger must have somehow caught the attention of a wandering fire elemental and it came in the form of the snake that you were focusing on. Sandy and I need to teach you how to harness your energy. Neverfall is a wonderful school, but you seem to have some pretty strong gifts and until you know how to separate your magic from your thoughts and emotions, life is going to be too dangerous for you and those around you. Will you work with us?" She had to *want* to learn, to want to control herself before we could teach her.

Jenna nodded. "I'm afraid of my own thoughts now. Please, help me."

"We can," Sandy said, "but the best way to prevent things like this from happening is to talk them out the minute you start feeling upset."

I glanced at the calendar. "We'll start on the next new moon."

Sandy nodded. "We'll be there. Jenna, you're a quick study, so this shouldn't take long." She paused, glancing at me. "I suppose we'll have to plan out a Cord Cutting for Derry. She didn't belong to any formalized group, but she definitely had a lot of friends around the area." She glanced at Jenna. "Don't feel you have to attend. When you're ready, we can do another ceremony for you privately."

Jenna bit her lip, then let out a sigh. "I'm not ready. I may have hated her at times, but…"

"She was your mother," I said. "I understand."

Jenna started to cry, softly, and Sandy wrapped her arm around the girl. "I'm not going to say it's all right, because it's not. But I'm here, and so is Maddy, and we'll help you through this."

I motioned to Alex. "I'll just leave you two here

together. I imagine you have some things you need to talk about. Alex, help me out?"

Aegis had already withdrawn, so Alex leaned down for me to wrap my arm around his shoulder and, holding me by the waist, helped me out to the dining room, where Aegis had poured himself a drink. He poured me one too—a snifter of brandy. I usually drank wine, but right now, the sharp heat of the liquor seemed just right.

I eased myself into a chair at the table and cupped the brandy snifter in my hands, warming the drink. "How bad is the storm now?"

"Worse. It's rattling the island. I don't know that I trust the 'Vette to get us home in one piece." He glanced at the lights as they flickered.

Alex crossed to the massive double-sided fireplace that divided the dining room from a parlor. He struck a long match and then held the flame to an already prepared stack of wood and kindling. The fire caught, and blazed to life. Then, taking a long lighter, he swiftly began lighting candles around the room. He moved quickly, but not quite quick enough to beat the lights flickering one last time before they died. But we had the firelight to see by, and Alex finished lighting the rest of the candles.

As I was sitting there, Mr. Peabody waddled over and rubbed against me. I leaned down and caught the skunk up in my arms, cradling him as I stroked the soft fur.

"How are you feeling, Mr. Peabody? Is life treating you good?" I scratched him under the chin, just where he liked it, and he squirmed a little, letting out a squeak of joy. After a moment, I set him back down and he hustled over to Aegis for more attention.

A few minutes later, Sandy appeared, carrying a flashlight. "Jenna's taking a nap. I got her calmed down. I don't think we'll have any more unexpected reptilian guests, but we really need to teach her how to master her emotions."

I sipped my cognac. The heat burned a trail down my throat, warming me from the inside out. "I agree. She's extremely talented. I don't think Neverfall has quite caught on to just how much power she has. Probably because she didn't present favoring any particular element to begin with."

Sandy motioned for Alex to pour her a drink and sat beside me. "I'm starting to think she may be a shadow witch."

"You know, you might have something there." Shadow witches worked on the astral, more than working with any particular element. They were often more powerful than other witches, and they were definitely a rare breed. "You can ask Neverfall to test her. It's not a routine test at the school. The tests aren't easy, I gather."

"They aren't. I'll call the headmaster tomorrow and set something up for next month. I think she needs time to process Derry's death first."

We sat in silence, listening to the crackle of the flames, sipping our drinks. Alex brought over a plate of fruit and cheese, and Sandy motioned for him to sit with us. Outside, the wind howled a frightful row. I shuddered, closing my eyes. The storm was alive; there was a sentience to it that I could feel, even inside the house. It was searching for something, or someone, and it wasn't going to rest till it found them.

"Ralph had to take George to the hospital," I said, remembering that Sandy didn't know about what had happened. "George was nearly drained by a vampire."

At that, the wind raised another row, rattling the windows.

Sandy asked Alex to close the storm shutters. Then she turned to me. "This series of storms the past few nights—you know they aren't natural. You know somebody's behind them and you know who."

I had been trying my best not to think about it, but at her words, I broke down and let the possibility come flooding into my mind. I fished in my pocket for the bronze pentacle, and sat it in front of me, on the table. "Yeah, I know. But the question is, when will she arrive? And what will she be like? And the most important question—why has she returned?"

"I suppose we'll find out when we find out. Unless you want to ask Auntie Tautau if she knows anything about it." Sandy caught my gaze, holding it steady. She was as worried as I was.

I thought about it. Auntie Tautau might know something, but whether she would give us any useful information was definitely up for debate. But then, something clicked. A memory. I closed my eyes as the words replayed themselves over and over again.

Auntie Tautau had provided me with a means to procure an herb that had saved Sandy's life. I had asked her, "Is there a price?" Because I knew full well that when you dealt with the Aunties, their help was never free.

She had said to me, *"There's always a price. You have already paid it, though you don't realize it yet. You'll know, when the time comes, what that price has set into motion."*

"I know why. I don't know the reasoning behind it, but I know why she's returning."

Aegis and Sandy leaned in, staring at me.

"It was back when Garret was helping me find the thistlestar." I told them about going to Auntie Tautau and what she had said. "She told me I'd know what the price was, when it was set into motion. This is it. In the depths of my gut, I know. What I did somehow wove Fata Morgana back into our lives."

Sandy let out a long breath. "We both set it into motion. You wouldn't have been looking for the herb if you hadn't been trying to save me. Well, then. I guess…now…we just wait."

And with that thought, we fell silent again, listening to the wild keening of the wind as it rolled and rattled and tore through the island, toppling trees and shaking down rooftops and sweeping up trash bins to scatter them through the streets.

CHAPTER NINE

We waited out the storm at Sandy's. The wind clipped along at a good forty miles an hour sustained, and the gusts had to be sixty to seventy, as predicted. Alex brought us all warm blankets to curl up in, and we went into the parlor—to the other side of the fireplace—and snuggled up on the sofas. Jenna came out, looking ragged, and Alex found a sleeping bag and she curled up in front of the fireplace and soon fell back into a deep sleep.

"Trauma wears a body out," I said, staring at her slumbering form. "She's certainly had to deal with more than her share."

"Where's Max?" Aegis asked.

"He was due home tonight. I hope to hell he isn't on the ferry." Sandy pulled out her phone, biting her lip. "I don't want to seem clingy."

I could tell she wanted permission to text him. Sandy had no desire to play the clinging vine, but sometimes that worked to her detriment. "Call him already. See if he's holed up in Bellingham or Seattle."

She sucked in a quick breath. "All right." As she put in the call, Aegis and I shifted position. The ottomans fit squarely against the sofa, creating a queen-sized bed, and Alex had brought us an egg crate mattress to put over the top. We were comfortably stretched out, and I felt my eyes threatening to shut. The day had been too long, too full, and there was too much still ahead of us.

After a moment, Sandy was talking to Max. "I was worried. Are you still in Bellingham?" She paused, listening. "Shut down? Good, I think it would be a horrible mistake for them to run tonight." She paused again. "I love you too. I've got a lot to tell you, but that will keep for later."

She tucked her phone away. "He's in Bellingham, at the Golden Door. He said that the ferries have all shut down for the next few hours, so he'll catch the first one out as soon as he can."

"Given what the water must be like, that's a wise move." I yawned. "I'm sorry, but I can't keep my eyes open any longer. Do you mind if I zonk out?"

"Go ahead. I'm beat, too." Sandy flipped her recliner so that it was almost straight. "If you need anything, just wake me up."

"Or ask me," Alex said, settling down in an overstuffed armchair. "That's what I'm here for."

With Aegis watching over us, we drifted off to the crackle of the flames, which seemed to barely hold back the dread howl of the wind.

I woke around four in the morning to find the storm had died down to a steady patter of October rain. The wind was silent, and my vertigo seemed to have magically lifted overnight. Everybody else was awake and gathered in the kitchen. The power had come back on around three o'clock, so Alex was making a pre-dawn breakfast of bacon and waffles, with Jenna helping him. We gathered around the table for breakfast.

"How are you feeling?" I asked Jenna.

She shrugged. "Tired. I'm not used to getting up this early, but I was hungry so Alex said he'd cook breakfast. I'm better than last night, but I feel…kind of numb."

"Don't sweat it, Jenna. Feel exactly how you need to feel." I paused, feeling like I sounded like every other adult who talked to children. "Just be wherever you need to be right now."

"Thanks, Aunt Maddy." She gave me a pale gleam of a smile, but it vanished again, as she contemplated her waffle.

Without warning, the door swung open and Max came dragging in. He tossed his coat over the back of a chair as Sandy rushed into his arms. Max was about five-ten, burly and strong, with wheat-colored hair and deep brown eyes. He had a scar that traced down the left side of his face from his temple to his chin, but it only gave him a roguish look.

"The ferries working again?" Sandy reached up, stroking his hair out of his eyes.

"Yeah, and I had set my app to sound an alarm for when they came back into service. I caught the first one I could."

"You must be exhausted," Sandy said, steering him toward the table.

"Me? You all look pretty wiped out, too." After greeting Sandy, he tapped Jenna on the shoulder. "Do I rate a hug?"

"Yeah, Uncle Max." She slid out of her chair and he gave her a sound hug.

"How's the smartest girl at Neverfall doing?"

She blushed and ducked her head. "Not so hot, I guess."

Max glanced at Sandy, who shook her head and mouthed, "Later."

"Well, then, we'll have to do what we can to fix that." He glanced at the table. "Do I smell waffles? And bacon?" His eyes gleamed.

Alex laughed, peeking out the pass-through window. "I'll put some on for you, too."

"Thanks. I didn't bother with food at the hotel, since I figured I'd be heading out early. I didn't realize it would be the middle of the night, but hey." Max waved at us. "I see you all had a slumber party. Bummer I missed it. I'm going to go wash up. I'll be back down in a few."

As he headed toward the bedroom, it struck me how comfortable the three of them seemed around each other. Jenna, Sandy, and Max *fit* in a way that was undeniable.

I finished my second waffle and motioned to Aegis, who was on his third. "We should get home to see if there was any damage. And you have to get into your lair before sunrise."

He nodded, pushing back his chair. "I hate to eat and run, but Maddy's right."

Sandy flashed me a grateful smile. She had to tell Max

about Jenna and the snake, and that wasn't going to be an easy concept to explain to someone who didn't use much magic. Weretigers weren't as gun-shy of it as werewolves, but they still didn't tend to mess around with the arcane rites much.

I stood, testing my balance. "I think somehow last night wrung the last drop of vertigo out of me. Thank the gods, because I was getting damned tired of having to be helped everywhere."

Aegis gave me a stern look. "Feeling better or not, I'm still going to make certain you reach the car in one piece, and no driving today, either. Tomorrow, if you don't have any more vertigo, all right, but with me in the car. Or Kelson, I guess, given if I tried to help out in the daylight I'd be one hell of a crispy critter."

We made our farewells and were halfway to the car by the time Max opened the window to yell a quick goodbye to us.

As we drove home in the darkness, Aegis cautiously skirted downed boughs and trees that lay strewn across the roadways. More than once, we had to turn onto a side road to avoid a tree that was blocking the way. The island looked like it had come through a hurricane. We passed two houses where tall firs had been uprooted, crashing through the roofs. Tall timber had shallow root systems, and in the Pacific Northwest, it was by no means unusual for trees to topple like dominos after a major storm, where the ground had become so saturated with water that it couldn't hold the tree anymore.

"Come first light, this is going to be one heck of a sight." Aegis focused on the road. "You must be tired. I was awake, of course, but you and Sandy were out like the dead. Alex twitched a lot in his sleep, and poor Jenna, she was having some sort of nightmare. I wanted to wake her up, but then thought the better of it. She knows who I am, but being woken up by a man you're not used to being around doesn't inspire feelings of safety."

"Watch out!"

Aegis stepped on the brakes and we came to a screeching halt, two yards away from a confused-looking cougar standing in the road. As the car idled, the cougar gave us another look, then bounded back into the ravine next to us, disappearing into the undergrowth.

"I guess the storm disrupted everybody." Aegis hesitated. "You think it's an animal or a shifter?"

I watched the big cat bound out of sight. It stopped once to look at us over its shoulder, its eyes gleaming in the night. "I'm not sure."

We were almost home when I saw flashing lights down a side road. Something spurred me to ask Aegis to turn so we could find out what was going on. I wasn't usually one to put myself in the middle of matters better left to the police, but a little voice inside urged that we needed to be there.

As we pulled up, I saw Delia's new Expedition. She had bought the SUV about three weeks ago, and her customized license plate—SHERIFF—proudly announced her presence.

She glanced up as we eased onto the shoulder. We were next to Brackenwood Park—a small hiking park that offered one or two parking slots, but was used mostly by horseback riders, hikers, and biking enthusiasts. She headed over to the car as I rolled down my window.

"We were headed home from Sandy's. What's going on?" I glanced at the scene. There were at least two other squad cars present, as well as the medical examiner. That boded ill. He didn't come out unless somebody died.

She leaned against the door, looking worn out. "I was called out about an hour ago. A couple of teenagers who pulled in here to make out during the storm happened to find a dead body. Man around fifty, sprawled in the middle of the parking lot. Or what there is of it."

I held my breath, waiting.

"Another vampire kill, Maddy. We've got a serious problem on our hands." Delia pressed her lips together, looking like she wished she was anywhere but here.

THERE WASN'T MUCH I COULD DO BUT PROMISE TO CALL Essie again, so we headed for home. On the way, I pulled out my cell, surprised to find a strong signal. Flipping to my contacts, I tapped Essie's name. Three rings later and Shar-Shar answered.

"Sharlene, please tell Essie that Maddy Gallowglass is calling and that it's urgent. Don't give me any BS about her being out, either. In this storm, I'd doubt it if you told me Thor himself was out and about." I used my no-nonsense tone of voice. Surprisingly, Shar-Shar reacted quickly.

"One moment, Maudlin." She put me on hold, and then, less than a minute later, Essie picked up.

"Maddy, why am I not surprised to hear from you again? What happened?"

I was as uninterested in small talk as she was. "Two things. One, another vampire kill tonight. Second, Ralph Greyhoof's brother has been drained by a vampire. We're not sure he'll make it. We think he's in thrall."

"Shit." Essie seldom swore, but the fact that *shit* was the first word out of her mouth told me she wasn't blowing this off. "You're sure?"

"Does a fish swim?"

"I'm going to send out my spies. There isn't much time till morning, but we'll do whatever we can to track down whoever it is and take care of him. Her. Whoever. One kill can be a slip. Two? A habit." She paused, then added, "I'll call Delia right now."

"She's at the scene of the latest kill. You should be able to get hold of her."

"All right. I'd say thank you, but—and don't take this wrong—I'm not particularly thrilled by the news." She hung up before I could say anything else.

"I did my duty. I called Essie. She's sending out her spies. I really don't think she's behind any of this." There wasn't much more I could say. We were facing a potential crisis and it wasn't something that could be easily dealt with behind the scenes. I thought about my silver dagger and stake back home, and decided I should probably start wearing them again. Aegis wouldn't necessarily like it, but we were facing a storm of a different kind now, it seemed.

As we pulled into our driveway, Aegis turned off the engine and then, before opening his door, turned to me. "Maddy, you do what you have to. I know what you're thinking, and I know that we can't let this get out of hand.

If you have to dust off your old skills, I'm not going to complain or feel threatened."

I nodded, letting out a long breath. "Thanks. Because I fear it may come to that." And then, with him holding me by the elbow, we headed into the house, back to what felt like safety.

AEGIS AND I ATTEMPTED TO MAKE LOVE WHEN WE GOT home, but to my chagrin, the room started to spin in a not-so-good way, and he insisted on stopping. After tucking me in with an admonition to "Sleep in and don't drive," he headed downstairs. I was thoroughly surprised when I immediately fell back asleep and slept like the dead until ten.

I managed to make it downstairs on my own, to the kitchen where Kelson had my latte ready. She had made it a strong one.

"By the time I got home last night, you and Aegis were gone. Was everything all right?"

I couldn't even remember if I had left her a note. "There was an emergency over at Sandy's, but luckily Aegis had just woken up and was able to drive me over there. The storm got so bad that we just stayed until early morning. We got back around four-thirty or five. How is George doing? Was Jordan able to give him a transfusion?"

"I stayed until he was out of danger, so I could bring Ralph home. George is still in the hospital, and Jordan still has some concerns about him. He'd been low on blood for a while, and that affects the internal organs. Or something like that. Anyway, for now he's out of immediate danger, though it's still touch and go. I brought Ralph home at around nine-thirty last night. Mr. Mosswood had done the dishes and made sure everybody had snacks. He told me that you and Aegis left abruptly after a phone call, and he also told me that you fainted standing at the sink doing dishes."

"I didn't faint, exactly. I just got dizzy. But the vertigo was almost gone this morning, and I was able to make it downstairs on my own, you'll notice."

"I did notice," she said. "Do you think you can drive?"

"I think so, but I promised Aegis I wouldn't until tomorrow. I suppose I could just take the car out and not tell him, but that's not the kind of relationship we have." I poked my nose in the fridge. "I feel like eggs and toast. I had waffles and bacon at around four A.M., but I'm hungry again." I handed her a carton of eggs and a loaf of bread, and then decided to sit down. I was still a little weak in the knees and I didn't want to push myself too hard. "When is Jordan going to pick up his car?" He had parked out front instead of in our driveway and I assumed his car was still there.

"He already did, early. He took a cab over and drove off at around eight o'clock."

"I suppose I should go check on Ralph today. That's what a good neighbor would do."

"You don't seem very enthusiastic about the idea." She popped a couple slices of bread into the toaster and cracked three eggs into the frying pan. "Are you sure you don't want anything else with this?"

"Do we have any fruit?" I asked. "I could go for some melon or a berry cup."

"I can pull you together one of those." She flashed me a grin.

"I should buy a home gym. It would be so much easier to work out if I didn't have to go all the way down to the gym every time and then Wilson wouldn't yell at me for missing as many workouts as I do." My trainer was hard to please, that was for sure.

"Um hm," Kelson said, sliding my toast and eggs in front of me. "Fruit's coming right up."

"No, really." I waved my fork at her. "Aegis could train me here. And then I could meet with Wilson once a week. There's plenty of room in the basement. We're partway through sorting out all the stuff that was left down there. We could put an air cleaner down there, and paint, and turn it into a workout–hangout space."

"I think it's a great idea, actually." She poured herself a cup of coffee and joined me at the table. "Several of the clients who've stayed here have asked if you had a good recommendation for a gym. If you had the space in the house for them to work out, it might spur on reservations. You'd have to ask them to sign a waiver of liability, of course."

"That's a good point." I thought about it for a moment. "Let's do it. That means we need to get our asses in gear and clear up the remaining crap down there. It will only take a week or so if we make a concerted effort on it."

"There's one other issue I wanted to talk to you about." Kelson looked around, as if to see if we were alone.

"Franny do something?" I kept my voice low. It was always hard to tell when she was hanging around, listening to the conversation.

Kelson shrugged. "I'm not sure, but I caught sight of

her and Mr. Mosswood in the hall, having what seemed like an intimate discussion. After that, and lunch yesterday, I think there might be something going on between them, though I'm not sure how that would work."

I leaned back with a groan. "I wondered about that. I've noticed some odd familiarity between them. How the hell, though…I mean, they're both adults—but he's alive and she's a spirit." I couldn't very well forbid her from seeing him. On the other hand, was that the reason he was hanging around? Had he fallen in love with Franny? If so, the only way he could see her was to stay here, since she was trapped in the house. "This all makes my head hurt."

"Mine too, but I thought you should know."

"I don't want to know." I let out a long sigh. "I guess I don't mean that, either. I'll have a talk with him. Or her. Or both. So, back to the home gym idea. What's your day like?"

"Well, Ralph's twins left to go see him this morning. I think they're hoping for a play date, if you know what I mean. Henry went out to do some research. So while everybody is out, I'm going to take the opportunity to clean up their bathrooms and put fresh sheets on the beds. We aren't expecting any new guests for a week, so other than that, it's general cleaning. I should be done by two. What would you like me to do?"

"I suppose we can get a start on the basement this afternoon." I paused, staring outside. Near the patio, an owl was perched on one of the low bushes. I recognized the bird. Not only had it come flying around me when Sandy had been hurt, so much that I wondered if it was an actual owl or a shifter instead, but I had seen it in the trees out back a number of times. Now, something urged me to go outside to greet it.

I cautiously walked to the slider, but there was no dizziness that I could sense. The eggs and toast had settled my stomach. I quietly slid open the door, making sure Bubba and Luna weren't around to follow me out. Closing the screen door behind me, I turned to the rhododendron the owl was perched in, and slowly advanced on it.

"Hi there. I recognize you. What are you doing here, especially in the daytime?" I spoke in an even voice, keeping my movements as smooth as I tried to keep my voice. I didn't want to spook the bird.

The owl looked at me, its unblinking eyes focused on my face. It was about sixteen inches tall, and it was a barred owl with mottled brown—almost gray—markings. The bars of color extended down its wings, and it remained calm, waiting for me as I drew closer.

"You've been following me for some time. What do you want?" I cautiously sat down at the patio table in one of the chairs that had managed to avoid being blown across the lawn. The grass was littered with boughs from the storm, and from here, I could see one of the trees along the side of the lot had lost a large branch, which had splintered off onto the ground.

The owl ruffled its feathers briefly, then took wing and flew over, landing on my shoulder. I sat very still. I wasn't afraid—the owl obviously had something to say to me—but I wasn't sure exactly what to do next.

I let out a long breath and closed my eyes, reaching out to see if I could touch the aura of the bird. A moment later, a flash surrounded us both and I could feel the energy loud and clear. The bird was magical. It wasn't a shifter, but it was definitely a familiar and it wasn't bound to anybody. It touched my thoughts and I sensed a question hanging between us. Almost an anticipation.

"You want to be my familiar? Is that it?"

A moment later, a warm glow surrounded me. The owl nestled itself into my energy and there was an odd moment that I had never experienced before. It was as though our auras entwined, and we became part of the same core, the same energy. At that moment, I could sense the thoughts of the owl, although not in a language I was used to. It was more of an impression whose meaning was crystal clear.

My name is Lanyear. I've been waiting for you.

I floated in the sensation for a moment before focusing my thoughts. It was more about focusing on emotion, or a concept rather than thinking *at* the bird. I focused on acceptance, on welcoming, because the overwhelming sensation that I felt was one of good fortune, of luck and of companionship.

I'm Maddy. How long have you been around?

I've been waiting since you first arrived. I'm here to work with you.

Bubba flashed through my mind. He wasn't my familiar—he was an entirely separate being. But I wondered how he would take to another creature joining the household. He had brought Luna in, but Luna was his girlfriend. This was not only a different species, but a *bird*. And the cat part of Bubba might not be too happy about Lanyear.

Do not worry, we'll make this work.

And with that, Lanyear settled himself on my shoulder, and—still rather overwhelmed—I headed back inside.

Kelson took Lanyear's appearance in stride. I called to Bubba and he came running in, followed by his ever-present shadow. Luna adored Bubba, and Bubba adored Luna, and they were almost always together.

"Bubba, I want you to meet somebody. Kelson, you too. This is Lanyear, and he's apparently my familiar. I think Arianrhod sent him, because when I first met him, I was asking her for a sign. That was a few months back."

Bubba gave me a long look. "*Mrrf?*"

"*Really*. You need to tell Luna not to mess with Lanyear. He won't hurt you as long as you don't try to hurt him." I glanced up at Kelson, who rolled her eyes and suppressed a snicker.

Bubba gazed at Lanyear, who let out a low hoot, and then turned, swishing his tail back and forth, and marched off out of the room. Luna gave Lanyear an inquisitive gaze, but followed Bubba.

"Well, that didn't go over very well, did it?"

Kelson laughed. "Did you really expect it to? At least neither of them made a jump for him." She glanced around the kitchen. "May I suggest we put up some tall perches—high toward the ceiling, away from any of the shelves Bubba and Luna can climb?"

"I think that's a good idea. Meanwhile, I'll ask him to stay right outside until we get those installed. No use asking for trouble."

I carried him back to the door and held out my arm.

He flapped his way from my shoulder to my wrist. Once again, I closed my eyes and felt for that connection.

Lanyear, until we make it safe for you—and safer for Bubba and Luna—you need to stay outside in the yard. Will you be all right?

Again, the whisper-soft flutter of wings on my thoughts. *I will. Call when you need me.*

I opened the door and he flew off my wrist, out to a tall tree near the house. As he took up a perch there, I thought how odd this year was turning out to be. But even as I was contemplating Lanyear and what the future would bring with him, a low rumble of thunder echoed as the sky darkened. I stepped out and watched as a huge thundercloud raced in. Lanyear flew lower in the tree, hiding beneath a branch thick with needles. There was something unnatural about the storm, something almost terrifying.

"Maddy! Maddy!" Sandy burst out of the kitchen and raced to my side. In the coming thunder, I hadn't even heard her drive up. "I drove like a maniac on the way over here. I had the terrible feeling that something is wrong. What's going on?"

I shivered, folding my arms across my chest. "I'm not certain, but I imagine it has to do with that." I nodded toward the cloud.

Sandy shaded her eyes, gazing up at the towering plume that rolled in on an updraft of wind. "The storm's alive."

"That storm's hiding something," I said softly, a prickling at the back of my neck. "Or *someone.*"

Sandy caught my arm, leaning close, as the clouds overtook the sky. Dark and frothing, forks of lightning rippled through them as the clouds lay siege to the island. An army in gray, they marched to the rumble of low thunder. My stomach twisted, but I couldn't turn away. I wrapped my arm through Sandy's as we waited for the storm to break. Kelson darted out the kitchen door to gaze up at the gathering tempest.

"What *is* that?" she whispered.

"I think…"

I paused as lightning streaked across the sky, forking out in all directions. Thunder ripped through the air and in that moment, the world seemed to freeze. A stillness fell over the area, as if the world had stopped. I huddled closer to Sandy. *One beat…two…three…*four beats passed and then, the clouds swirled into vortex, touching down in the woods behind my house. The trees churned as the funnel cloud spewed out moisture, and the clouds opened up to drench us with icy rain. The lightning crashed again, skipping from cloud to cloud.

The funnel cloud vanished, whipping back into the air as a figure emerged from the glade. Clad in a long black dress and billowing cape, her hair was flame red, as though it had been set afire, and even from this distance, I could see the glittering blue of her eyes.

"She's back," Sandy whispered.

I could only nod as Fata Morgana came striding toward us, returned from the ocean after two hundred years.

CHAPTER TEN

Fata Morgana.
 As she strode toward us, I let go of Sandy. We needed to meet her as an equal. One thing I knew about Fata was that she had a tendency to take over situations. Or at least, she had in the past and I doubted that had changed. No matter how I was feeling, I wasn't about to let her see my nervousness. Sandy seemed to sense my mood and she straightened her shoulders, and lifted her chin.

We waited until Fata was near, before moving forward to greet her. I wasn't sure what to expect, so I wasn't sure how to act. But Sandy stepped out in front, holding out her hands.

Fata Morgana paused, her gaze focused on me. For a moment, I thought she didn't even see Sandy. Then, slowly, she took a deep breath and said, "I'm back. Did you miss me?"

"Fata," Sandy said, withdrawing her hands when Fata

didn't meet them. "Welcome to Bedlam. Welcome to our home."

Only then did Fata turn toward Sandy and slowly smile. It was a feral smile, ever so slightly dangerous. "Cassandra, I wasn't sure whether you would be here. When Maddy summoned me, she woke me out of my slumber and I rose out of the ocean. I followed Maddy's call, and… Here I am."

A light flickered in her eyes that I didn't recognize. She was Fata Morgana, and yet, she wasn't. I reached out, searching for some familiarity. I knew it was her—there was no question of it. But she seemed distant and alien, like a sleeping princess who had been woken after a hundred years to find herself in a different land. I wanted to ask her inside, but I found myself a little afraid of what might happen.

Just then, Kelson opened the sliding door and Bubba ran out. He took one look at Fata, and dashed over and jumped into her arms. He had always liked her, and she, in turn, had been indulgent of him. Startled, she looked down, staring into his face for a moment. And then, the strange light flickered again and faded, and when she looked up we were staring at our Fata. At the Fata we had known and loved.

Bubba leaped down and wandered over to me. I picked him up, still worried.

Fata looked at the house and smiled. "So long, and yet, this house could have been around the last time I was out and about."

"It might have been. It was built in the early 1800s."

"What year is this?"

"2017. What's the last year you remember?" Sandy glanced up at the sky, which was whipping up another round of rain and wind. "Why don't we go inside?"

I nodded, motioning for them to follow me. Carrying Bubba, I led them into the kitchen.

Fata blinked at the artificial light. She took everything in, then shook her head. "So different. So many changes. I left in…it was a long time ago. It was after I left the two of you. I went over to Europe again, but didn't stay long. The call of the ocean was too strong."

"Where have you been all these years?" I asked. Bubba bounded out of the room, but before he left, he turned to me and let out a soft, "*Mrpp…m-row?*"

I gazed into his eyes. "I will, little guy. I will."

With another glance at Fata, he turned and silently padded out of the room. I slid a quick look toward Fata. She seemed to be calm and focused, but I'd have to be cautious. Letting her in the house was like letting a wild tiger enter my home.

Fata drifted over to the kitchen table and, running her fingers over it, slowly sat in one of the chairs. She leaned back, her face looking as young as the day she had left us. Her hair glistened, falling to her shoulders smooth and straight. She was completely dry, unlike Sandy and me, who were soaked through to the skin.

"Where was I?" Her voice was faint. She seemed to be a long ways away. "I rode the waves out to sea. Out to the wide, wild ocean. There was something calling me. To be honest, there's always been something calling me, since I was first born. I remember in my bed, as a child, I would close my eyes and hear the song of the ocean, beckoning me to come play. When we fought—oh, Maddy, how we fought that day. I was so angry with you. I wanted to drown the town and the two of you with it. But that was just the storm talking inside me. It wasn't me." She had closed her eyes and was leaning back.

I glanced over at Sandy, feeling totally creeped out. Fata Morgana had always been wild, but now, she felt barely constrained, on the edge of breaking into a fury. She was Fata, all right, but in the intervening centuries, something had definitely changed. Sandy licked her lips and gave me a cautious shake of the head.

After a moment, Fata spoke again. "What was I saying? Oh, yes. There was something calling me, and I summoned a wave. It came like the gentlest of horses and let me stand astride its back. And so I rode it out to the depths. For days, the wave carried me. When I was thirsty, there was rain, glorious rain, and I opened my mouth and drank straight from the heavens. When I was hungry, fish rose from the water, jumping high so that all I had to do was hold out my hand and they would land in my fingers. I ate them raw, alive, and the flesh was so sweet and so bright that I didn't want for anything else."

Fata opened her eyes, her lips wide in a brilliant smile. She was dazzling and beautiful, and she made me remember thoughts better left in the past. I shook away the vivid images that lingered in my mind, but when she caught my gaze, I had the feeling she, too, was remembering. She licked her lips slowly, then gave me the faintest hint of a wink.

"What did you do? You've been out of touch for nearly two hundred years." Sandy seemed to catch the nuances and intervened. I let out my breath, flashing her a silent thank-you.

"I dove deep, I swam in the currents, and became one with the Ocean Mother. She welcomed me in, kept me from drowning. When I was tired, I curled up in her underwater caves and slept deep—sometimes for decades. When I was hungry, there was always fish. When I was thirsty, the rains came. Until…sometime during the summer, when I seemed to wake out of a long dream. I heard you calling for help, Maddy, and I had a vision."

Pausing, she sniffed. "What smells so good?"

I cleared my throat. "Muffins, probably. Or soup. Kelson's making dinner. Are you hungry?"

Fata nodded. "I haven't wanted anything beyond fish for years, but now, my stomach aches. Do you have bread? And something hot? I don't care what, really. I just…it's been so long, but I need food again. Solid food."

She leaned forward, elbows on the table. "I'm confused," she said, and the sureness left her voice. She blinking, rubbing her eyes. "Where am I? What time is this? Maddy, how did we get here?" Fata asked frantically, a look of terror washing over her face. "I'm afraid."

Sandy jumped up, motioning to Kelson. "Get her some food. Something's happening."

I took hold of Fata's hands and held them tightly, trying to ground her. Sandy rubbed her shoulders, whispering words of comfort. After a few minutes, Fata seemed to relax. Kelson brought over a bowl of beef soup and a loaf of French bread with butter. Sandy slowly spooned the soup into Fata's mouth, and Fata swallowed, staring straight ahead.

After we had managed to get half a bowl of soup and a

slice of toast down her throat, Fata suddenly shifted in her chair, let out a soft cry, and fainted, slumping forward.

"Fuck. What the hell do we do? I suppose I can call Jordan." I wasn't sure what to think. I was absolutely unprepared for this.

"I think you better. Meanwhile, let's get her into the parlor and stretch her out." Sandy and Kelson carried Fata Morgana into the living room. They wouldn't let me help. I found a blanket and pillow, and we arranged her on the sofa, then tiptoed out of the room, but close enough where we could still keep an eye on her.

"I'm afraid of her," Sandy said in a low voice. "Call Jordan, now. This is Fata, but she's more than Fata, if you know what I mean."

I nodded. "Yeah, it's like she's got her memories and knows who we are, but she isn't alone in there." While Sandy watched Fata, I moved to the edge of the room and put in a call to Jordan. When he came on the line, he sounded a little bit harried.

"What's up, Maddy? I don't mean to rush you, but I was just heading out to dinner with my girlfriend."

I have no clue that Jordan had a girlfriend. He'd make good boyfriend material, for sure, but last I heard he wasn't involved with anybody.

Feeling guilty about interrupting him, I said, "What else? We have a serious problem. I don't mean to interrupt your evening, especially after calling you about George, but we have…a situation. I can't go into it over the phone. We just need you to look at somebody, and tell us what you think. And it has to be while she's still asleep. I know this sounds cryptic, but it would take far too long to explain what is going on."

Jordan paused, then let out a long sigh. "At least I know when you call me it's not hypochondria or some mountain out of a molehill. I'll be over as soon as I can. Is there anything I should know so I can know what instruments to bring?"

I glanced back at the sofa. Fata still seemed to be unconscious. "Have you ever heard me mention Fata Morgana?"

"Wasn't she the water witch that you and Sandy hung out with a few centuries ago?"

"Yeah. She's back, but there's something going on and we need to know what it is. She was always a little scary but now, Jordan, I'm afraid of what she could do to the town. She brought the storms with her. That much I know. There's more to Fata than just Fata. If that makes any sense."

"In a way. All right, I'll grab my bag and be over in twenty minutes."

I turned back to Sandy. "He's on his way. I wonder how long she'll stay out?"

"I don't know, but I hope it's until Jordan gets here. What should we do in the meantime? I'm not certain I want to leave her alone." Sandy gave me a long look that told me she was as frightened as I was.

"I suppose we just wait."

Sandy and I settled down at a small table near one of the windows in the parlor. Fata remained unconscious, and we did our best to keep quiet so we didn't wake her up. Finally, I caught a glimpse of Jordan's car pulling in and I hurried to the front door so he wouldn't ring the bell. As I opened the door, he took one look at my face and pushed past me.

"This really has you spooked, doesn't it?"

"Jordan, Fata was a force of nature when we knew her. I was running wild at the time, but she... Fata was beyond control. We were just lucky she never took it out on anybody who didn't deserve it. I'm not so sure she's still as selective." I let him into the parlor and nodded at the sofa. "We've tried to keep quiet. I suggest you move cautiously. I've no idea what she might do if she woke up and found you examining her."

Jordan stared at Fata for a moment, then set his bag of instruments down on the table next to the sofa. But he made no move to open it. Instead, he closed his eyes and held out his hands, running them through her aura as she slept. When he opened his eyes, the look on his face went from curious to startled, and he backed away, motioning for us to follow him into the hallway.

"I can tell you one thing right now. She's not fully a witch. She may have the DNA in her blood, but I'd swear to you she's a water elemental, bound in form. I've got a couple more tests I can do, but they're invasive. My ethics preclude me performing them unless I ask her consent. It's not like she's committed a crime or that the police are asking me to check her out. Do you understand?" He looked extremely uncomfortable.

I nodded. He was right. We were asking him to invade her privacy. And that didn't feel right, as worried as we might be.

"Yeah, I understand." I glanced at Sandy, who nodded as well.

"Do you want to wake her up and ask her if I can examine her? You could always tell her that she fainted, and you were worried about her so you called the doctor."

I rubbed my forehead. This wasn't going the way I had hoped, although I wasn't sure what I had actually expected. I think I had hoped Fata would just fade away and not bother coming back. She meant so much to me back then that I couldn't bear to see what she had become.

Sandy answered for both of us. "Come on in. We'll try, although I'm not sure how she'll respond."

I knelt by Fata's side and gently tapped her arm. "Fata? Can you hear me? Fata, it's Maddy. We want to make sure you're all right."

Fata stirred, ever so slightly, her eyes fluttering. She looked confused for a second, then brightened as she saw my face.

"It wasn't a dream, then. For some reason I thought I had dreamt that I had come back to you." She glanced over at Jordan. "Who are you? I don't remember you."

"Jordan is a doctor, honey," Sandy said. "We were worried when you fainted, so we called him. Do you mind if he examines you?" Sandy had a more winning way with her. I had to admit she had a diplomacy that I longed for, but never managed to attain. And it seemed to be growing the longer she took care of Jenna.

Fata blinked, still looking confused. After a moment, she said, "All right. If you think it's okay."

"Jordan is a good friend of ours, so you're in safe hands." I sat down on the sofa beside her as she swung her feet over to sit up. "We'll be right here, so there's no worry."

She seemed more like her old self as she nodded and smiled. When Fata smiled, she lit up the room. She reminded me of the stars, cold and beautiful and twinkling with an icy chill.

Jordan introduced himself, holding out his hand. "Hi, I'm Jordan Farrows. If you let me just examine you for a little bit, I promise I won't do anything that makes you uncomfortable. If you tell me I'm overstepping my boundaries, I'll stop." He opened his bag and pulled out a stethoscope and a couple of other medical instruments that I didn't recognize.

Fata looked puzzled when she saw them, but she just shrugged. "Go ahead."

He checked her lungs and her heart, and then he had her hold what looked like a quartz crystal ball, though I had a feeling it was more than just a regular crystal sphere. He was reading some figures off of a tablet as she held it. After a moment, he put away all of his instruments and closed his bag.

"Well, everything checks out. You work with water energy, don't you?"

Fata nodded. "Since I was a little girl, I was strong with the water element. Just like Maddy and fire, or Cassandra and the air. I think that's what brought us all together back then. We were at the top of our elements."

Jordan cleared his throat. "I know that Maddy and Cassandra are experts with their particular elements. But Fata—may I call you Fata?"

She gave him a nod.

"Fata Morgana, you have become so enmeshed with the water element that you have *become* part elemental. The water has taken over part of your essence. Did you know that?" Jordan was being extremely diplomatic with his tone. That alone told me that he was nervous.

Fata stared at him for a moment, her eyes wide. The crystal blue of her irises clouded over momentarily, and it looked like a storm was gathering in her gaze. And then it cleared again and she shifted, shaking her head as she leaned forward to rest her elbows on her knees.

"At times, I know. Then it fades and I seem to forget. And other times, I'm completely part of the Ocean Mother, and I forget my former life. I sleep within her embrace for decades before waking to ride the waves again. But something called me and woke me to my past. I knew Maddy needed help, and so I came."

She looked first at me, and then Sandy. "The three of us made a pact long ago that we would always be there for each other in darkest need. And even though we ended in an argument, that pact stands. I'm here because when Maddy called to me, I was given a vision, and I knew that she needed me. I came as soon as I could, although it took me a while to find you," she said, turning to me. "I've never been to this land. But I knew I needed to find you and tell you what I was shown while I was dreaming."

A lump formed in my stomach. I knew I didn't want to hear what she was about to say.

"The pact," I whispered. "We made it the day we raided the village. We stood around the fire and pledged blood to blood."

It was a windy afternoon, and we had been tracking the vampire village for months. And now, we were just a mile away. We were in Romania, having traipsed through Europe staking vampire after vampire. The humans knew who we were, and even though they were afraid of our magic, they welcomed us when they realized we were trying to help protect them.

There had been a particularly bad outbreak of vampirism in Romania and surrounding countries, and so we went where we were needed. I was still enmeshed in the blood thirst to destroy the creatures who had destroyed my sweet Tom, and no number of vampire kills could seem to assuage it.

Sandy and Fata Morgana had been by my side. The villagers called us the *Witches Wild*, and in truth, we were. Out of control, focused on one goal, we did whatever it took to accomplish our mission. There was always blood on my hands, blood on my skirts, blood on my dagger, blood on my silver stake.

As we stood above the village of vampires, I realized I was tired. My entire life felt like a river of blood that I continually waded through. I was tired of the coppery scent in my nose. I was tired of the dust that filled the air when the vampires crumbled.

But *here*, here we could make a major dent. I wasn't sure how many vampires were down in that village. Possibly a hundred. But I knew one thing for sure—there weren't any humans. The vampires back then didn't leave their victims alive. They were waging war on humanity, and we were the only ones standing in the way.

As we stood there, staring down at the village, Fata Morgana held out her hands.

"We have come through heaven and hell together, and we've been here for each other throughout these long years. I propose we make a pact, that the Witches Wild will always be here for one another. When any of us are in danger, we have only to call out and the others will come.

For once, let the blood we spill be our own and be healing, let it be a force for good."

Fata was in one of her more coherent modes, and what she said resonated deep within my heart. I took her hand and held out my other to Cassandra.

"Together we stand. Together we fight, together we play, together forever."

Cassandra took my hand, and then Fata's, and we formed our circle. "In for now, and for always."

I let go of both of them and took out my silver dagger. Auntie Berma had given me the pair—the dagger and stake. I held up my left hand and took my dagger, dragging it along my lifeline, cutting a superficial gash, but it was still strong enough to bleed. Fata held out her left hand and I slashed it as well, and then Cassandra's. I put away the dagger, and then the three of us joined our blood together, meeting our hands in the center of the circle.

> *Hand to hand, we join our blood,*
> *blood to blood, we join our hearts.*
> *Our powers band, in fire or flood,*
> *the sum of all, stronger than the parts.*
> *Wind, fire, and water make,*
> *a force that cannot break.*
> *Witches Wild, so we three stand,*
> *joined together, upon this land.*

Bound together by our sacred oath, we turned to the village waiting in the valley below. I conjured the fire, surrounding the entire village with a row of flames at the top of the hill. Sandy invoked the winds, and Fata

Morgana brought the rains to the surrounding areas so that the fire wouldn't get out of control.

With one last breath, I whispered the spell to send the fires racing down into the village just as the sun began to set. As the vampires came out, shrieking as they met their deaths, I realized this would be my last raid. As the scent of smoke and char began to fill the air, I fell on my knees, wishing the world would burn around me.

In the end, there was only dust left…the dust of vampires scattered to the wind. And in that dust, I left my anger behind. I was so tired of my fury that I could no longer sustain it. We turned and walked away from the remains of the village, and left our vampire hunting days behind.

I shook myself out of my memories. For good or ill, the three of us had bound ourselves together that fateful day, and we were still bound by sacred oath. Fata Morgana might be part water elemental now, but she was still the Fata who had stood by my side, who had run with me through the country, hunting my enemies.

"You said you had a vision?" I took her hand.

She seemed to settle back into herself. With each moment that passed, she felt like the Fata we had known, rather than the wild, hybrid creature who had raged her way to shore in the storms.

"I did. It was a vision, not a dream. One of the Aunties—I don't know which one, I don't even know if I've met her—told me. She whispered in my ear while I was being rocked by the Ocean Mother." She paused, then motioned for Sandy to come sit on her other side.

Giving me a hesitant look, Sandy took her place beside Fata.

Fata let out a long breath. "One of the oldest vampires has been awoken. I don't know who woke him, or why, but he's risen to walk the earth again. He's coming for you, Maddy. Someone, deep within the shadows, is out to end your life. And whoever it is, they've summoned Dracula to be their assassin."

I caught my breath, staring at her.

Dracula?

He was real, that much we knew. The book by Bram Stoker had been a simple retelling of a nasty encounter with him, but unlike the book—or the many movies made—Dracula had not met his end. He had vanished underground, hiding out till people began to question whether he'd ever been real.

Sandy caught my attention. Over Fata's head, she mouthed, "The Arcānus Nocturni."

Crap. Of course. If anybody was aligned with them, it would be Dracula. It *had* to be. He was one of the oldest of the old, as far as we knew. If they could wake him, of course they would. I was a danger because I knew about them.

The Arcānus Nocturni were the ancestors of the vampires. They were so ancient that nobody knew when they had been turned. And they had the ability to walk in sunlight, like the living, which made them a deadly menace. Few knew about them, and it was a good thing for vampires the world over, because if humans discovered that even a fraction of them didn't require downtime

—didn't necessarily have the vulnerabilities that everybody thought they did—the entire vampire race would be wearing bull's-eyes on their hearts.

Thanks to Essie, I had managed to catch a glimpse of an illustration of the Queen Mother of all vampires. I had also learned that said queen was bored. She wanted all vampires to be able to walk abroad at all times. Luckily, Essie didn't share the ancient queen's desire. Even though I didn't trust Essie, I could take this information to her and she would help. She didn't play well with other vamps, and bristled when she thought her territory was being challenged. Dracula would present that challenge.

Fata glanced at Sandy, then at me. "What? What are you two thinking about?"

I hesitated. Something was holding me back from mentioning Essie. Scrambling for something to say, I shook my head. "I was just thinking about how different Aegis is from Dracula." *Crap.* The words had just tumbled out of my mouth.

She froze. "Aegis? Who is Aegis?"

I bit my lip. "He's my boyfriend, Fata. We met when I bought this house."

The look on her face was unreadable. After a moment, she said, "Is he a witch, too? Or did you end up with a shifter?"

Once again, I hesitated. Finally, I decided that she'd find out sooner or later. I couldn't keep my relationship a secret from her forever. And with Jordan around, if she blew up, he might actually have something in that bag of his to knock her out.

"Aegis is a vampire." I wanted to add, "He's one of the

good ones," or some such qualifier, but it wouldn't serve any real purpose.

Fata stiffened. She glanced at Sandy, who shifted a little away from her. Then, her voice so soft that it terrified me, Fata asked, "You're dating a vampire?"

I nodded. "Yes, I am, and I'm in love with him. Vampires aren't like they used to be—the majority of them. Modern vampires have taken their place in the world and adapted to the times. They have become part of society."

"You expect me to believe that? *You*, who drove Cassandra and me across Europe, seeking the monsters who destroyed my cousin and your true love? You expect us to believe that everything is lovely with this vampire. You're fucking him? Sleeping with him? He's *dead*, Maddy —he's worse than dead. He's a mockery of whoever he was before he was turned. How can you do this? Mad Maudlin is sleeping with the enemy and protecting him?"

She pushed herself to her feet. Outside, the skies darkened. A low rumble of thunder echoed in the distance. I motioned to Sandy. We needed to calm her down. Jordan reached for his bag and unobtrusively stepped to the side table, where he began hunting through it.

"Listen to me. Times have changed. I'm the last person who expected to ever get involved with a vampire, but here we are. Aegis was a servant of Apollo. He angered the god and was thrown out after Apollo turned him into one of the Fallen. He's a good man, though."

Sandy tried to jump in and help me. "He *is* a good man. He's helped us all, more than once. And he treats Maddy like a queen."

"You say that now, but what about when he decides he

wants to turn you? What will you do then? What will you do when his thirst drives him to feed off you? You know how vampires are around witches' blood. We're a gourmet feast to them!" Fata was flailing her arms. She whirled to Jordan, who had pulled out a syringe. "Put that away, *healer*. You think I don't know what you plan on doing with that?" Her voice had turned to ice.

I glanced at the clock. It was noon. Thank gods Aegis wasn't awake yet, but I was afraid to let Fata find out he was staying in the house. She might take it into her head to hunt him down and stake him.

"Fata, stop. Come back to yourself." It dawned on me that when she faded out like this—when the ice and chill took over—the water elemental part of her was rearing its emotional head. And since Fata was already prone to volatile outbursts, the water was amplifying her anger.

She paused, slowly—visibly—reining herself in. "I need to go walk on the shore. I suppose you want me to meet him? This vampire of yours?"

I wanted to just skip the whole idea and say no, but we had no clue how long she was staying, and at some point, surely she would come in contact with him. "I wish you would, if only to realize you're jumping to conclusions. But *only* if you make me an oath-bound promise that you won't hurt him."

She simmered, but finally gave me a curt nod. "Very well. I won't hurt him as long as he doesn't try to hurt you or Cassandra." Turning to Sandy, she said, "Guide me to the shoreline. I can feel the water surging from here, and I need to sit beside the waves for a while."

Looking frightened, Sandy cleared her throat. "All right. You'll have to ride in what we call a car."

Fata shrugged. "A cart? I have no need. Just take me out and point me in the direction."

Still stuttering, Sandy led her to the front door. As I glanced out the window, I saw Sandy pointing in the general direction of the western shore, and then, in a whirl of sudden rain, Fata dissolved into vapor, and was gone.

CHAPTER ELEVEN

Sandy returned as soon as Fata vanished, an ashen look on her face. I turned to Jordan, who had quietly watched the entire affair.

"We have a problem." I slumped back into a chair. "You say she's part water elemental? I don't think she started out that way, though I didn't meet her until…it was 1659. Fata was twenty-seven and I was thirty. But now that I think about it, the first time I saw her, she came riding in on the ocean waves. When she hopped off of the wave, she danced around me on the shore, laughing. I wasn't afraid of her, not then. She told me her family had cast her out when she was thirteen. Her powers hit at puberty, and it scared even her parents."

Jordan pulled out his tablet. "I saved the readings on her. She has an immense amount of power, but it's all concentrated in one direction. Water, be it snow, rain, or ocean. She can do little else on a magical level, I'd wager. The element flows in her aura like blood in her veins. I doubt if she even needs to breathe when she's underwater. She's one of the Ocean Mother's chosen."

"Did you find out anything else?" Sandy asked. "We need every scrap of information we can gather on her in order to know how to proceed."

"I suppose she's vulnerable—every creature or force has its vulnerability. But be cautious. At this point, she could swamp the island with a small hurricane, I'm betting." He paused. "Let me call my girlfriend. I told her I'd be late and I know she worries."

As he moved to the side, Sandy turned to me. "So, not only is Dracula on the island and after you, but we have to keep Fata contained. I think we'd better ask Auntie Tautau for advice."

"I think you're right." I chewed on my lip. "I feel like we've got hold of a rattlesnake. Right now, it's biding its time, but at any moment, it could turn and bite us."

"I don't want Fata over at my house, and I don't want her knowing about Jenna. I'm responsible for her safety and frankly, yeah, the snake is in the henhouse, so to speak." Sandy gave me a pained smile, then sat down, staring glumly at the coffee table. "Should we dissolve the pact? We might be able to do it, the two of us."

I thought about it for a moment. If we were able to dissolve the oath we had made, would Fata feel it vanish? Then she'd have no reason to hold herself back if she got angry with us. On the other hand, we couldn't do anything to her while the oath held.

"We're in a tight place right now. I'm not sure which is the safest course of action."

"Let's talk to Auntie Tautau, then. I'll get my jacket, if you want to drive us over there." I turned to Jordan, who was once again listening to our conversation. "You aren't under any sort of oath like we are. Will you look for a way to neutralize Fata? What about your stasis chamber? It's magic-proof."

He thought about it for a moment. "I think that might hold her, but I can't be entirely certain. Meanwhile, I'll work on some ideas. Don't tell her. I won't endanger my lab or the medics who work there with me." He gave me a stern look. "Understand?"

I nodded. "Yeah, I do. Thanks, Jordan. Enjoy your afternoon."

"How can I, now that I know what's loose in Bedlam?" He shrugged his coat on, then gathered his things and headed out the front door.

"Let's get moving. I don't like that Fata knows where I live." I warned Kelson to be cautious should Fata come around again. Then, Sandy watching me to make certain my vertigo didn't strike again, I climbed into her van and we headed out to talk to Auntie Tautau.

AUNTIE TAUTAU WAS ONE OF *THE* AUNTIES. AND THE Aunties were a particularly interesting group of witches. They were ancient, well beyond the concept of old. Whether they were witches like Sandy and I were, nobody knew. But they watched over the magical community, and they stepped in when things needed to be put to rights. That didn't necessarily mean they were *helpful*, but they focused on keeping the balance.

Auntie Tautau lived in a cottage that was a little ways outside of the main part of town, on the outskirts of

Bedlam. Tucked back in a thicket of vegetation, the cottage was surrounded by an old-fashioned wraparound porch, the walls covered with ivy. Bushes and shrubs crowded the sidewalk, though by this late in the year many of their leaves were littering the ground. The yard had that windswept, not fully kept-up look, although I suspected it was because Auntie preferred it that way, rather than out of any neglect.

During summer the yard was filled with flowers, but with the arrival of autumn they had died back and the grass peeked out, green from the constant moisture the island got. The spiders were still in sight, giant orb weavers fat from a summer of insects, who crooked their jointed, striped legs as they waited in their webs. But the walkway was clear of them, and they stayed on the sidelines, watching us as we made our way to the porch.

Auntie Tautau opened the door as I raised my hand to knock. She always knew when company was coming, and if she answered the door, it was because she was willing to talk to you. She waved us in, glancing at the thunderheads that were gathering over the island. I could only wonder what Fata Morgana was up to, because the clouds had all the mark of a temper tantrum. Maybe Thor would step in, irritated that someone was stealing his thunder, so to speak.

"Come in, girls. A little bird told me you would be visiting me today, and so I put on the kettle and baked up some pumpkin loaf. It's a cold day, so come in and warm yourself by the fire." The bird on her hat—a crow named Mr. Merriweather—squawked.

Entering Auntie Tautau's house was like stepping back a century. Her cottage was filled to the brim with knickknacks and curios, but nothing seemed overcrowded. It felt like an old Irish cottage, and Auntie Tautau was the grandmother always waiting for you.

She motioned for us to sit on the sofa and we did. The few times I had offered to help her carry tea trays from the kitchen, she practically chased me back to the living room. Now, I played the good guest and stayed where I was told. As we sat down, I breathed a sigh of relief. Auntie Tautau's place was the one place I felt truly safe. A nuclear bomb could go off and I would feel like we were protected and covered there. Sandy seemed to feel the same way, because she let out a sigh of relief.

She turned to me. "Do you think Fata Morgana knows we're here?"

I shook my head. "I doubt if anybody knows who Auntie Tautau shelters under her roof, unless she wants them to. Fata Morgana may be part water elemental, but Auntie Tautau is an *Auntie*. There's not much that can trump that."

Sandy nodded. "Well, I'm not going to argue with that."

Auntie Tautau reemerged from the kitchen, a tea tray in her hand. She set it down on the coffee table. The tray contained three mugs of hot chocolate with whipped cream and marshmallows, along with a pumpkin loaf. Three saucers and forks were waiting beside it. She served the pumpkin loaf, and the smell of cinnamon and cloves spiraled up to whet my appetite. As she handed around the mugs of hot chocolate, a knot in my stomach unwound. I took a long sip of the bittersweet drink, and let out a soft sigh.

"This is so good. I didn't realize I needed this." I bit

into the pumpkin loaf and the soft sponge melted in my mouth, a mixture of pumpkin and spices and all things good.

"Remember, the Aunties know what you need before you do. Now, you're here because of Fata Morgana, aren't you? What is it you want to know?"

Auntie Tautau took a long slurp of her chocolate, patting her lip with a napkin. She let out a happy burp and leaned back in her rocking chair. She was wearing a cheerful ivy-patterned house dress, cinched with a red belt. Her straw hat was perched as usual on her head, and Merriweather, her crow, was perched on the hat as usual. I had begun to wonder if Merriweather ever sat anywhere else. When I had first met Auntie Tautau, I assumed Merriweather was fake. But now I knew he could talk and reason as well. I had my suspicions that Merriweather hadn't always been a crow, but I wasn't brave enough to ask.

As to what we wanted to know, I wasn't entirely sure, but I decided to start with the first question that entered my mind.

"Is Fata Morgana dangerous? I mean, we *know* she's dangerous but is it safe to let her roam around Bedlam?"

Auntie Tautau laughed. "You might as well ask if the ocean is dangerous. Because Fata Morgana is part of the ocean now. As for letting her roam around Bedlam, what do you expect to do in order to get her off the island?"

Well, that answered another question.

"Do you have any suggestions about getting her to go back to where she came from?" I felt vaguely like a traitor, but we had to know. The Fata we had known and loved had always been a little crazed, but now that she had merged with the water elemental, I wasn't sure if *our* Fata even existed anymore, except in fleeting glimpses.

Auntie Tautau nibbled on her pumpkin bread. After a moment, she cocked her head to the side. "There are ways to entice her to leave, but it is not time. There are things that must happen before she goes back to her watery realm. In the meanwhile, I advise you to watch your step with her. She remembers certain things from your time spent together, and those are almost programmed into her at an instinctual level. Anything contrary to those concepts—the values you lived by—may register as an alarm to her."

"She can't understand how things have changed," I said, beginning to understand.

"True enough. The times have changed. The world has changed. Fata Morgana has changed. But she has been out of touch with the world outside of her element. When she says she has slumbered deep in the depths of the ocean, she means it literally. The Ocean Mother rocked her gently, shielding her from everything going on in the outer world."

I caught my breath. "Will she ever again be the Fata Morgana that we knew? Is she still our friend?" I felt a well of sadness rising up in my chest. People had come and gone out of my life over the decades and centuries, but no one had I regretted losing as much as Fata Morgana. Even my sweet Tom—even his loss was easier to handle. I understood it better.

Sandy reached out to take my hand, holding it tightly.

In a choked voice, she asked, "How did things get to this point? We were the Witches Wild, we were feared and loved across Europe. You were Mad Maudlin, and you led us on a wild hunt. We saved hundreds of people, perhaps thousands." She began to cry. "The world is so different, and I love it in many ways. But I suddenly feel like I've left part of myself behind. We were so alive back then, Maddy. Fata Morgana is still alive, she's still taking the world by storm. What are we doing?"

Auntie Tautau watched us, saying nothing.

I turned to Sandy and reached out to wipe away the tears from her cheeks. "We are doing more than you can imagine. We can't ever go back to the past. I learned that the hard way. And the truth is that I don't want to run through the country chasing vampires again. Hell, I hate that I have to pull out my stake and spike again. I don't *want* to sleep on the ground and freeze in the winter like we did. I don't want to ever have to stay one step ahead of the witch hunters again."

"I suppose you're right," she said.

"You damned well know I'm right. Remember, back then people like us *died*. When they caught us, they tortured and burned us in the name of religion. Remember all those innocents who *weren't* witches, the ones the Inquisition burned at the stake? *I don't want to go back to those times.* Life evolves, and we're evolving with it. We may not run as wild as we used to, but we still dance under the moonlight. We still work our magic and now, we don't have to be afraid to do so."

Sandy nodded softly. Auntie Tautau held out a packet of tissues to her and she took one, drying her eyes. A cough and a sip of hot chocolate later, and she smiled.

"I don't know what came over me. I haven't felt like that in a long, long time."

"It was Fata Morgana," Auntie Tautau said. "Remember, water rules over emotions. You have a volatile water elemental in your midst, and you are both connected to her by a pact that you made long, long ago. Is it any wonder that your emotions are on edge?"

"She's right," I said. "Just being around Fata is going to send us into a tailspin." I turned back to Auntie Tautau. "Is there a way we can get her out of Bedlam safely?"

"Yes, and when it's time you may do so. When it's time, you'll know it and you'll know what to do. For now, watch her closely, don't let her around any of the vampires in the village without supervision, and try not to make her angry." With a soft laugh, she refilled our plates with more pumpkin loaf, and proceeded to chat about the upcoming Samhain celebrations.

By the time we left Auntie Tautau's, it was going on two P.M.

Sandy drove toward the center of town. "How about stopping at Chicken Chicken and getting some lunch? Pumpkin loaf and hot chocolate are tasty but they aren't substantial. I could go for some popcorn chicken or something."

"That sounds good. There's not much we can do until Fata Morgana decides to come back from the shore. I wonder where she went. I hope she didn't head toward one of the marinas. I'd hate to see somebody upset her."

"Auntie Tautau seems to feel she's here for a reason that hasn't come to light yet, so there's nothing we can do until it's time for her to leave. But I have an idea." Sandy pulled over to the curb. "Lihi? Lihi! I need you."

Lihi popped into view. A homunculus, she was bound to Sandy by a mutual contract. Sandy paid her in crystals, which were a common currency in the realm in which Lihi lived. Lihi was twelve inches high, about the size of a fashion doll. She had bat wings and bat ears, and was terribly cute. She had a rat-like tail and wore hot pink shorts and a halter top. I wasn't sure if I had ever seen her in any other clothes.

"You rang? What can I do for you?" Lihi was pretty much at Sandy's beck and call, doing whatever she asked her to do. In return, Sandy never asked her to do anything dangerous or illegal, at least as far as I knew.

"You know who Fata Morgana is?"

"Yes, I was watching this morning when you met her. I decided it was safer to stay in hiding."

"I need you to find out where she is. I want you to keep tabs on her. You don't have to get close, but just keep her in view. And keep me updated."

"As you wish." Lihi vanished.

"You know, seeing you interact with Lihi makes me wish I had a homunculus to work with. But with Bubba and Luna, and now that Lanyear the owl has decided to become my familiar, I'm not sure how I'd manage it."

"Lanyear? What's this about an owl?"

I forgot, I hadn't told her. As we drove to Chicken Chicken, I explained what had happened.

We pulled up to the drive-thru. I ordered a six-piece chicken tenders meal, along with mashed potatoes and a biscuit. Sandy ordered popcorn chicken, baked beans, and a biscuit. It was too stormy to sit outside, so we pulled into one of the parking stalls and ate in the car. Sandy's van was actually comfortable, and she had installed some nice upgrades. A narrow table pulled out between the seats and we were able to set our meals on it.

We were just finishing our lunch when Lihi popped back in.

"Look, over there! You wanted to know where she was." The homunculus pointed across the street, toward the town square.

Fata Morgana was standing there, staring at the fountain. She reached out, and the water suddenly turned a vivid brilliant blue, then purple, and then silver. The water cycled through colors, then froze into a massive ice statue. Even from here we could hear Fata's throaty laugh.

"Well, she seems in a good mood, at least." I wasn't sure exactly what to do about it. She wasn't hurting anybody, but if Delia saw what was happening she might come on a little strong. I decided it was time to call her and warn her.

"Lovely," Delia said in a dry voice when I explained. "But I'll take Auntie Tautau's advice and stay on Fata Morgana's good side. You say she's part water elemental now?"

"Yes, and she's likely to affect the emotions of anybody who comes into contact with her. So emotions may be running high. Hopefully the satyrs will stay away from her, and the centaurs too. They're already volatile enough as it is. Which reminds me, Jordan said that George is still touch-and-go. He thinks he's stabilized, but said that it's still too early to tell. And another piece of information that you should know. Fata Morgana brought me a message. I know who our vampire murderer is."

"I'm not going to want to hear this either, am I?" Delia's breath whistled between her teeth.

"No, in fact you're going to want to hear this about as much as *I* wanted to hear it. Apparently the Arcānus Nocturni have decided to send an assassin after me. So they woke up Dracula."

The line went silent. I worried that I had gone too far and thrown her into a permanent state of shock.

"Are you there? Delia?"

"I'm here. I heard what you said. I'm just trying to take it in."

"Well, take it in as quick as you can because we have to figure out what to do. I can tell you right now he's going to be difficult to catch, and *he* can walk abroad in daylight. Because if he is the anointed one of the Arcānus Nocturni, you know that he has their power."

"I was afraid you were going to say that. Why can't Bedlam ever just be a nice quiet place to live?"

I began to laugh. "You really want me to answer that?"

"No, smartass. So what do we do? How do we take down Dracula? Is it even possible?" She paused, then added, "Should we ask Essie to help us?"

It didn't escape me that the sheriff of Bedlam was now routinely turning to me for advice pertaining to matters with the local vampire crowd. On one hand, it was flattering. On the other hand, I could do without that kind of flattery.

"Yeah, I think we should. Essie's not going to be happy that he's in her territory. She may not be the biggest fan of humans, or witches, but I'd bet next year's profits that she'll be willing to help us."

"What do you think the Arcānus Nocturni will do if you kill Dracula? Isn't that like killing off royalty?" Delia sounded a little hesitant, and I understood why.

"That occurred to me, too. It didn't take much more than that to start World War I, did it?"

"No, and some of my family were around that area during that time. Like Jack-Az, my family hails from the Black Forest area of Germany. Trust me, not a fun period to live there in."

"I'll talk to Aegis. He may have some ideas. And I'll go over to Essie's tonight. The three of us should get together soon. We need to hammer out some new regulations for rogue vampires visiting Bedlam. But right now, I've got to figure out how to avoid Dracula's attention. He's out to kill me, and I don't fancy laying odds against his ability to do it." I hung up.

Sandy stared at me, shaking her head. "Do you remember what I said a little while ago about wishing for the old days? Scratch that. I'll gladly stay in the twenty-first century. Twentieth century? I'm not sure which it is, to be truthful."

I laughed. "You and me both. I've had my fill of sleeping on the ground and waking up in the cold rain. It's one thing when we go camping, but we can always come home to where it's dry and warm." I paused, flashing back to the years when we chased vampires. In a quiet voice, I added, "I think I'd better start carrying my silver stake again. And my dagger."

Sandy's smile faded. "Did you ever think you'd see this day come?"

"No, I thought I was done. Thanks to the Arcānus Nocturni, I'm apparently not." I glanced over at Fata Morgana, who was still playing with the fountain. "And I never thought I'd see the day that she would actually return. I feel like a traitor. I loved her so much in so many ways, and then she was gone. And I thought our friendship was over. She was so angry at me. Do you really think Aegis is safe around her?"

Sandy watched Fata for a moment, then shrugged. "She loved you, you know. Back when we were all hanging with the satyrs. She loved you with all of her heart. She would have followed you into hell if you had asked her."

"I know," I said. "And I loved her. But Sandy, even though we had a lot of fun together—all three of us—I couldn't give her my heart the way she wanted me to. She wasn't meant to walk among society the way you and I are. And I… I just couldn't return her love the way she wanted. She never forgave me. I tried to be gentle, but I guess there is no gentle way to say *I don't love you the way you love me*. I wonder if she even remembers that time? I wonder if she remembers the way she used to feel about me? She was pretty upset when she heard about Aegis. "

I never talked about it. In fact, I preferred to pretend that it had never happened. But when one of your best friends falls in love with you and you can't return the feeling, the relationship can never be the same. And so Fata had left, after the blowout of blowouts. She had returned to the ocean to mend her heart, which I had shattered.

"You did what you had to, Maddy. It would have been far worse if you had pretended just to make her happy. You know it, and I know it. And I think, deep in her heart, Fata Morgana knew it. Come on, let me drop you off at home. And then, I need to get back to Jenna."

"How is she doing?"

"Better than I expected, but she's still so upset. I mean, her mother just died and she's going through all of this guilt over how she feels. I don't expect her to get through this without a few more upsets."

"I know how she feels, in a way. When Zara died, I felt such a mix of emotions. For so long, I didn't care if she died. Then I found out what really happened, and I wanted her to be here for me, but it was too late. I don't ever want it to be *too late* again with anybody else. You know what I mean?"

Sandy nodded. "I know what you mean. I'm struggling with that myself. Max has broached the subject of marriage."

Grateful for the sudden change of subject, I clapped my hands together. "You two are perfect together!"

"Well, you certainly don't have any opinions on the subject, do you?" She laughed. "I'm not sure, but he says he'd be happy to make a life with me and Jenna. We'd make quite the blended family, wouldn't we?"

"Can I give you a piece of advice?" I asked. Without waiting for an answer, I added, "Think very carefully before you say no. Don't lose one of the greatest things that has happened to you in a long time. He's a good guy, Sandy. And you two make a great couple. And Jenna loves you both to pieces."

"I'm thinking about it," Sandy said. She gave me a little smile as she started the ignition. "And yes, he is a great guy."

Sunset was running about 6:20 in the evening at this point, and right on the dot—even before Aegis was up—I was on the phone to Essie. Shar-Shar must've heard the urgency in my voice, because she put me right through without trying to play gatekeeper.

"Essie, I know who our killer is. Who the vampire is. I need your help. And I guarantee, you're going to *want* to help me when you hear this."

"Oh, really?" Essie sounded intrigued. "Do you want to talk in person, or will the phone do?"

"Oh, this needs to be talked about *in person*, in private. As soon as Aegis is ready, we'll be over." I paused for a moment, then added, "This one scares me, Essie. And with good reason."

"When the famous Mad Maudlin is scared of a vampire, then whoever he is, he's big and bad. I'll be here. I'll see you in about an hour?"

"An hour it is." I ended the call just as Aegis came through the basement door.

"Hey, love," he said, sweeping me into his arms for a tender kiss. "How are you feeling today? How's the vertigo?"

"I'm feeling good, the vertigo's gone, but we have to talk. And we have to talk to Essie again, and we're headed there within the hour." I wrapped my arms around his neck, reveling in the feel of his body against mine. Now that the vertigo was gone, I was hungry for him. It'd been too long, and I wanted the smooth chill of his skin next to mine. "Are you interested in something quick before we go?" I gave him a crooked grin and licked my lips.

"I'm always interested in something quick with you, although I prefer stretching it out," he said, a salacious smile on his face. He slid his hands up my back slowly, pressing against the material of my sweater. "If we are going to have any fun at all, let's get upstairs. I think we can manage something in less than an hour. It only takes fifteen minutes to get to Essie's."

"I don't think it will matter if we're a few minutes late." And so I took his hand, intending to lead him upstairs, but he picked me up and carried me up to the bedroom.

CHAPTER TWELVE

As we entered the bedroom, Aegis gently kicked the door shut with his foot. He carried me over to the bed, depositing me gently on the comforter and then, using his phone, switched on the stereo. A blast of music filled the room and we were surrounded by the siren songs of Shriekback and the Kills. We both liked edgy music, and sex made it even better.

I looked up at him, my blood boiling through my veins. His scent, his eyes, the feel of his hands, the silhouette of his broad chest, the low throbbing of his voice—everything about him made me hungry for his touch. I had never found a man so compelling. Not even Tom, I thought, then brushed the thought away. Why compare? Finally, with Tom, it felt like the past was the past and the present was the present, and I could focus on my relationship now without dragging him into it.

Aegis stepped back, his entire focus centered on my face as he slowly unbuckled his belt. He was wearing black jeans that cupped his ass, and a low V-neck sweater that was a brilliant cobalt blue. He was a gorgeous man, as beautiful as the god to whom he had been bound. And knowing he was a demigod, that his father was Hermes, made me wonder just how brilliant and beautiful the gods really were.

I slipped off the bed, lowering myself to my knees in front of him. "Let me do that," I said in a husky voice, my breath heavy in my chest. I pushed his hands away and began to slowly lower his zipper, inch by inch by inch. He let out a faint moan, dropping his head back as his cock sprang to attention. I took him in my hands, pressing my lips to the tip of his shaft. He pressed forward, gently, as I tightened my lips around him. By now I was used to the chill of his skin, and sometimes when we used flavored lubricant as a toy, it was a lot like sucking on a Popsicle. Only *so much sexier*.

"You give great head," he said in a throaty voice. "Don't stop, please don't stop."

"I have no intention of stopping," I said, running my tongue up and down his length. His pre-cum was salty, even though he produced no actual semen. "You taste good."

He reached down, gently holding me by the sides of my head as he thrust harder. I began to work him faster as he slid between my lips, forcing them apart with his girth.

"Babe, would you mind tit-fucking me?" His voice was ragged now.

I knelt back, then made my way up on the bed, pulling my shirt off as I sat down. I reached back and unhooked my bra, tossing it to the side as my boobs bounced gently.

He stepped toward me as I leaned forward holding my breasts together, rubbing the nipples as I formed a channel around his cock. Placing his hands on my shoulders, he began to thrust up and down as I tightened my breasts around him. I glanced down, staring at the head of his cock as it rose and fell between my breasts, licking my lips as I anticipated that lovely shaft driving itself inside me.

"I'm going to come, babe," Aegis said with a grunt.

I leaned back, spreading my arms as he aimed his cock at my breasts, coming hard. With most men, I wasn't particularly fond of the cum shower, but with Aegis it was different. I loved giving him pleasure, just like he loved giving me pleasure. I slowly rubbed my breasts, spreading his essence over me.

"You drive me crazy, woman," he said, stripping off his shirt and his pants. He had to stop to take his boots off first, giving me time to undress. I had barely wiggled out of my panties when he landed on the bed next to me, hard again, and grabbed me by the waist. He laid me back, whispering, "I want to eat you out. I want to taste you. I love your smell, I love your taste. I love everything about you."

I bent my knees, spreading my legs. Aegis slid between them, spreading my lips wide as he leaned in and began swirling his tongue against my sex. He knew how to make that tongue work, how to exert just the right pressure to drive me out of my mind. I moaned as the sex haze washed over me. All I could think about was his tongue on my clit, and how I didn't want him to stop, how I could barely breathe. As I shifted, he pressed harder and I gave in, coming so hard that I let out a peal of laughter, throwing my head back as I reveled in the release.

Aegis joined me, barking out a low throaty laugh, and he crawled up, his eyes focused on my face. He cupped my breasts and squeezed, hard, and I let out another cry. Pain mingled with pleasure, and I growled, so hungry for him that I caught hold of his waist and pulled him down beside me. I rolled him over and straddled him, sliding down on his cock, relief spreading through me as the length of his shaft penetrated deep.

"Now I get to ride you," I said, leaning forward. "Buck up, cowboy."

He held my waist and rose to meet my downward thrust. As he sped up—vampires had amazing speed and stamina—I raised one hand over my head in a fist and let out a loud cheer.

"Yes, that's my stallion!" I laughed again, grinding against him. "Fuck me, bloodsucker."

"You want fucked? I'll give it to you good, witch."

His eyes gleaming, he rolled me over and drove deep inside me as I wrapped my legs around him. And then one of my favorite songs came on—"Sour Cherry" by the Kills—and I lost what little reserve I had left. I began to stutter, and then let out a shriek as I came again, harder than before. Aegis continued to drive as I spiraled over the crevice, falling into an orgasm so hard it gave me a cramp in my side. Before I could ask him to pause so I could ease the spasm, he groaned again, leaning his head back as he came once more, shuddering into my arms.

As the music continued to blare, we held each other, riding the waves of our passion, creating a private little bubble in a world that was too fraught with danger.

Surprisingly, we headed out the door only ten minutes later than we should have. A quick shower together left us fresh and clean, and I was happy to find I could walk down the stairs by myself without getting too dizzy. But the memory of what I was facing swept over me. For a little while I had been able to forget, but now that it was dark outside and *anything* could be lurking in the shadows, a sudden shaft of fear struck me.

"I'll be right back." I ran back upstairs.

In the back of my closet was a small chest. I opened it and stared at the silver spike that lay there, gleaming softly in the light. I slowly withdrew it and the matching sheaths, one of which held my dagger. I strapped them on, one to each thigh. As I slid the dagger and the spike into place, it felt like a shadow from the past washed across me and I realized that—no matter what happened from now on—I had to let the part of myself that had been Mad Maudlin back in.

As I returned downstairs, Aegis took a quick look at my legs, and then into my face. He stood there, unafraid, and opened his arms as I snuggled deep into his embrace, cautious not to touch him with the silver. His jeans would protect him, to a degree, but I didn't want to hurt him at all.

"I have some things to tell you, on the ride over."

"I figured as much," he said with a whisper. "Let's go. And if she bitches, then she can come outside to talk to us by the car."

On the drive to Essie's, I took a deep breath and told Aegis about Fata's return. He listened in silence, until I came to the part where she had freaked out about me loving a vampire.

"She tries to stake me and she's got a fight on her hands," he said. He meant it. Aegis could bluster like any man, but there was an edge that came into his voice when he was serious. "I *won't* have her browbeating you, either."

"Be cautious, love," I said. I hated to admit it, but Fata scared the hell out of me. "She's part water elemental and, as such, has incredible strength and power. But she came to deliver a message to me. I have to be grateful for that. And that leads us to my second piece of news for the day. And why I broke out my stake and dagger. The vampire running around killing people? I know who it is."

Aegis glanced at me, then back at the road. "Who?"

"Apparently the Arcānus Nocturni has decided I'm too much of a threat. They woke up Dracula and sent him after me."

Aegis screeched to the side of the road, parking abruptly on the shoulder. "You're fucking with me, right? Fucking *Transylvania* Dracula?" But by the shaking of his voice, it was obvious he knew I wasn't joking.

"That would be the one." I shook my head. "I talked to Auntie Tautau. Sandy and I went over there after Fata decided to go sightseeing. We can't ask her to leave until it's time, and we won't know when that is until it happens. As for Dracula, I'm going to have to walk softly on this one. If I take him down, I'll be killing a cultural icon, and that's never a good thing."

Aegis was silent for a moment. The only sound in the

car was the sound of my breath. Finally, he said, "This is one of those damned if you do, damned if you don't situations. If the Arcānus Nocturni went to the trouble of waking him up, then you're on their radar in a really bad way. They mean business. I can guarantee you, we can't possibly take on the entire organization. Their members are spread worldwide, hidden right out in the open. These are vampires whose lineages extend thousands of years, even before I was turned."

My breath felt caught in my throat. I stared through the window into the darkness.

"You're just a ray of sunshine, aren't you?"

Aegis was right. The Arcānus Nocturni were scattered worldwide, and they were all but invincible. With the power their members had, and with no clue of how many of them existed, our best chances were to try to fly under the radar. But now, I was on their shit list.

He said nothing for a moment, then reached for my hand.

"Maddy, I'll stand beside you. Hell, I'll stand in front of you if you want. But we can't just go on hope that this will blow over. We have no choice but to destroy Dracula. And yet, if you do, well…as you said, you'll be destroying a cultural icon. One of the fathers to the vampire race. Destroying Lucifer—"

"Please, call him Luke."

I didn't even want to *think* about Lucifer. A messenger for the gods, he had gone too far out among the stars and returned with vampirism. The illness had fallen on him while he was deep in space and he carried it back. And the goddess Nyx had forced him out of the sky, throwing him down to earth much like Apollo had tossed Aegis out after turning him into one of the Fallen.

Luke had been there when we had destroyed the village in Romania. He escaped, and had tracked me down, out for revenge. But Aegis and I had prevailed, and he was dead, a pile of dust that scattered to the winds. *Of course* the Arcānus Nocturni wasn't going to forgive that. He had been one of their greatest members. And I was responsible for his death.

"Whether we call him Luke or Lucifer or Lucian, the fact remains that by destroying him, both you and I cemented our places on their hit list. We had best get over to Essie's and tell her the news." He started the car again, shaking his head. "I suppose we owe Fata Morgana a debt of gratitude for letting you know. But it feels like we're sandwiched between her and Dracula, and I'm not sure which one I'm most afraid of."

"On that matter, I totally agree with you." And still, I felt like a traitor for saying so.

AS WE EASED INTO ESSIE'S DRIVEWAY, I WONDERED HOW SHE would take to me being armed. When I stepped out of the car, I heard a gasp from the shadows.

"Are you crazy?"

I recognized that voice. "Hey, Ruby."

Ruby had helped Essie kidnap me at one point, and we had developed an uneasy regard for one another. I had the feeling that Ruby could easily turn out to be like Aegis—a vampire with a conscience. But as long as she lived in Essie's nest, that wasn't likely to happen.

I knew she felt the silver. "I'm armed because I need to be armed," I told her. "Essie will understand when I tell her what happened. But I need to go in feeling protected. I give you my word of honor I won't hurt anybody in there who doesn't try to hurt me. Witches' oath." I held my left palm upright and tapped it with my other hand. A universal symbol among witches and those who knew them that we had given our oath.

"All right, but I don't guarantee she's not gonna bite my head off. *After* she bites yours off." Ruby slipped out of the shadows into the floodlight that spread across the driveway. As usual, she was dressed in jeans and a turtleneck. She was tall and slim, and must have been in her thirties when she was turned. Her long hair was the color of burnished copper and she had pulled it back into a braid. Her pale skin and eyes seemed almost translucent in the brilliant floodlight.

"Well, come on. Let's get this over with."

I found it oddly comforting that she walked in front of me, seemingly unafraid. I honestly didn't want her to fear me—at least not as long as she was on my side. If Fata could see me now, she would probably turn in disgust and run back to the waves on which she had come.

Aegis wrapped his arm through mine, tugging me closer to him. The brooding look on his face told me he was worried.

As we entered Essie's house, I blinked. She had redecorated since the last time I was here. It had been a goth fantasy house, but now the walls were painted a pale blue, and the furniture had been changed out to New England cottage-by-the-sea. I forced myself to keep a straight face. The thought of the Vampire Queen of the Pacific Northwest living in a New England Cape Cod–style cottage seemed awfully strange.

Ruby led us into the parlor, motioning for us to sit on the navy and white print sofa. She vanished out the door after telling us to stay put, and a couple moments later, Essie entered, sans her usual guards.

"Ruby tells me that you're wearing some very interesting weaponry." Essie gave me a long look, her gaze fluttering to my thighs. "I see she wasn't exaggerating."

"You'll understand when I tell you why we're here. I don't feel safe without my weapons right now."

"Do you mean in *my* house in particular?"

Oh great. I had just insulted her.

"No, Essie. I do *not* mean just in your house. I told you on the phone that I know who the vampire is who's been murdering people. Do you know the name Fata Morgana?"

Her eyes widened. A crimson ring formed around her irises. "Are you talking about the Fata you use to run with? I know of her. I know all about your connections with her, because I've looked into your background."

"Right. I'm not surprised. So, today Fata rolled back into town. In fact, she's here in the village now, so tell your nest to be careful. She's not exactly running reasonable at this point. But she brought me a message, and I've verified it with Auntie Tautau."

"And what was that message?" Essie held my gaze and I shivered. While she couldn't charm me—witches couldn't be charmed by a vampire's hypnotic gaze—her very stature demanded respect and attention.

"The Arcānus Nocturni woke up Dracula. They've sent him after me and he's here on the island, now."

Essie let out a hiss. This was the first time I had ever seen true fear in her eyes. Oh, I had seen her cunning, and wary, and I had witnessed her nervousness around a member of the Arcānus Nocturni, but I had never seen Essie Vanderbilt truly afraid.

"*Dracuul*? They woke up Dracula? *The fools.*"

"What I don't understand, though, is since he's after me and he's been on the island for a while, why hasn't he tried to kill me already? If he's as powerful as I think, why hasn't he attacked yet?" I had been toying with the question since Fata first told us, but it only fully formed in my mind within the past hour.

Essie hesitated. She glanced at Aegis, who gave her a nod.

"Why do you think Dracula has survived so long, when so many people have hunted for him? He's one of the oldest vampires, and he's made so many enemies over the years that you would think *someone* would have managed to take him down by now. He's the most famous vampire in the world. So answer me this, how do you think he's survived?"

I was smart enough to realize that she was offering me an answer with her question. She was also giving me the chance to figure it out for myself. At times, Essie liked to play teacher.

I thought about it for a moment, mulling over the possibilities in my mind. I had long been a fan of the Evil Overlords List, a fun little list I had found on the Internet about how to be an effective evil overlord. The basic concept came down to: Don't give your enemies a chance. At first opportunity, take them down. But was that always the right choice?

"I assume that the Arcānus Nocturni gave him as much information on me as they have, but that doesn't necessarily mean that he knows everything he wants to know. He could be studying me. It would make sense. Study your enemy, find out all you can about them before you go in. Especially when they're living with another ancient vampire, one who may not be as old as yourself, but who could still be extremely dangerous?"

Essie smiled. "You do not disappoint me, Maddy. Yes, Dracula has always taken his time. Stoker's book was on point, and more of a biography than most people realize. He had a friend whom Jonathan Harker is modeled after. Dracula is crafty and cunning, and he plans ahead. Dracula's also been asleep for at least a hundred years, so he's going to want to know what kind of world he's dealing with. And my guess is that he's not at full strength yet." Here, she paused.

"You might as well tell her, or I will," Aegis said.

"I thought you might have already done so."

"I would have, except I just found out about this on the way over." Aegis leaned back in his chair. "Essie, I know you don't care for me because I refused to join your nest. I have nothing against you, and I hope you won't hold anything against me. But you should know, anything that might affect Maddy's health or safety is my concern. I'll give her any secret, any information that I need to in order to ensure her safety. And that's just something you have to accept."

Essie's eyes narrowed. After a moment, she gave a little shrug as though she didn't care. I had a feeling that wasn't her true feeling, but she didn't want to press it.

"I can understand why you would do so. At least

Maddy seems to have a discreet tongue." She turned back to me. "When a vampire has been asleep for a very long time—figure fifty or sixty years, or more—they tend to be weak when they awake. Their strength returns a little with each kill, or feeding if you like. It can take up to two weeks to a month before they reach full power again, depending on how long they slept and how weak they were when they went to sleep."

I frowned. "Don't all vampires wake every sunset? I thought you wake when the sun disappears, and sleep when it rises. Except, of course, for the Arcānus Nocturni."

Essie held up one hand. "One moment," she said, rising and moving to the door. She peeked outside to make sure no one was around, then quietly closed it and locked it and returned to the table.

"What I am about to tell you is information you'd best keep to yourself. I realized that Aegis could have told you, but since I am here now and party to this, it means that I could be in grave danger should anyone find out that I've opened my mouth on the subject."

She leaned across the table and took my hand, turning it over so that it was palm up. I tried not to pull away from her. With her other hand, she motioned toward my leg.

"Your dagger, if you will. I am going to require a blood oath that you keep this silent and to yourself. No telling Delia, no telling Cassandra or anyone else. Will you abide by the pact?"

"If Aegis would tell me without forcing me to make that pact, should I give you my oath? It doesn't really make sense now, does it?"

Essie squeezed my hand hard enough to hurt. "Oh, Aegis would tell you what I am about to, but I have information that even he does not. Remember, I run in a circle that Aegis has never entered. The nobility of the vampire nation doesn't let in the *riffraff*." With those words, she glanced at Aegis.

If her insult bothered him, he chose to ignore it.

"Do you think I should?" I glanced at him. "Whatever you say, I'll trust you."

Aegis gave Essie a sarcastic smile. "Oh, I'm sure she has the dirt on other people within the nobility. All the royals are corrupt that way. Go ahead." There was a gleam in his eyes that told me he was up to something.

I turned back to Essie and nodded. "Very well, I'll seal it with my blood. But you don't get to drink it. No, you get to prick your own finger and blend it with mine. And not on my cut directly. I don't want any of your blood absorbing into me. We squeeze out at a few drops into a bowl and when they mingle, then my promise mingles with yours. We can seal on a handshake if you like, but those are *my* terms."

Essie looked disappointed, but she agreed. I pulled out my dagger and pricked my finger with it. The blade was extremely sharp, and all it took was a little flick and the cut was done.

Essie grimaced as she held out a finger and I realized how much she trusted me at this point. Here I was, holding a silver dagger in her parlor, without any guards around, and she was trusting me not to stab her in the heart. Feeling like I had just forged another inroad, I made certain to keep the cut on her finger light and quick. She let out a hiss as the silver touched her skin and smoked, but it was over and done within a matter of a few seconds.

We squeezed drops of our blood into a trinket dish on her table. Ironically, it was in the shape of a heart. And then, after wiping my hand with a towel, I offered her a handshake and she took it.

"I swear on my blood, I will not reveal to anyone what you tell me here about Dracula."

"And I swear to give you the information that I know." Her expression was a mixture of mingled relief and fear.

"All right, dish it out."

Essie's eyes glimmered. I had the feeling she was enjoying this, in a perverse way.

"Very few people know this. I only found out through a…shall we say…clandestine friendship. Dracula takes far longer than other ancient vampires to heal. He may be one of the Arcānus Nocturni, but before he went into hibernation, he was wounded, severely. His heart was nicked by silver, though not pierced through. The wound wasn't enough to shatter him into dust, but it was enough to permanently scar him."

"Can he walk in the sunlight?"

"Yes, but if he doesn't feed on a regular basis, he quickly loses strength. And here's something that not even the Arcānus Nocturni know. Don't ask me how I found out, because I will not tell you. I have my ways."

Aegis and I shared a look. Essie was one hell of a detective.

"Dracula has developed a disease that affects a very small percentage of vampires. Think of it as an autoimmune disorder. Dracula is allergic to witches' blood. He knows he can't kill you. He doesn't dare feed on you—or any other witch. That alone would kill him. So he must find another way if he's going to kill you. And that's why he's being extremely cautious. He must know about your past. And given you aren't just a vampire hunter, but a witch, you loom as a larger threat in his mind than you would to most vampires."

"You say the Arcānus Nocturni doesn't know about this illness?"

"You think they'd send him out after you if they did? I'm not even sure if they know about the close call he had. And he can't afford for them to know about his weaknesses. They'd quietly stake him as a liability."

I nodded. "So they think they've sicced an ancient terror on me, but in reality, he's vulnerable."

"Vulnerable, yes, but don't underestimate how crafty he is."

So Dracula was allergic to witches' blood. It wasn't exactly as though we could use it as a weapon, and I didn't envision myself offering up my throat trying to entice him into feeding off me just so he would die. But I was thinking linearly. There had to be an answer here.

"Is he just allergic to drinking my blood? To ingesting it?"

Essie's expression darkened. "In for a penny… No, you see, there's the rub. If you get enough of your blood on his flesh, it will burn him. Remember, I only know this because I did some extremely in-depth research at one time, and I know vampires who aren't very happy with the Arcānus Nocturni. This isn't something vampires would make public knowledge, even among their own kind. We aren't always the most trustworthy bunch."

As I mulled over the thought, Essie returned to the

door and unlocked it, opened it, and called for tea. I looked at Aegis, but he shook his head and held his finger to his lips. I wasn't sure what he was planning, but I had the feeling that he had just managed to pull the wool over Essie's eyes. And I wanted to know how.

CHAPTER THIRTEEN

"So, was that information worth your oath of secrecy?" Essie just had to get the last word in.

I nodded, still saying nothing. I was trying to process everything that I had learned. After a moment, I asked, "Two questions. First, how did he sleep for so long if he needs to feed regularly?"

"Good question," Essie said. "I'm impressed. When a vampire lowers himself into stasis, that need fades as well, until they wake again. All vampires will be weak when they first wake after hibernation, but with Dracula, the need for blood will be extremely strong."

"You have an exceptionally good source of information, it seems," Aegis said.

"You had better believe it." Essie snorted. "You know my past, I'm sure. Philippe had an interesting stash of information and when I staked him, I stole every document I could find. He was responsible for turning me. He was damned well going to fork over the information I needed to survive in the vampire nation. If it took staking him to procure what I needed, so be it."

I grinned. Essie could be downright scary, but she was also good for a laugh at times. "Fair enough. Second question: do you have any idea of where Dracula is? Or where he might hang out? He can walk in the daylight, but will anybody recognize him? Would he dare to go out in public in the daytime?"

"I sincerely doubt that Dracula is going to be walking around the streets of downtown Bedlam, or going to Chicken Chicken. As to where he might be hiding, there are so many niches and nooks on this island. Caves, abandoned houses, even deep in the forest. He could be anywhere, Maddy. But you can be sure that he's watching you, so he's probably not far from your house. Especially if he drank from Ralph's brother. And if Ralph's brother turns, he's going to be an amazingly tough vampire. A vampiric satyr? Sired by Dracula himself? Consider that a very dangerous combination. I'm afraid if George does turn, you're going to have to employ your old talents. Unless Ralph has the balls to do it."

Could Ralph actually kill his brother? Even if George did turn into a vampire, I wasn't sure that Ralph had the courage or heart to dust him. Which meant if Jordan thought that George was dying, we were going to have to keep Ralph away from him. And that would be a problem, given the funeral rites among satyrs.

"I'm afraid you're right. Do you mind if I give Jordan a call? I want to ask him what George's condition is."

"Be my guest."

Just then, Ruby brought in a tray with the tea on it, and scones, and delicate watercress sandwiches. Aegis flashed me a sideways smile, not letting Essie see him. The British delicacies seemed totally out of place, especially now that she had redecorated into the New England cottage by the sea decor. I punched in Jordan's number, stepping aside to talk in private.

Jordan answered on the second ring. "Maddy, are you all right?"

I was getting tired of him asking that every time I called, but given the reasons I called, I couldn't blame him. "I'm fine. I was wondering how George is doing."

"He's in crisis mode right now. Ralph is with him right now. I think I might be able to stabilize him, but George was so low on blood that it's amazing he was even walking around. If it wasn't for the fact that he was a satyr, he would have been dead. And, I think, turned. We were able to get enough information out of him to confirm that he drank the vampire's blood."

My heart began to pound. I let out a sharp breath. "If it looks like he's going to die, get Ralph out of the room. And call me immediately. There are aspects to this case that make it absolutely necessary that we do not allow him to turn."

"Because he's a satyr, right?"

I paused, trying to remember if Jordan had overheard us talking about Dracula. I didn't want to ask him, in case he hadn't. "Right. Please, keep the knowledge that he was bitten to yourself for now. It's vital we don't stir up panic on the island."

"All right. If George makes it through the night, I think he'll survive. But it's going to be touch and go. Keep your phone turned on."

"Will do." I disconnected.

"How is George doing?" Aegis had picked up one of the watercress sandwiches and was eating it. He politely shook his head when Essie offered him another.

"Not good. Jordan says that if he survives the night, he'll be all right, but the chances of that aren't spectacular. And George was forced to drink from Dracula. So if he dies, we'll have a vampiric satyr on our hands. I suppose we should get home."

"Yeah, we have a lot to do."

I turned to Essie. "Thanks, Essie. I'll keep my word. If you think of anything that can help us find out where Dracula's hiding, call me. I'll keep my phone on all night." I paused, then said, "Why *are* you helping us? Dracula is one of your kind. I know why Aegis is helping me—but he lives a different lifestyle than you."

Essie gave me a frozen smile. "Because the thought of the Arcānus Nocturni taking over this world scares me spitless. I like my title, and I like my place in the vampire nation. I don't want anything or anybody upsetting the apple cart. I have my eye on a higher prize, and I'll do whatever I must to get there."

It occurred to me as we left that it was a good thing Essie was on our side. Well, as much she could ever be.

Jordan didn't call during the night, and the first thing I did when I woke up was to contact him. "Did George survive the night?"

"I can't believe it, but he did. I think he'll be okay. Which means if he survives for sixty days, the disease will vacate his blood and he won't be in danger of turning when he dies."

Although I was relieved to hear the news, it occurred to me that we didn't know if that particular rule played through for the members of the Arcānus Nocturni. Could their blood be more potent? Could the disease stay in the body longer? It was something I needed to ask Aegis, but I wasn't going to be able to until he woke up.

"I'll stop by Ralph's this morning and talk to him. Do what you can to keep George alive, because you do not want to meet the vampire who tried to sire him."

"Will do. Thanks for calling, Maddy."

I turned around to see Bubba and Luna waiting for me. I hadn't had much time the past few days to pay attention to them, given all the crap that had been going on, so I sat back on the bed and patted the comforter.

"Come on up, you two." As they leapt on the bed, both of them purring loudly, I felt a stab of guilt. "I'm afraid I haven't been a very good mom, have I?" I leaned back against the pillows as Bubba crawled on my chest and Luna snuggled by my arm. With one hand I petted Bubba, and with the other I pulled Luna toward me in the crook of my elbow.

"Bubba, I have a problem. I'm not asking you for anything, and I'm not wishing anything, but I need to talk."

He blinked at me with those deep beautiful eyes. The cowlick on the top of his head poked up as usual, giving him a slightly silly look. I scratched him behind the ears, then under the chin.

"*M-row?*" He blinked at me.

"I'm okay, but no, everything *isn't* all right. Fata scares the hell out of me, and Dracula's after me. I'm not sure which of them scares me most."

Bubba rubbed his head under my chin and then sprawled out on my chest, his feet and tail stretching down my thigh. He was huge, fifteen pounds. And he was so fluffy that he looked almost twice that size. I gave myself ten minutes of just petting them before forcing myself to get up and take a shower.

Dressing, I pulled on a long tiered skirt, hunter green with burnished leaves embroidered all around the hem. Choosing a wine-colored V-neck sweater and a pair of knee-high leather boots with stacked heels, I finished dressing, put on my makeup, and then remembered to look for Aegis's note. I almost always checked when I woke up, but I had slept so deeply that I wasn't fully clearheaded yet.

Aegis had left a note telling me he would keep watch during the night, and that he was going to contact some old friends to see what they could find out about the situation.

As I clattered down the stairs, Kelson met me at the bottom.

"Delia's waiting for you in the kitchen. I can tell you right now she's in a nasty mood. I'm not sure why, though I tried to pry it out of her. How many shots do you want in your latte?"

"Better make a quint for me. With a whole lot of chocolate and peppermint."

"So, a five-shot mocha?"

"Ten points to the winner."

She laughed and nodded toward the kitchen. "You better go see what teacher wants."

I followed her into the kitchen. Delia was sitting at the table, stewing about something. Her eyes were flashing dark, and as I entered the room, she straightened.

"How late do you sleep, anyway?"

"Well, that's a cheery greeting. And how are *you* today, Delia?"

She let out an exasperated sigh. "I'm sorry. How are you doing, Maddy?"

"Just fine, thank you. I would be better if I didn't have Dracula on my ass. What's going on? You look fit to be tied."

"Your friend is raising havoc in town and I need you to do something about it. Fata Morgana flooded the town square this morning. She got so excited about that stupid fountain that she made it pour until it was like a geyser. The city's going to have one hell of a water bill, I can tell you that. It was like there was a broken water main. The water was ankle-deep in some lower parts of the town square. I don't know what the hell she was doing, but when I told her to stop, she threatened me."

Well, that wasn't the best news of the morning. "What did she say?"

"She told me that werewolves weren't her favorite type of dog, and that I should mind my own business." Her voice grated over the words, and by the tone of her voice, I knew that Fata had pushed it well over the line.

"I can talk to her, but I'm not sure if I can control her." I paused to accept my mocha from Kelson.

"Well, if you can't control her, you need to find somebody who can. Because if she stays in Bedlam much longer, she's going to hurt somebody."

I nodded, swallowing the desire to say, "If you can find a way to get rid of her, I'd be happy to help."

Delia picked up her hat. "I know she's an old friend of yours, but Maddy, I don't think she's who you think she is."

"Fata's changed—she's part water elemental now, and that changes her entire nature. And you know how hard it is to control an elemental creature. She might as well be part goddess."

As she headed toward the front door, Delia glanced over her shoulder. "If she's a goddess, then heaven help us all."

I DECIDED TO GO OVER AND TALK TO RALPH. I WASN'T SURE if he'd be at the hospital, but with George out of danger, he might be taking a break. It was storming again, pouring down rain, so I grabbed my keys to my CR-V. The vertigo was gone, and I was tired of waiting around for other people to help me.

Kelson glanced up as I headed toward the kitchen door. "Are you going out?"

"Yeah, I'm going over to Ralph's for a little bit. I am not about to walk in the rain, and I'm perfectly fine now. So I'm driving. No discussion." I gave her a look that brooked no argument.

She held up her hands, shaking her head. "You seem fine to me."

"I'll be back in a little while. If I have to go somewhere else, I'll give you a call. I need to find Fata Morgana as soon as I can, but I'm not exactly jumping for joy over the prospect."

Kelson gave me a sad look. "I'm sorry, Maddy. I know how close you were at one time. It's always hard to walk away from friends. I've had to do it myself in the past."

I paused, my hand on the door handle. "There was always part of me terrified that she would return. Somewhere deep in my heart, I knew that she had changed enough so that we wouldn't be living in the same world. And I was right. For the sake of the gods, I wish I was wrong. The Fata Morgana I loved and knew is long gone. Oh, she's in there, there's a flicker of recognition, but she's buried under the weight of two hundred years of living in the Ocean Mother's realm. Once the ocean takes you, there's no going back."

And with that, I headed out to my car.

Ralph's car was in the driveway, and the tree that had been downed was now a massive pile of kindling and firewood. I cautiously edged around it, not wanting to puncture any of my tires on stray splinters. I glanced up at the roof, hoping that Ralph had managed to have it fixed already and that we could deposit his twins back with him, but the tarp was still stretched across the shingles. I let out a long sigh, realizing it would be a few more days before we could escort our guests back to where they belonged.

As I dashed through the rain, up the porch steps and to the door, a gust of wind rattled past, almost tipping me off my feet. I held onto the railing and, for the first time in a long time, found myself longing for calmer days. I usually loved autumn and winter best, but with Fata back, my enthusiasm had waned for the time being.

I opened the door and slipped inside. There was no one at the receptionist desk, but I heard laughter coming from the next room. Since Ralph's guests frequented the living and dining rooms, I had no qualms about wandering in to see if he was there. As I did, I got the shock of my life. There, sprawled on the sofa, sat Ralph. And on his lap, laughing, was Fata.

"I see I've come at the wrong time." My shock didn't keep my mouth from working, that was for sure. My first reaction was to turn and hightail it out of there, but I forced myself to stay put. What the hell was Fata doing with Ralph? Granted, we had partied hearty with the satyrs a long, long time ago, but really, *Ralph*?

Fata, who was dressed in a short black dress that left very little to the imagination, glanced over at me. The smile on her face was cunning and a little crazed.

"Maddy, come over here." She motioned for me to join them on the sofa.

I took a few steps closer, but stayed standing. "Ralph, I hear your brother's going to make it after all. I just came to tell you I'm happy that George will be all right." My voice fell flat, and I wasn't exactly sure of what to say next.

Ralph nodded. "I'm cele…cel…celebrating. Hey, Fata tells me you two were an item, and that you partied with my kind for years. She was just tellin' me 'bout some of your exploits." The look on his face was lascivious and he sounded stoned.

"So you're spilling my secrets, Fata? Don't you think

you should ask me about that?" I didn't want to start an argument, but the fact that she had been telling my history to Ralph without my permission pissed me off.

Fata's eyes flashed dangerously. "I thought you weren't *ashamed* of your past?"

"I'm not, but my secrets are mine to tell. Not yours."

I felt like I was dealing with an incredibly powerful and spoiled teenager. Fata had been reborn a daughter of the Ocean Mother, who had given her everything she needed. Now Fata expected to get anything she wanted from us.

Fata pushed herself off Ralph's lap. He looked dazed. He also had an immense hard-on, which was extremely visible since his pants were open. His knobby red cock stood erect, slick. I realized just exactly *what* Fata had been sitting on.

"What have you done to Ralph?" While I had no interest in Ralph sexually, neither did I want to see him become a pawn in whatever game she was playing.

"Only what you and I used to do to the boys. Remember, Maddy? Remember the parties we had? You, and me, and Cassandra. And those five beautiful satyrs that we stayed with for almost a decade? They were *in* us, in every combination you could think of. And you and I made love for hours, day after day." She held out her hand, crooking a finger at me. "Come, give me a kiss. We could have all of that again. Right now, right here. Sure, Cassandra isn't here, and we have only one satyr, but we can share him. And we have each other. That's enough, don't you think?"

The next moment she reached out and grabbed me by the hand, dragging me to her. She was immensely strong and I realized I was absolutely terrified.

She pressed close to me. "Kiss me, Maddy. Remember what it was like? Your lips against mine? It can be that way again. I'll forget that you drove me away, that you broke my heart. Your vampire can't kiss like I can. And I'll bet he can't fuck like me, either."

With that, she planted her lips on mine, kissing me deep. My body responded before my mind. I wrapped my arms around her, kissing her back, and then I realized what was going on. She had me in thrall with her emotions. Water elementals were incredibly seductive by their very nature. I pushed her away,shaking my head.

"No, Fata. *Stop*. I'm not ever going to be with you again. And I'm not sleeping with Ralph."

Fata laughed. "Who said anything about sleeping?"

"You know what I mean. Let Ralph out of your thrall right now. He doesn't deserve this. If you give a damn about me, even one little iota, stop using him as a pawn." I was angry now, my fire rising in my belly.

"If I let him out of my control, will you love me?" Her red hair crackled with energy, the static electricity rising around the room.

"I will *always* love you, *as my friend*. Do you know why I told you I couldn't return your love back then?"

Her eyes narrowed as she threw herself into a chair and crossed her legs, staring at me intently. "Does it matter? All I know is that you *rejected* me. I've torn ships apart on the ocean because of my anger at you. Do you realize how many deaths you're to blame for?"

"It's not my fault that you killed other people out of your anger. Don't you *dare* try to put that blame on me. Fata, I rejected you because I knew that you and I would end up at each other's throats. I was still in love with Tom.

I loved you because you were my friend, and I cared about you. But I wasn't *in love* with you. We had a wonderful time, carousing with Ralph's kind. But I burned out on it. I needed something more."

"You could have had something more with *me*."

"How could that have *ever* worked? You and I are so different. We're literally fire and water, and fire and water don't mix. You were always the wild one, Fata. They called me Mad Maudlin, but that was only because they didn't know who you really were. And there's nothing *wrong* with that. But I needed a break. I needed something else. You aren't the type to settle down. You'll never be the type. I'm not being mean. I'm just being honest. You know you're part water elemental. The Ocean Mother has changed you, she's taken you in as a daughter, and that is a blessed thing."

I wasn't sure if I was getting through to her. Finally, I decided to end the staredown.

"Leave Ralph alone. And stop messing with the town. Make me happy to see you. Please, don't make me regret that you've come back." I strode out, praying she wouldn't take her anger out on Ralph.

I was almost to my car when I heard her calling behind me.

"Maddy! Maddy? Please, Maddy, stop and talk to me."

I turned around to see her running down the steps, hair askew. She was crying.

"What do you want? What can we possibly have to talk about?"

"I'm sorry," she said, dropping to her knees. "I'm sorry that I angered you. Please, don't walk away from me. It's been so lonely in the ocean. At times I thought I'd go crazy. The Ocean Mother kept me locked up in her embrace. Oh, she talks to me, but she'll never understand how lonely it can get."

I wanted to break away, but the heartbreak in her voice was too much. I looked down at her, kneeling in the mud, and I began to cry, too.

"Maddy, I miss you so much. And I miss Sandy. I don't know what comes over me. The anger wells up and then she—the Ocean Mother—encourages me to let it out. Then, I rage and riot, and break ships and send waves over islands. When I see what I've done, I can't face myself, so I go back to sleep. I don't *want* to hurt people but I don't know how to stop. I don't know how to be the person I'm becoming. Help me?"

My stomach lurched, my heart thudding in my chest. What the hell was I going to do? How could I help Fata Morgana learn how to control herself? I knelt and gathered her in my arms, kneeling in the mud as she pressed against me, weeping as though her life was ending.

I brushed her hair back out of her face and kissed her forehead. What I had said was true. I had never been in love with her, even though she had fallen for me. But I did love her. And when she had left, it had broken my heart that I had driven her away. I had carried the weight of that knowledge inside me, never wanting to face it, because it was something that I couldn't fix. Sometimes, you can't fix what you break.

"I don't know how to help you, but we can try to figure it out. You have to control yourself, though. You have to stop messing with the town, and you have to stop manipulating people." I pushed her back, staring into her eyes. "Will you promise me that? Will you promise to be on your best behavior while we try to figure out how to help you learn how to deal with this?"

"Yes," she said, dipping her head. "I promise, on my oath. I promise on my blood. Just please, do what you can to help me. I don't think I can live with myself if I have to go back into the ocean and stay there. And yet, she calls me and my blood responds."

I gathered her to her feet. We were both covered with mud and soaked through to the skin.

"Wait here. I need to check on Ralph. I'll be back in a moment, so don't you go anywhere."

She nodded, her eyes wide. I ran back inside to find Ralph looking confused, staring down at his open fly.

"Maddy, what happened? I can't remember."

"Zip your fly up, and go make yourself some coffee. Then, you probably want to go check on your brother at the hospital. I just dropped by to tell you I'm glad he's going to make it. Keep a close watch on him, though, all right?"

Still looking dazed, he nodded and zipped up his pants, carefully tucking his penis back inside. "All right. Do you know why I was…" His gaze flickered to my face, and he blushed.

"You are probably just worried and trying to relieve some stress," I said. "I'll see you later." I turned and dashed back outside. Fata was waiting right where I had left her, and I bundled her in my car and drove back home, wondering what the hell I was going to do to help her.

CHAPTER FOURTEEN

I wasn't certain where to take Fata. Of course, I could take her back to my place, but I wasn't sure what good it would do. And then it hit me—Auntie Tautau's. If she wouldn't help me, I'd have to reconfigure my plan, but at least I could try.

Fata stared out the window as we sped along the road. The storm had backed off, though it still was buffeting the island with impressive gusts. She leaned her head against the seat.

"Are you happy with him?"

I thought about my answer. I wasn't about to gloat in her face, given our past, but I had to be honest.

"I'm happier than I thought I could be. I'm happier than I've been with anybody, even Tom. And that's saying something. I loved your cousin more than I loved anybody in this world," I said. "But Aegis makes me happy, and he's truly a good soul. Not all vampires are evil, so I've found out. Sometimes the world makes you wear a mask. My mother died a few months ago, Fata. Would it surprise you to know that I'm mourning her loss? Would you ever have believed me if I told you that I miss her and I wish she was still alive?"

She stirred. "Are you serious? About your mother, I mean?"

"I found out all too recently that Zara was living a lie imposed on her by Granny. I have a half-brother in England. We haven't met yet. In fact, he's supposed to call me when he processes the fact that I exist. Granny forced Zara to give him up when she was barely of age. My grandmother didn't like Zara's lover. So she excised him and my brother out of my mother's life. Zara had no choice, and everybody continued as if Gregory—my brother—never existed. I never knew until Zara came here a few months ago and told me she had Winter Syndrome, and that Gregory was her firstborn. And because of that, she always felt guilty for loving me. She felt like she was betraying him because she felt she had abandoned him. And in the short time she was here, we discovered that we actually did love each other. And then I lost her."

I clutched the steering wheel, cautiously maneuvering the slick road. Traffic was light at this time of day, but I was so fresh off the vertigo and still so emotional about my mother that I didn't trust myself. I eased over to a turnout that overlooked the ocean.

"I never knew. I would never have guessed. Your mother always seemed so distant and so critical." Fata straightened up and turned to me. "I'm sorry for your loss. I'm sorry that you found out how you felt too late."

"At least I found out soon enough to tell her I loved her. At least I found out in time to be able to say good-bye. But if I had turned away because I assumed she was just the bitch I always knew her as, I would never have found out about my brother. Or how Zara was treated. She wasn't beaten, or battered, but she was emotionally manipulated and used. My father didn't help. He knew about it, but he never wanted to talk about it or let her talk."

"What are you trying to say?"

"I suppose I'm saying," I said, choosing my words carefully, "watch out when you assume things about others. Until the day I met Aegis, I thought most vampires were only out to kill. He broke my assumption. And a couple other vampires I've met on the island have also opened my eyes. Maybe they aren't always the best or most ethical people they could be, but they're a lot better than some of the mortals still walking around living. That's why I want you to give him a chance."

She pressed her lips together, still looking so lost and alone, but then nodded. "I see what you're saying. It's hard to process, but I'll do my best. I meant it when I said I missed you. And I meant it when I told you I've been so lonely. I'm not certain what to do next. I don't know where I belong."

I started up the car again. "I'm hoping that the person I'm taking you to see will be able to help us on that issue. It can't hurt, that much I know. And Fata, one thing I've learned over the decades is that we're all just stumbling around, looking for the right path. Sometimes we luck out and find it. And sometimes, we just keep trying, because that's all we can do."

By the time we got to Auntie Tautau's it was going on two o'clock. I couldn't believe that the time had flown so quickly, but as I parked and cautiously got out of the car, it occurred to me that perhaps time speeded up when we were intensely focused on something.

As we stepped up on the porch, Fata looked around, avidly interested in the multitude of birdfeeders and flowerpots and gardens that surrounded Auntie Tautau's house.

"Who lives here?"

"Auntie Tautau. I've gotten to know her over the past few months and I really like her. I like her better than I liked Auntie Berma. Auntie Berma was a little too opinionated for my tastes. Auntie Tautau, well, she can be a lot of fun and extremely compassionate."

I knocked again, wondering if Auntie Tautau was going to come to the door. I was about to give up when I heard something inside, and then the door clicked open and Auntie Tautau peeked out.

"We need your help, Auntie Tautau. I need your help with Fata. You said I'd know what to do when it came time, and all I could think of was to bring her here." I didn't think it was time for Fata to leave and yet I wasn't sure what to do with her until then.

Auntie Tautau motioned us in. She gave us a once-over and shook her head.

"You look like you've been mud wrestling. What on earth were you girls doing? And you're both soaked to the skin. Come in, sit by the fire. I'll get some towels and robes." As she turned, Merriweather crooked his head, looking back at us.

"So the ocean comes to the Auntie," he observed. "Not

all goddesses live in the sky." And with that the crow shut his beak and Auntie Tautau disappeared through the door.

"I wonder what he meant by that," I said absently.

"I don't know if I want to know," Fata said. Her eyes were flashing again, but she seemed lethargic, as she knelt near the fire and rubbed her hands in front of it. "You always loved the fire, and I always loved that spark in you. You're so vibrant and alive, Maddy. And I always felt like I was hiding in a swirl of mist, dancing on the edge of the ocean and sometimes on the edge of my sanity. The world seems to constantly move and shift like the waves, and I never know whether I am seeing things correctly, or viewing them from a distance. Sometimes it feels as though I look at life through a microscope, and other times it feels like I'm part of every single grain of sand on the ocean shore. As though every single drop of water has a part of me in it, and it makes me feel stretched and thin."

"I wonder if you were always part of the water," I said. "I mean, I know you and I and Sandy were all born to our elements, but I wonder if there isn't a spark of water elemental or siren back there in your bloodstream somewhere. Something that allowed you to tune into your element more than Sandy and me due to ours. I love the fire, I can bathe in it and I feel it in my blood and bones, but not the way you connect with the ocean. Jordan said that you were part water elemental, so when did everything shift and change? While you were sleeping on the bottom of the sea, snug in Ocean Mother's arms?"

"I suppose," Fata said. She stood up and shivered, her dress covering very little of her skin. "I don't usually feel cold anymore, but right now I feel it to my very core. I wonder why."

"Because," Auntie Tautau said, returning with two large towels, washcloths, and two bars of soap. "In my house, very little of the outer world has any effect. The oceans pull on you? Here she still will, but never to the degree it does when you step outside my front door. Here, you can remember more of yourself. Wash up. Maddy, why don't you go first. There's plenty of hot water in the shower. I can run your clothes through the washing machine while you're here."

I wanted to say that I wouldn't be staying that long, but I decided not to argue. If Auntie Tautau could help us, I would stay as long as she wanted me to.

Fata glanced at me as I picked up the robe and towel and washcloth and headed around the corner, but she said nothing. Once I was in Auntie Tautau's bathroom—a cozy room, complete with a walk-in shower, a vanity, and an extremely clean toilet—I let out a long breath. It felt like I had been holding it since I first walked into Ralph's living room.

I stripped off my clothes and slipped into her shower. The hot water felt soothing against my skin, and by the time I got out and dried off and changed into the robe, I was breathing easier. I knew it wasn't polite of me to let Auntie Tautau handle Fata Morgana without me, but I desperately needed a break. Staring at myself in the mirror, I splashed some more water on my face and finally gathered up my clothes and made sure that the bathroom was clean, and headed back out to the living room.

Auntie Tautau took my outfit from me, and Fata's

dress, and while Fata took her turn in the shower, she bustled off to put them in the washing machine. When she returned she was carrying cups of hot chocolate, and a plate of cookies. Feeling grateful, I dove into my chocolate and sipped the hot, minty foam that frothed atop the drink.

Fata returned shortly after. Her eyes lit up at the hot cocoa and cookies, and she ate like she hadn't eaten in years. I ate three cookies but she finished the rest of the plate. Auntie Tautau returned to the kitchen and when she came back she was carrying another plate of cookies, along with a round of Gouda, and the pot of hot chocolate. She refilled our mugs, and sliced the cheese, handing us thick wedges.

"I wasn't planning on stepping in at this point," Auntie Tautau suddenly said to me. "I have a part to play, but it's not yet time. However, Fata Morgana can stay with me for the night. We'll take it one day at a time. She'll be safe here, both from herself and from harming others."

Fata had discovered some of Auntie Tautau's figurines. She wasn't even listening to us, so rapt was her attention on the ceramic dolls. She wasn't touching them, but stared at them as if they were the most miraculous thing she had ever seen.

I realized there was so much that Fata had missed out on in the outer world, so many things she knew nothing of that Sandy and I had experienced and seen as we watched the years and decades go by, changing ourselves to match the times. In a sense, Fata had been plucked right out of the past and dropped in the present, without any chance of acclimating herself.

"You'll be okay with her here?" It was a stupid question. After all, Auntie Tautau was one of the Aunties, but I still felt pushed to ask.

"I'm not the one you'd have to worry about, my dear," she said that gleam in her eye. "If I wanted to, Fata would be gone and never ever seen again. All I'd have to do is shift the web, and all that takes is for me to desire that it be. There's much you have to learn about the Aunties still, but then—you could live a lifetime and never know a fraction of what and who we are.

"Now, scoot yourself on out of here, Maddy. You have things to do, and you still have a deadly killer after you. I would help if I could, but it's not my vision to see where he is."

I started to say good-bye to Fata, but she was still engrossed in all of Auntie Tautau's curios. From the door, I blew her a kiss, knowing she would never see it. Feeling like a mother leaving her child at nursery school for the first time, I turned and walked away. The storm had lightened, and a ray of sun broke through, filtering in from low on the horizon. I took it as a good omen as I got in my CR-V and headed home.

THAT EVENING, AS AEGIS AND I WERE TRYING TO PUZZLE out where Dracula might be staying, the doorbell rang and Kelson answered it. It was Sandy and Max, and they headed into the kitchen, where we were sitting around a pot of tea.

"I'm so glad to see you," I said, jumping up to give Sandy a hug. I waved at Max and he blew me a kiss.

Aegis clasped his hand, and they did a manly shake. I tried not to laugh, but Sandy snorted.

"Oh hush, woman," Aegis said. "There's so much estrogen around here that we have to have some traditions. Let us have our handshakes, and back pats."

"Just long as you don't pat each other on the butt like they do in football," Sandy said with a giggle.

Kelson, who was finishing up a stew for the next day, carried over a bottle of wine that she knew Sandy and I liked, along with goblets and a bag of chips. "That's all we have for snacks right now, because Aegis forgot to bake tonight."

"They'll just have to do with ready-made muffins for breakfast. We're dealing with a serious issue and you know it." Aegis gave Kelson a long look.

"Of course I know that, and you should realize I'm just giving you a hard time." She wriggled her nose at him.

I poured the wine as Sandy and Max settled around the table.

"Where's Fata? Do you know?" Sandy glanced around, looking nervous.

"I left her at Auntie Tautau's. She's there for the night, and I don't think she's going to be going anywhere without permission. We had an interesting incident at Ralph's today." I told them about what had happened, feeling almost embarrassed to recount the discussion between Fata and me. But they had to know, especially if she had been running around, telling my secrets to everybody.

"So you and Fata were involved?" Aegis looked at me, his eyes wide. He didn't look upset, just startled.

"We were lovers, yes. And we were lovers with the

satyrs. And Sandy was right there with us." I suddenly stopped, afraid that Max didn't know about Sandy's past. I was positive she had told him, but the words had slipped out before I could make sure.

"Oh crap, did I say anything I shouldn't have? Or does he know?" Even when I tried to fix my gaffe, I seemed to be putting my foot in it.

Sandy let out a long breath. "Max knows about our past. I didn't tell him about you and Fata because it was in the past, until the past showed up on our doorstep."

"Here's the thing," I said. "Fata was in love with me. I loved her, but I wasn't *in love* with her. That's why she left. We had a big row, and the truth slipped out. She summoned up such a tempest that it shook the entire woodland where we were staying. And she stormed off to the shore. Sandy and I followed her, begging her to be sensible. But you can't ask the ocean to stop raging, and you can't ask a water witch to favor logic over her emotions. She accused me of breaking her heart, of doing it deliberately. She accused me of using her. And then she told me that I had actually broken her heart the day I picked her cousin over her. That made me angry—so angry. I had never known how she felt until we started hanging with the satyrs. When I met Tom, we fell head over heels in love, and Fata seemed so happy for us. She kept saying that finally, she had a sister. Tom was her cousin, you know. When I heard that, I hate to say it, but I began to wonder about his death."

"You can't mean it, can you?" Sandy leaned forward. "Do you really think she would've done that to her own cousin?"

"She was the only one who knew where he and I were

that night. She was the only one we told where we were going. I suppose the vampires could have been tracking us, but it seemed so convenient that Fata was the one who told us to go to that grove. So, you see, I don't know whether she would have done that to Tom, or to me. I don't suppose I'll ever find out, and right now, I don't know if that matters."

"Well, it certainly explains a few things," Aegis said. When I looked at him, he shrugged. "I meant about the way she's acting. But back to the topic at hand, where could Dracula be hiding?"

I desperately wanted to tell Sandy about Dracula's weakness, but I had pledged my word to Essie and I couldn't break it. I glanced over at Aegis.

"I can't talk about some things," I began.

He held up his hand. "Maddy made an oath that she can't tell anybody something she found out. But Maddy, you'll notice that *I* didn't take any such oath there. Essie forgot to bind me to silence. So I can tell them exactly what we learned."

I let out a little gasp and half rose out of my seat. "I never thought about that."

"I'm a smart cookie, you have to admit." Aegis looked so pleased with himself that I jumped up and threw my arms around his neck, giving him a big kiss.

"Tell us what?" Sandy asked.

Aegis turned to them. "It seems as though Dracula has developed an allergy to witches' blood. The touch of it can burn him, and ingesting it can kill him. So he has a definite vulnerability. The question is, exactly how do we exploit it?"

"Actually," I said, "the first question is where do we

find him? We can't kill him if he doesn't show himself. And frankly, I don't feel like running around on a wild goose chase, putting myself in danger, playing hide and seek. What about the Durholm estate? We know that has secret tunnels beneath it."

"Possibly, but he would have to evade everybody who's there and we know that the Winter Fae keep tight control over who gets in and out of that place." Sandy brought out her tablet. "Let me call Bjorn and ask him about abandoned houses in the area. It would have to be one with the basement, so that may narrow it down a little bit."

"Good thinking, and while you're at it, ask him if he knows of any tunnel systems throughout the town. I'm sure there are, but we don't have time to go looking for them right now. Although I suppose we have as much time as it takes before we can find Dracula."

While she called Bjorn, a local fox-shifter real estate agent, I found my silver stake and dagger and put them on the table, carefully keeping them away from Aegis. They had seen so much action over the years, been party to so many deaths. And yet, now they called to me like they hadn't for a long, long time. Auntie Berma had given them to me, on a day that I would never forget.

When I emerged from the Faerie Barrow after the faerie warrior had carried me away into it, I was unaware that twenty years had passed. The area looked overgrown, a little wilder, and I felt dazed. I had cried a good share of the time when I was inside, but I had learned from the Fae.

They had taken me under their wing, and taught me tricks with the fire that I would never have known. They also taught me to use faerie fire, a skill that I felt best kept hidden, because it brought me too close to the realm. There were so many times when I thought it would be easier to give up and stay inside with Bubba, but he kept me grounded. He reminded me of the world outside, and while I was content there, after a time I realized that I needed to go home. Finally, the tears slowed and I approached the warrior, whose name was Tia, and asked her to let me out. Carrying Bubba, I followed her to the door and she opened it.

"We will miss you," she said. "You could make a life here with us. Tom knew it would be a safe haven for you. If you ever want to come back, just call for me and I'll hear you." She gave me a tiny silver whistle, which I tucked in my pocket.

"I'd love to stay, or at least a part of me wants to. But I need to go back. I need to find Tom. Surely, he had to have escaped, don't you think?" In my heart, I knew I was clinging to false hope. But I didn't want to admit it, because then the reality of what had happened would hit home. I had spent so many days in tears, missing my Tom, and worrying about him. What if all those tears had been in vain?

I turned to Tia. "How long has passed since I came here? Since you rescued me?"

I had asked the question a number of times, and in all the time I had spent here, no one had ever answered me. They would just smile and say, *Not enough time*.

Tia held my gaze and for a moment I thought she still wouldn't answer. But finally, she took a deep breath and said, "Twenty years. Twenty years have passed in the outer world. May I give you a word of advice?"

I was still stuck on the twenty years' part, but I nodded.

"Don't expect to return to your old life. You can't. Things have changed in the outer world, and you've changed from being in our world. Be prepared to pick up a new direction. Best of luck, Maudlin. We would have you stay with us if you like, and the invitation is an open one." And with that, Tia opened the door and I walked out into a new world.

The first thing I did was head for home. They probably thought I was dead, and I wondered if my mother would finally show some sign of being happy I was alive. Bubba ran at my feet, pouncing on butterflies and grass and anything he could get his paws on. He had seemed content in the Faerie Barrow, and I hoped he didn't mind that we had left there.

When I arrived home, I suddenly felt shy, and I knocked rather than go right in. My mother's voice echoed from inside, bidding me to enter. As I opened the door she glanced up, looking harried at the stove, where she was making a stew. She dropped her spoon and backed up a couple steps, a look of fear sweeping across her face.

"Maudlin, is it you?"

I nodded. "I was in a Faerie Barrow."

She seemed hesitant. "We thought you were dead. We thought the vampires had turned you as well as Tom."

In that second all my hopes and dreams crashed to the floor. I had known in my heart that the vampires had taken him, but I had wanted to believe that it was just worry, that he had somehow managed to escape. And then what she said hit home.

"*Turned him?* You mean, they didn't just kill him?" A new horror washed through me. I had hoped and prayed that he had managed to escape, or at the worst, that he had died at their hands. But if they had turned him, then it was worse than anything I had dared imagine.

"Oh, they turned him, all right. While you've been hiding yourself with the Fae, the vampires have been on the rise. Their numbers are growing, both here and in Europe. The vile creatures are growing bolder with every night." She picked her spoon up again, and rinsed it in the dish bucket. Then, returning to her stew, she began stirring it slowly, looking like she wanted to say something.

"What is it? I can tell there's something else."

"The witch hunters have been on the rise as well. They're blaming some of the vampire kills on the witches. For you to suddenly appear again seems suspicious, and it would not bode well if anything caught their eye. I suggest that you look for a new place to live. You can stay here the night, but you'd best move on in the morning."

It didn't escape my notice that she hadn't even hugged me, nor welcomed me back. In fact, she seemed troubled to see me. At that moment, I realized that nothing for Zara had changed. She was still callous and cold.

"No, thank you. You obviously don't want me here so I'll be on my way. If you see him again, say good-bye to Father for me." I motioned to Bubba to wait for me outside. "I'll just get some of my things from my room—"

Zara cut me off in mid-sentence. "When I thought you were dead, I sold your things. Except for a few of your ritual items. They're in the trunk over there."

I pressed my lips together, unable to say a word. If I spoke, it would be to break her down as much as I could. My own mother didn't care that I was alive. And now, she was sending me out into the world without so much as a blessing.

I opened the trunk, relieved to see that she hadn't sold my wand, or the few crystals I had collected. Stones had power, and actually I was surprised that she hadn't decided to auction them off. I pocketed them, then slid my wand inside my cloak. At least the Fae had outfitted me with a gorgeous purple gown, and an indigo blue cloak. The material would last through time, given it was woven on a magical loom. There were pockets inside the cloak for a number of things, and as I passed by the table, I picked up two of the rolls that were sitting in a basket.

"I trust you won't begrudge me a bite of bread," I said, holding Zara's gaze.

She shrugged. "Of course not. Maddy…" A look crossed her face that I couldn't read, but then she stopped and shook her head. "Best of luck."

I couldn't accept the lackluster apology. Zara could never say she was sorry, but this was going too far. I turned and headed out the door, shutting it behind me. I wouldn't speak to my mother for another thirty-two years.

I made my way over to Auntie Berma's, praying that she was still there. That she hadn't decided to bug out. Sure enough, the ivy-covered cottage was still looking as neat and tidy as ever. I raised my hand to knock on the door and she opened it before I could touch the wood.

"You're back," she said with a smile. "I wondered how

long it would be before you would decide to enter the world again."

"You knew I was away? That I wasn't dead?"

She motioned me in, pointing me to the table, where I took a seat. Before she answered, she filled a bowl with hot soup and slid it in front of me along with freshly baked bread, and an entire apple pie. The Fae had fed me, all right, but the food in the outer world seemed more rich and vibrant. I dug in immediately, feeling like I would never feel full.

Auntie Berma poured herself a cup of tea and sat down opposite me. "Of course I knew, what do you think I am, some garden-variety witch? I'm one of the Aunties, and don't you forget it."

"A Faerie warrior saved me. Tom summoned her and she carried Bubba and me away. By the way, can you give Bubba something to eat?"

Bubba let out a little *purp* and jumped up on the bench beside me. Auntie Berma picked out a few choice morsels of chicken from the soup and put it on the table, motioning for Bubba to eat. She also put out a bowl of water for him, and poured me a glass of mead. I drank it down, and she poured me another.

"You're a lucky woman, to escape a Faerie Barrow. Most people who go in never come out."

"They liked me. They invited me to return whenever I want, and said I can stay there. I'll remember it, in case the world grows too tiring."

As I mopped up the last of the soup with the bread, and then started in on a slice of pie, Auntie Berma crossed to an armoire. She opened it and pawed through one of the drawers inside. When she returned to the table, she placed a silver dagger and a spike in front of me, as well as their corresponding sheaths.

I stared at the dagger, unable to take my eyes off of it. Something about it sang to me, with the silver engravings and embellishments on the hilt, and the blade that gleamed with an inner light. The spike seemed to be its match, engraved with the same runes and ornamentation. Hesitantly, I reached out and ran my hands over the top of the blade. I didn't touch it. It was sacrilege to touch a witch's dagger unless she gave you permission. But the energy emanated off of it and it tickled my fingers with a spark, running up my arm like tendrils of ivy.

"What's this? May I touch it?"

Auntie Berma nodded. "Of course you may touch it, because it's yours. You'll need these in the coming years. You'll need them far longer than you think you will, so even when you think you're done, do *not* give them away. These are your cornerstones, Maudlin. Your destiny is beginning to unfold in front of you. And these—the dagger and stake—will be your comfort, your curse, and your blessing. Take them, and bind them to you. For they are sacred tools, ancient and priceless."

I picked up the dagger. It felt right in my hand. As I picked up the stake in my left hand and held both out in front of me, it felt as though the universe trembled, as though a piece of the puzzle had fallen into place.

I looked up at Auntie Berma, a dread decision sweeping over me.

"I'm going to find the vampires that turned to Tom. And I'm going to destroy them. If they're terrorizing the countryside, I will hunt them down and turn them to ash."

And with those words, I sealed my fate.

Sandy got off the phone, shaking me out of my reverie. "Bjorn gave me a list of five houses where he thinks a vampire might be able to hide. They all have basements, and they're all empty. Two of them are almost in the center of town, so I think that probably eliminates them as possibilities. I really doubt if Dracula would choose a place with high visibility. But the other three, they're all in the general area, and they're on back roads. He said he can get us in to check them out during the day, which might be the best idea."

"No," I said. "Remember, Dracula is part of the Arcānus Nocturni, and he can walk about in the sunlight. Going after him during the day would simply leave us a man down, given Aegis can't go with us. We can start tonight."

The doorbell rang, and Kelson headed into the living room to answer. She returned, her face pale.

"Essie Vanderbilt is at the door. She can't come in, unless you give her an invitation. But she said she needs to talk to you now."

"Oh crap," I said. I really didn't want Essie visiting me at home. "I'll go talk to her." I glanced at Sandy and Max. "Don't tell her that Aegis told you about Dracula's allergy."

Both Sandy and Max nodded, and I headed to the front door. Sure enough, Essie was standing there, wearing a long green dress and a brocade jacket with gold buttons. She had on the feathered hat that looked straight out of *Downton Abbey*.

"Essie, what brings you here?" I wasn't about to invite

her in until I knew what she wanted. And even then, I had my doubts about the wisdom of the idea.

"I thought you might want to know something. And I didn't trust any of my messengers to deliver this information." She leaned closer, her face pale under the porch light. "I think I might know where Dracula is hiding."

And with that, I actually invited Essie Vanderbilt into my house.

CHAPTER FIFTEEN

I called out to Aegis, Sandy, and Max to join us in the living room.

"Essie Vanderbilt, meet Max Davenport. You know Sandy, and of course Aegis." I turned to them as they took their places on the sofa. "Essie said she thinks she knows where Dracula's hiding."

"Actually, I said I think I *might* know where he's hiding. We can't guarantee it, but it occurred to me that you might not know about the catacombs."

"Catacombs? That sounds like a barrel of laughs. I didn't know we had catacombs on Bedlam." All I could think of were the catacombs of Palermo, Sicily. Containing nearly eight thousand bodies, the catacombs were a grisly tribute to death.

"If you're thinking of mummies, then you're a little off-base. These catacombs were created around two hundred years ago, before vampires were officially let into Bedlam. Once again, I'm breaking tradition by telling you. I don't think they're used much by anybody anymore, so I doubt if I am revealing any secrets. But it would be just the place for someone like Dracula to hide."

"You wouldn't be interested in going with us, would you?" I held her gaze for a moment, though I knew what her answer would be.

Essie laughed. "Oh, Maudlin. Somehow I don't think that would be the wisest thing for me to do. But in the interests of being a good neighbor, and I do consider us neighbors, although we live in completely different neighborhoods, I thought you might want to check it out." She stood, smoothing out the skirt of her dress. "I'm off. I have things to do."

"Thank you," I said. "And I hope you don't take this the wrong way, but I'm disinviting you from my house."

"I'd think you were stupid if you didn't. No offense taken," she said as she swept out the door.

I shut it behind her, turning to lean my back against it. "Oh hell, I forgot to ask her where the catacombs are."

"We can find out from Delia. She's sure to know." Aegis handed me my phone.

"Good idea." I called her, but there was no answer. When I called the station, Bernice, the receptionist, told me that Delia was over on the mainland for the evening. She had left instructions that only emergencies were to be forwarded.

"Well, hell. You wouldn't happen to know where the catacombs in town would be, do you? The entrance, that is?"

Beatrice cleared her throat. "No, I don't happen to know that."

"No problem. I'll find out a different way." I bit my lip, thinking as I hung up. Then, snapping my fingers, I jumped up. "Henry! He's writing the history of Bedlam. I'll bet you he knows!"

Aegis clapped his hands. "Of course. You know, we need to remember we've got quite a resource under our roof." He stood up. "I'll go see if he's in his room."

"Be sure to knock," I said. "Henry and Franny have been getting awfully friendly lately, remember. I have some suspicions that something's going on between the two of them. Not that I know how that could happen, logistically."

Aegis rolled his eyes, but gave me a nod. "I'll be polite. I promise I won't pry."

As he took off toward the stairs, I turned back to Max and Sandy. "Now that you know about the witches' blood, I can talk to you about it. I was thinking about pulling a raid on the blood bank, though I'm not sure that's exactly the best way to go about this."

"I'm certainly not giving my blood to Dracula, that's for sure." Sandy let out a snort. "What do you think would happen if news got out that Dracula's running around Bedlam?"

I thought about it for a moment. The groupies would go crazy, and if anybody from the clubs like the Vulture Underground, or even the Utopia, found out, we'd have such an influx of goth girls and boys that it would clog the ferries and road system. That alone might be enough to drive him away. Except, with so much fresh meat on the island—and some of them willing victims—it might be enough to make him stick around.

"So," Max said, "if he's allergic to witches' blood, how much will it take to kill him?"

"I'm not sure. Essie didn't say, but you can bet that

since she told me, it has to be an amount that I can get my hands on. Essie does nothing without forethought. She's probably got one of the most streamlined ulterior agendas that I've ever seen. She is intent on working her way up in the vampire nation, and she'll do anything she can to get there. Even cavorting with the enemy. My guess is she's hoping that we'll kill Dracula for her, and that will be one less of the old guard to stand in her way."

Sandy walked over to the bar and poured herself a snifter of brandy. "Want one?"

"I thought you'd never ask." I paused for a moment, then added, "I'm still not sure what to do about Fata Morgana. Today, I saw a side of her that made me want to weep. She was so willing to use Ralph to get to me, and then when I turned my back on her, it was painful to see her grovel at my feet. She's lonely. The Ocean Mother may take care of her and may have changed her, but Fata's still inside of that incredibly powerful water elemental."

"Do you think Auntie Tautau will do anything?" Sandy handed me a snifter of brandy and I sipped the fiery liquor, closing my eyes as it trickled down my throat.

"I don't know," I said. "She seems to think Fata's presence here is vital, though for how much longer, I don't know." I caught Sandy's gaze and held it. "Do you think I'm to blame for her going away? Did I really lead her on? Those days are such an incredible blur. After so much blood, after so much pain…the freedom and booze and sex…it was like a feast after famine. I barely remember any of it, I was so stoned."

"You had to let go of all the death. You were steeped in it, Maddy. I remember days where all we did was run, stop, kill vampires, then run again. They were a plague, and you singlehandedly prevented them from devastating the continent." She shook her head. "Fata loved you because you were strong. You burned so bright, you were like flames to a moth. And even then she was drifting on the tides. Did you ever ask her where she was born? How she came to be Tom's cousin? Because I did, once. And she had no answer. She couldn't trace their lineage together. Did you ever ask Tom about her parents?"

I blinked. "I never thought about it. He said she was his long-distant cousin, but he never once mentioned how they came to meet." I searched my memory. Fata had introduced me to Tom, had said they were cousins, but that was about it. He didn't contradict her, and I didn't think to ask. "I have no clue if they were actually related, now that you mention it."

Sandy drained her snifter and refilled it. I held out mine and she poured me another shot. "I'm just saying this: you saw her come in on the waves, from the ocean. What if she's always been part elemental and just never knew? Or had somehow forgotten? What if she was never Tom's cousin but he thought she was?"

I slowly eased myself into the rocking chair, breathing shallowly. If Fata wasn't Tom's cousin, why had she told me she was? What would she get out of it? And then, I thought, what if she hadn't expected Tom and me to get together? What if she had regretted her decision to introduce us? Could she have sicced the vampires on us out of jealousy?

"Oh, Sandy. I can't think about this. I can't let myself even begin to believe this. The ramifications could mean…"

"But you *have* to think about it. You have to pay attention because your life could depend on it. She still loves you. Her behavior makes it obvious, but now she seems even more dangerous than she did back then. When did you meet? I can't remember."

I thought back. "I met her in 1659, even before I saved Bubba. So I knew her for over a hundred years before we fought and she left."

Max cleared his throat. "I don't want to interrupt, but I see where this is going. If she lived among people—be they witches or humans—for a hundred years, she was influenced by you, and quite possibly the elemental side of her nature calmed down. But now, for the past two hundred years, she's been back in the ocean, back in her element. She's forgotten the social niceties."

"Social niceties like not killing people and not playing with people as pawns." Sandy winced, settling on the sofa near me. "I love Fata, but the more this unfolds, the more terrified I am of her staying here. What if we can't control her?" She turned a pale face to me, tears flecking her eyes. "I can't believe we are having this conversation."

"We have to break the pact we made—" I stopped as Aegis returned.

"Henry and Franny were having a heart-to-heart, and they looked serious. I said nothing, but I have the feeling both of them were relieved when I got my info and left. Anyway, Henry told me that the catacombs in Bedlam have several entrances, but the nearest is down at the base of Beachcomber Spit. We can be there in fifteen minutes." He stopped, glancing curiously at me. "Are you all right? You and Sandy both look like you've seen a ghost, and I'm not talking about Franny."

I suddenly burst into tears. Aegis, looking confused,

opened his arms as I rushed into them. He closed his arms around me, kissing my head as I leaned against him, crying, the jagged sobs wracking my body. The next thing I knew, Sandy tapped him on the shoulder and he backed away. She pulled me down onto the sofa and, crying with me, took my hands. I curled up on the sofa, my head on her lap as she stroked my hair and brushed it out of my eyes.

I was crying for Fata, and for me, for Tom and Sandy and for all those years we ran steeped in blood. I closed my eyes, and the visions of my dagger slashing through one vampire and another and another and another filled my thoughts. There was blood on my hands, blood on my soul. I could taste it, smell it, until it merged with the fire within me and then—then, for a time, all that mattered was blood. Until the night on the hill, and the flames raged so brightly that there was nothing left the next morning and we were hip-deep in ash. And that had broken the rage.

After a time, the tears slowed. I was breathing out of my mouth, my nose was so stuffed up. Sandy slowly eased me into a sitting position and I panted raggedly. Max found the tissues and handed them to both of us.

I caught my breath, then blew my nose. "I've needed to do that since I first felt her on the wind, returning. I knew in my heart this wouldn't be good. That it would be better for everyone that she stay out in the ocean depths. I wish she would have forgotten about us. About me."

"But the Aunties seem to feel she needs to be here," Sandy said, resting her hand on my arm. "So we accept their decree, and we ask Arianrhod for protection. Because we need all the help we can get." She accepted the water that Max brought for both of us. "Thank you. We have to be clearheaded when we go after Dracula. The question is, do we draw some blood in advance? If our blood will burn him, shouldn't we siphon off a few vials that we could use as a weapon?"

"I'll bathe my stake in my blood. Then I'll drive it into his heart and see if that eats him." A fire was burning in my belly now, warming me after what felt like a long, cold winter. "I'm not sure what ramifications that will bring, but we have no choice. I don't like being hunted." I stood. "I'm going to call Jordan and ask him to swing by. He's looking into a way that we can contain Fata, should we need to."

I straightened my back, realizing that I couldn't think about her as the person I once believed her to be. I could love her to pieces, I could love the memories and hate the memories, but I had to be clearheaded and face the fact that she was a powerful entity who could destroy the island if she got angry enough. And I was the High Priestess whose job it was to watch over Bedlam. I couldn't let my emotions endanger us.

Sandy seemed to pick up on my mood. "I'll do it. You call him so often I'm sure he'll be happy to be interrupted by somebody else. Meanwhile, guys, gather the equipment you think we'll need to go hunting the big D."

An hour later, Jordan was once again driving off after he had drawn off a pint of blood from both Sandy and me, leaving us with the warning, "You do not want to let anybody else get hold of this, but then you know that."

Blood was life. Blood was power and control. Sandy and I were both extremely aware that somebody with access to our blood could do some serious damage if they were experienced enough as a magician or witch.

We sat at the kitchen table, using a funnel to siphon the blood into small vials. They were glass, easily breakable, and as we fit the stoppers into the tops, it suddenly occurred to me that we had to have a way to carry them. I didn't want them jostling around together in a fanny pack, where they could jar against each other and possibly smash.

"We need a way to transport these where they aren't going to get broken or be hard to find. It would be ideal to have a belt that we could hook them onto, but I haven't got anything like that."

Sandy laughed. "I hope not. I certainly hope you don't make a habit of carrying around blood vials wherever you go. I'm coming up with a blank. Max, Aegis, either of you have any suggestions?"

Aegis was staring at the blood that he was pouring into the vials. "I'm just doing my best not to take a taste. You have no clue how good your blood smells to me. Both of you."

I rolled my eyes. "I know that witches' blood is an aphrodisiac for you, but dude, that sounds creepy when you say it."

Max laughed. "Creepy is as creepy does. As long as he doesn't put the fang to your throat. Say, why not wrap a piece of packing foam around the center of each vial? Then even if you put them into a container together, they won't be rattling around. And it should break just as easily if you throw it."

"That's actually not a bad idea. Kelson," I called, "can you find us some packing foam or bubble wrap?"

Max's idea worked like a charm, and we loaded the vials into four separate belt pouches and strapped them on. Then Sandy and Max armed themselves with makeshift stakes and we headed to my CR-V. Sandy had suggested her van, but my CR-V took steep grades better than her retro hippie-mobile. We were as ready as we'd ever be, so I eased out of the driveway and we headed toward Beachcomber Spit.

Beachcomber Spit was another shoreline park, accessible by a narrow road with a steep grade. To get there we had to drive up Sidewinder Road to an outcropping that overlooked the eastern side of the island. A turnoff led into a small parking lot, where a one-lane road offered access down to the shore. There were hiking trails down the cliff as well, but I wanted a faster escape route, and that came with wheels. The rain was splattering down, steady and constant. The wind had calmed, but I could still smell a storm on the horizon.

"So exactly where are the entrances to these catacombs?" I asked.

"Henry told me that there are two entrances on Beachcomber Spit, one beyond a large pile of rocks against the cliffside. He said you couldn't miss them. The other is underwater a little ways down the shoreline."

"I wonder how come we never hear about them, if there are entrances around the island," Sandy said.

"I asked Henry that too. He told me that while there

are several entrances, and he knows where they are, they aren't all that easy to see unless you're actually looking for them. They camouflage well. Once we get beyond the pile of rocks, we'll have to do a little bit of searching. Henry apparently went looking for them, and he said that the one we're headed toward is covered up by a tangle of tall sea grass and other shoreline shrubs. I hope somebody brought flashlights, because it's not going to be easy in the dark."

"I always carry a couple of them in my emergency kit in the car. But I thought you and Max brought whatever supplies you thought we would need?"

"We did," Max said. "I brought some rope, and we did bring flashlights, Aegis. I also brought some chalk in case we get in there and aren't sure where we're going. We can mark large white arrows on the wall."

"Have you been reading Hardy Boys mysteries?" Sandy asked.

"Believe it or not, I was part of the Raven Scouts when I was a kid," Max shot back. "I held badges in tracking and scouting, and in hunting."

"What the hell are the Raven Scouts?" I had never heard of them. Then again, I hadn't heard of many groups, given my belief that any group that would have me probably wasn't a group I wanted to join. The coven not included, of course.

"The Raven Scouts are a multi-Otherkin organization for young shifters of all types. Think of a supernatural Boy Scouts–type of group, minus the homophobia. Members learn all sorts of survival skills, as well as socialization skills. Trust me, young weretigers *need* to be socialized with other shifter types. We can be a handful when we're little, given big cats are solitary by nature. I was always getting in spats when I was a little kid, and I don't know how many times I had to take interspecies communications remedial courses."

I couldn't help but smile. There were so many different issues that surrounded members of the Pretcom, and I was mostly familiar with those of witches. It kind of tickled me when I heard things like what Max had just told us, because to me, it pointed out the similarities between races and species, rather than the differences. Every child needed to be socialized. Young witches needed to be taught not to misuse their magic, apparently Weres needed to be taught how to interact without striking out at others, and I was sure that the Fae had their own forms of childhood misbehavior.

As I pulled into the parking lot at Beachcomber Spit, I hoped that we wouldn't find anybody else there, and for once my hopes were answered. I paused at the top of the road, trying to ascertain whether there was anybody coming up it, before easing the CR-V onto the graded lane. It wound down and around, big enough for one car with a very narrow shoulder, and a guardrail that had seen better days. Maybe I should bring that up in the next town council meeting, I thought. We should check all the guardrails around the island and make certain that they were strong enough to stop a car that might careen over the edge.

In the distance, the faint sheen of silver waves crashed onto the shore, spurred on by the breezes coming in off the strait. We were one night away from the new moon, and combined with the cloud cover, it was dark as pitch. My headlights were the only guiding force we had at this point, and I flipped them to brights so that I could see better as we crept our way down the road. Finally, after bending to the left to follow the edge of the cliff, the road opened into a small parking lot next to the sandy shore.

Rocks and pebbles littered the shore, as with almost every Washington beach. The mud flats were exposed, and one huge driftwood log sat to our right, chained into the cliff. The tides along Bedlam Island were strong, and like a number of Washington shorelines, giant logs—tall timber that had washed into the ocean—often rolled in with the tides. Driftwood logs could be dangerous, since the waves would toss them around like matchsticks and they could kill beachcombers when the storms grew violent.

I parked in the spot furthest up the shore, hoping the tide wasn't coming in yet. I hadn't consulted any of the tide charts so I wasn't sure. I slipped into my jacket, which was hanging over the back of my seat, and then, motioning to the others, stepped out of the car and looked around.

Without the headlights, the only light we had was from the silver glint of the waves. I hesitated to turn on my flashlight in case anybody might be around—namely, Dracula—but I realized that we could easily break an ankle as we searched for the opening.

"I suppose we better get a move on," I said, finding myself reluctant now that we were here.

"I take it you want to do this as much as I do," Sandy said.

"Yeah, but it's better to be proactive rather than have him show up on my doorstep. All right, I'm going to turn on my flashlight so everybody take a deep breath and be ready in case we're being watched." One hand on the hilt of my dagger, I lifted my flashlight with the other hand and flicked it on, training it against the cliffside as I swept the beam from side to side.

The pile of rocks that Henry had told Aegis about was right where he said it would be. A large jumble of boulders and stones rested near the foot of the cliff, concentrated in one area. I wasn't sure if it had been an old quarry, or if someone had just taken it into their mind to gather all the massive stones into one area. Whatever the case, at least we had our direction pegged.

Aegis took the flashlight from me and moved to the front.

"I'm going first," he said. By his tone, I knew it was futile to argue. Max took up the rear, to keep watch behind us. Sandy and I walked side by side, sandwiched between them.

We crept up the shore, toward the base of the cliff. The overlook must have been a good sixty to eighty feet above us, if not more. The slope leading up was so steep it would have been difficult to climb. It was obvious that several landslides had occurred over the years, a common occurrence when the slopes and hillsides around Western Washington were stripped of their vegetation so that unthinking people could enjoy the view. Erosion was exacerbated by the heavy rains that we had, leading to a number of houses toppling over the edge. At least with Beachcomber Spit, there weren't any houses to come crashing down should the hillside decide to give way.

The pile of rocks sprawled about twenty feet wide and five feet deep, looking for all the world like what I referred to as "nature art." As far as I could tell in the beam of the flashlight, it wasn't meant to resemble anything, and it certainly didn't spawn any emotion in myself except curiosity. Perhaps that was what it was meant to do, I thought. Artists tended to focus on inspiring questions and curiosity. Then again, maybe somebody just wanted the fun of making a big old pile of rocks.

As we cautiously skirted our way over the rocks, careful not to twist any ankles or go faceplanting on the smooth, weatherworn surfaces, I tried to scan again the base of the cliff, looking for an entrance. But Henry had been correct. Massive stands of beach grass, some waist high or taller, covered the expanse between us and the rock surface. And beach grass had a nasty habit of slashing into the skin, the gashes stinging like paper cuts. I was glad I had worn jeans and a turtleneck and a jacket. Sandy was in her yoga pants and a sweatshirt, thinner material but still able to stave off the worst of the razor-sharp blades.

Aegis suddenly stopped. "I hear something coming from that direction," he said, pointing to the left, beyond a waist-high patch of grass. "It sounds like wind whistling through a tunnel."

As we headed in the direction he pointed out, the blades whipped back and forth with the rising wind.

"I wonder if Fata is having a nightmare," I said. "We get a lot of storms on the island, but I have a feeling that most of them this week have been due to her."

"You're probably right," Sandy said. "Hopefully, Auntie Tautau will be able to help her."

"I have no clue, but I have to admit, I'm hoping Auntie Tautau will help her find her way back to the ocean before long." I stopped as Aegis motioned for us to be quiet.

We broke through the thicket of grass, into the shadow of the cliff where everything was so dark it was hard to see even with the flashlight. But then Aegis shone it a few feet to the left, and there, behind a large outcropping, we could see a dark shadow against the base of the precipice. It looked like the opening into a cave. We had found the entrance to the catacombs.

CHAPTER SIXTEEN

Aegis was right. The currents of air flowing into the cavern created a soft symphony, almost sounding like voices on the wind. We crept forward, my stomach knotting as we went. I had had my share of nerve-wracking adventures, creeping into caverns to look for vampires, but it had been a long time since then, and the edge I had during my hunting days had faded into a soft blur. But I was stronger than I was a year ago, and I had more stamina. Even so, delving deep into the catacombs that ran beneath Bedlam didn't promise the excitement that I valued.

"Follow me," he said, glancing over his shoulder. "Be cautious. Max, keep an ear open for anybody who might take a mind to swing in behind us. It will be difficult to tell if there are secret passages inside, and we might miss some of the side tunnels. I don't want anyone looping around behind us to catch us unawares."

"Do you really think we're going to find Dracula

here?" I asked, both hoping and yet fearing that he might say yes.

"This is the sort of place he would hang out. Dracula is an old-school vampire."

"So is he truly Vlad the Impaler?" Max asked from behind.

"No," Aegis said. "Although Vlad actually idolized him. Dracula was around long before Vlad. That said, Dracula *is* his ancestor. I know the two met *and* that Dracula refused to turn Vlad into one of the Fallen. They had a blowup about it, and Dracula left. The two looked so much alike, rumors started that Vlad was actually Dracula. When he was captured, they cut off his head and impaled him through the heart, thinking to destroy the vampire. His body was buried in a tomb that still remains hidden, once his body was returned to his family. His head was burned. So while Dracula is a relative of Vlad's, he existed long before the Impaler took his name and his throne."

"I didn't know that," I said. "When our hunt swept through Romania and Transylvania, people there seemed to think they were one and the same. I suppose old rumors die hard, and sometimes they become legends. And those legends become truth. At least as far as the general public is concerned." I thought for a moment. "Is there anything we should know about Dracula that Essie didn't tell us?"

"I've never met the man, but I do know that he's ruthless and cunning. He has several weaknesses, however. He likes fame, and he likes his legendary status. If he could handle modern living, he would probably be up and still running through the world. I doubt, though, that he would choose to have woken if the Arcānus Nocturni hadn't brought him around. In fact, I wonder if he wasn't trying to die."

"What do you mean?" Sandy asked. "Vampires can't die, not like we can. If he wanted to die, why didn't he walk into the sun?"

Aegis turned to stare at her for a moment, his expression thoughtful in the glow of the flashlight beam. After a few seconds, he gave her a small shrug.

"Do you realize how terrifying it is for a vampire to even think about walking into the sun? Those who do are usually desperate. For one thing, the fire burns with a searing pain that is almost beyond imagining. And Dracula, as old and as tired as he probably is, isn't desperate. He doesn't regret his nature, he isn't ashamed of who he is. The killing, the blood drinking, it's part of his very essence. No, I think he preferred to sink into a sleep from which he would never wake up. He didn't expect the Arcānus Nocturni to wake him up."

"So he's ruthless, has an allergy to witches' blood, and a ego to match his legend. He's also weaker than normal, one factor in our favor." I tried to think of anything else, but other questions eluded me.

Aegis turned back to the passage, his finger to his lips.

We followed him silently as he led us deeper into the tunnel. The walls were rough and sharp, formed by pickax and hammer rather than nature. Here and there, we saw wooden beams and cross-pieces shoring up the passage. I tried to look for side passages, but it was so dark that we could barely see the floor in front of us. Sandy had another flashlight and as we went along, looked for anything Aegis might have missed.

The smells in the passage were dank, filled with mildew and dust, and the scent of decaying seaweed. I wrinkled my nose, but tried not to sneeze. I found myself thinking how vampires had used these passages early on, to come and go into Bedlam as they chose. And now, the Vampire Queen of the Pacific Northwest was living out in the open and everyone accepted her.

It truly was a changing world, and these would not be the last of the changes. My kind—witches—could live upward of six or seven hundred years, or more. Most of us only had one or two children in our lifetimes, and many, none at all. We were still rare in the world of humans and other Pretcom, but I wondered if that would change as well.

I was caught up in my thoughts when ahead, a sudden noise startled Aegis into stopping. I ran into his back. Sandy grabbed my wrist and pulled me back beside her as she turned off her flashlight. Aegis had already turned off his.

That will teach me to keep my mind on what I'm doing, I thought.

A gust of wind hurtled through the passage and I caught a fetid scent on it. It was familiar in a distant sort of way, and I tried to remember where I had smelled it before. Suddenly, I knew what it belonged to.

Goblins. We hadn't seen any for quite some time. Since I had moved to Bedlam, I hadn't had any run-ins with the creatures. But every now and then they made an attempt to sneak into our community, and we kicked them out as soon as we found them.

Goblins were of an ill nature, creepy little creatures who thought only of gold and silver and themselves. Most of them were thieves, and more than a handful were murderers as well. Usually, goblins didn't think twice about offing somebody when they wanted what their opponent possessed. Greedy and lecherous, they were one species we could do without.

"Goblins," I whispered to Aegis.

Sandy overheard me. She stiffened.

Aegis motioned for us to back up. I realized that we were near a juncture in the passage. Which way led to the goblins was hard to tell, the smell was so rank and filled the air so much.

"Get back—" Aegis started to say, but was interrupted when four goblins came dashing around the corner, running headlong toward us.

Goblins were bipedal, like humans, but there, any resemblance ceased. Their eyes were narrow and dark, evolved for seeing in the dim light rather than sunlight. They were lean and stretched thin at around five feet tall. But their size cloaked their strength. Goblins were strong, and wiry quick. Most of them generally wore their hair pulled back in a braid or ponytail, leaving the sides of their scalp to show. The hairline started at the middle of the skull, and their teeth were sharp and razor-like.

"Just move back slowly and don't turn around," Aegis said. "Do you know if goblins speak English?"

"They're nasty, not stupid," I said. I was trying to see their expressions in the beam of Aegis's flashlight, but it was difficult to read their faces and I had no clue whether they understood us or not.

"So what the hell are we going to do now?" Sandy asked. She rested her hands on her hips, staring at the goblins in front of us. "Maddy, can you use your fire?"

"I suppose I could try, but I have no idea exactly what would happen. I've never used it in such an enclosed place before. What about your wind? Can you drive them back with it?" Sandy was extremely powerful with air magic.

"I can try," she said. She took another step back, separating herself from us so that we wouldn't take the brunt if her spell backfired. I pressed myself against the side of the cavern, digging my hands into the nooks and crannies formed by the rock. Max noticed what I was doing and followed suit.

Sandy cleared her throat. She held out her hands, and began to sing.

> *Waves of wind, waves of air,*
> *gather here, flow to there.*
> *Shake and rattle, rage and storm,*
> *a funnel cloud, please to form.*
> *Aim be swift, aim be true,*
> *chase them down, and pursue.*

A massive gust raged through the corridor past us, shaking the walls as it began to form into a ceiling-high funnel cloud. I dug my fingers deeper into the nooks and crannies that I was holding onto, and Aegis braced himself against the storm. Max flattened himself against the passageway wall, and we watched as the miniature funnel cloud touched down in the center of the tunnel, spinning toward the goblins. I wanted to clap, but I didn't think that would be a wise move, given that I was still trying to hold on and not let the wind suck me into it.

"That's one nasty funnel," I said.

Sandy, who was focusing on controlling it, merely

nodded. She was making maneuvers with her fingers, and I realized she was controlling the pathway of the storm. The funnel cloud raged down on the goblins, and they scattered, turning tail to run back into the other passage. A tangible snap echoed as the cord between Sandy and the funnel cloud broke, and she let it go, spinning it ahead into the hallway. It rounded the curve. Without another sound, it turned the corner and vanished from our sight.

"Well, I have a feeling they aren't going to bother us for a while." I grinned at Sandy. "Nice funnel cloud. We should remember that next time somebody gets in our way at the supermarket."

Sandy snorted. "It's nice to have a reason to use my spells, you know? Sometimes I feel like we don't get enough practice with our more powerful magic. We should go out in the country and let 'er rip."

"Let's save that for after Fata goes home. I don't want to see *her* let it rip. Not after the storms have been buffeting the island." I tapped Aegis on the arm. "Should we continue?"

"I suppose," he said. "Although I'm not certain that Dracula would be using the catacombs if they're filled with goblins. By the way, isn't there a law against goblins coming into Bedlam?"

"Yeah, and I need to talk to Delia about that. She needs to bring a force down here to clear through the catacombs, now that we know they're hiding out here. But since Essie thinks Dracula might be down here, we'd better press on."

We continued on until we found ourselves in the middle of the juncture. It was a triple fork in the road, with passages branching off to the left, the right, and continuing straight ahead. I skirted around Aegis and walked a few steps down the passage ahead, sniffing deeply. When I returned I shook my head.

"The goblins have been that way, so I doubt if we want to continue straight until we search the other two. Let's start with the left." I backed up behind Aegis again, resting my hand against the chiseled wall.

We headed deeper into the catacombs. I was relieved that we weren't facing a bunch of mummies. Even the non-animated ones were spooky, and the few I had seen over the years who *had* been resurrected through necromancy were terrifying. They were fast, they never tired, and you had to burn them to stop them, unless you could somehow reverse the spell that brought them to life. In fact, *most* of the undead were better off left in Halloween stories. More often than not, they turned on those who had given them back what resembled a life force. And except for vampires, none retained any semblance of the person they had been in life.

The path began to slope downward, the grade steepening as we descended farther into the cavern. The air thickened, and while it was still breathable, it felt stale and musty. I found myself thinking about miners, and the canaries they took into the shafts to tell them when the air went bad. I couldn't do that—I couldn't ever use another being as a guinea pig—but I understood why they did what they did.

The passageway began to narrow as we continued, and my nervousness grew proportionately. As the tunnel became too narrow for us to walk side by side, Sandy had to swing behind me. Here, I could extend both my arms, and my fingertips on either side scraped the sides of the tunnel. Ahead of me, Aegis slowed down, holding up his hand for us to stop. I motioned to Sandy and Max and we all froze. I tried to peek beyond him, but I could only see what seemed like a never-ending tunnel deep in the cliffside. I wanted to ask what he had heard, because he had cocked his head to the side, sweeping his hair behind his ear as though to listen.

The only sounds I could hear were the sounds of Sandy, Max, and me breathing. I closed my eyes as we stood there, reaching out, trying to touch the energy around me. It seemed to roll in like the mist, thick and viscous, almost cloying. Inhaling slowly, I drew a deep lungful of breath and analyzed what I could smell.

Dampness, of course. *A sense of mold and mildew from deeper in the tunnel, the sting of salt water in the air. And... something else. Something pungent, like freshly turned soil on a rainy day.*

I'm not certain how long we stood there, but it seemed like a very long time until Aegis straightened up again. He leaned toward me, cupping his hands around my ears as he whispered.

"I thought I heard the sound of moaning up ahead. Now, I can't hear anything. Try to be quiet as we go. Tell Sandy and Max, but do it quietly."

I turned, holding my fingers to my lips and motioned for Sandy and Max to close in toward me. Max leaned over Sandy's shoulder, and I leaned forward so that I could whisper to both of them. It felt oddly intimate.

"Aegis thought he heard something up ahead—a moan or something. He's not sure now. He asked us to be quiet as we go. So watch your step."

They nodded, and I turned back and tapped Aegis on

the shoulder, giving him the go-ahead. We started on again, in what was beginning to feel like a never-ending journey.

Another ten minutes in, and Aegis stumbled. He froze, bracing himself against the wall. A moment later, he turned the flashlight beam on the floor ahead of us to show an abrupt slope, where the passage suddenly took another steep decline. One more step and he would have tumbled down the slope.

Aegis started forward, cautiously testing the tunnel floor as he went. It was rocky and slick, and now extremely steep. As I came to the edge and realized that there was about a twenty-foot descent that would be fairly treacherous, I regretted not bringing some sort of walking staff. Aegis glanced back at me and immediately jogged back up the slope to hold out his hand and help guide me down.

Once we passed the entryway to this portion of the passage, I saw that there was a dropoff of about twenty feet to our left. The rock wall continued to the right. The path had narrowed considerably, now about two feet wide, and it looked harrowing in the light of the flashlight.

The floor was so rocky that I was inching forward, clinging to the wall, afraid of slipping over the edge. Finally, Aegis picked me up and, resting me over his shoulder, carried me down the slope, setting me down at the bottom. Then he returned for Sandy and carried her down as well. Max made his own way down, though he was cautious and looked like he might topple over the edge.

We found ourselves in a chamber, about the size of a

small ballroom. It was hard to tell whether there were any other doors or passages along the circular wall, and the floor here was smooth, at least where we were standing. The flashlight's beam only penetrated so far into the gloom. For all we knew, Dracula could be standing on the other side of the chamber and we wouldn't be able to see him. But if anybody was down here, they could surely see us by now.

"What now?" I was growing more wary all the time. I had the feeling we were walking into a trap, although I didn't see how it could be. Unless Essie and Dracula had made a pact together, and I had my doubts about that.

"You stay here while I circle the wall. Keep your weapons ready. I'll make sure you know it's me when I'm on the way back." Aegis took off to the right, edging along the wall. We could see him for a little while and then he vanished into the gloom, his flashlight a vague flicker in the air. My only consolation was that if we were having a hard time seeing Aegis and he had a flashlight, then anybody else here would be having a hard time seeing exactly how many of us there were.

"I can't believe I'm standing here with a fanny pack full of my own blood," Sandy said.

"I can't believe that I'm standing here wearing a fanny pack packed with your blood either," Max added.

I smiled, grateful for the light banter. I was tired and weary, and I really wasn't looking forward to a fight with the godfather of vampires. At least *one* of the godfathers. We waited in silence, until a few moments later, Aegis's voice echoed out of the darkness to our left.

"It's me," he said before stepping into the circle of light from Sandy's flashlight. "I found two other passages leading farther into the cliffside. I think we're underneath the Gull Springs area." Gull Springs was a neighborhood not far from Beachcomber Spit. It was inland a little ways, and it was one of the older neighborhoods in Bedlam.

The name tweaked something in memory.

"Hold on, I think I remember something." It had happened earlier, I realized, something that we had been thinking about doing. And then, I remembered.

I snapped my fingers. "One of those abandoned houses we were talking about is in Gull Springs. I wonder if there's a secret passage leading from the house down to here. I just can't imagine Dracula hanging out down here, except to use the tunnels to come and go by. The impression I get is that he's a snob. And snobs don't hang out in dark caverns."

"Well, there's one way to find out," Aegis said. He took off across the chamber as we hurried to keep up. When we approached the other side we saw that, yes, there were two exits to the chamber. I walked up to the left one and leaned inside, sniffing deeply and closing my eyes. It smelled more fetid and dank than where we were. Then I approached the other and did the same. There was a flicker of movement in the air, and I inhaled again. This time I could smell rain and chill weather.

"This way. I can smell it. I smell rain and the outdoors. This must come up near a house or something. Shall we go?"

Aegis took the front again. "Be cautious. If we *are* near Dracula's hideout, we're likely to come up in the basement or someplace close to that. And he's probably living in the basement, given the fact that we need protection from the sun."

"No," I said. "Remember? Dracula can walk abroad in the sunlight. He's one of the Arcānus Nocturni."

"Damn it, I forgot," Aegis said, an angry look on his face. "My mistake could have gotten us all killed. Please, be careful and don't rush into anything. Go quietly."

He led us into the tunnel and immediately the floor began to slope up. The ascent was as steep as the descent, but it was easier going because there were handholds along the side and the rocky outcroppings gave us a place to steady our feet and hands. We weren't exactly rock climbing, but it felt close to it. Ten minutes later, we were nearing the top. Aegis shut off the flashlight and we were plunged into darkness.

"I don't want to alert anyone who might be up there. Wait here, and I'll be back in a moment." He began to creep up toward the opening, and though I couldn't see him ascend, I could hear the faint movement of his boots against the rocks. We waited for what seemed like an eternity before he returned.

"It lets out into a basement," he said. "Just like you thought it might. There's a door that leads to the outside, and it's open. The basement looked deserted, although I did see a coffin there. It must be Dracula's, but I didn't see any sign of him. Either he's out, or he's upstairs in the main house. Whatever the case, be very cautious when we arrive at the top."

We continued to climb in darkness, and a few moments later, we came to a trapdoor that was open. The smell of rain and wind rushed through, a welcome change from the fetid air of the caverns. Aegis went through the trapdoor first, and then a moment later he reached down and pulled me through. Sandy came next, easily slipping through the trapdoor and out on her own. Finally, Max followed.

The room was dimly lit from a single bare bulb overhead. It looked like a typical basement, with tools hanging on a corkboard against one wall, and dusty old trunks against another. The furnace was to one side, and a workbench next to it. And in the center of the room, a coffin sat on sawhorses. It reminded me of Aegis's setup downstairs in the Bewitching Bedlam. I had tried to convince him to change it out for a bed, given the sunlight never penetrated his lair, but he told me that he wasn't comfortable falling asleep outside of his coffin. There was too much vulnerability involved. I understood and had dropped the subject.

"Should we just wait?" I glanced around and saw another staircase leading upstairs, probably to the main floor of the house. Thinking quickly, I pulled out my phone and brought up Bjorn's email with the house addresses on it. Sure enough, when I looked at my GPS, we were in the last one on the list.

"We *are* in an abandoned house, like I thought. This is one of the ones Bjorn told you about." I glanced at Sandy.

"I'm not sure whether I'm glad to be right or not," she said.

"At least we know there isn't a family involved, at least not any that we know of. I'd hate to think there was a lineup of corpses up there. And you know, with Dracula, that's what we would have." My fingers itched, and I absently reached for the stake. I was fiddling with the handle, when I realized that my entire body was tingling, and I felt an adrenaline rush that I hadn't in a long, long time.

"Crap," I said. "Get ready, my intuition tells me he's coming."

I barely managed to pull out my dagger in one hand, my stake in the other, before the door at the top of the stairs opened. There, looking larger than life, stood a dark-haired man in a black suit. He was wearing Armani, that much I could tell from a glance. There was no penguin suit, no flying black cape behind him, but the feeling of dread was so strong that I almost dropped my weapons and ran. I hadn't felt anything like this in a long time. I heard a faint whimper behind me, and I realized Sandy was feeling the effect of his glamour as well. His energy was so strong and magnetic that it rippled through the air like heat waves, encompassing all of us. Aegis seemed the only one who wasn't affected, and he stiffened and let out a slow growl.

Dracula said nothing as he slowly descended the stairs. He kept his eyes fastened on me, never wavering, as though he could glue me to the spot with just his gaze. I sucked in a deep breath, trying to force the butterflies to a remote corner of my stomach so that I wouldn't panic and screw up. I held my stake high, and my dagger firm as he approached.

He stopped just out of arm's reach, and held out one hand toward Aegis. With a flick of his fingers, Dracula muttered something under his breath and Aegis went flying back, slamming against the workbench so hard that the left leg of the bench splintered, and the large circular saw that had been sitting on it slid off, narrowly missing Aegis's head. He looked dazed as he struggled to his feet.

Crap. Dracula knew magic.

Instantly, I jumped back, slipping my dagger back into

its sheath. The stake might work, but I'd never get close enough to him to use it and I knew it. Instead, I quickly unzipped the fanny pack and pulled out a vial of my blood. There was only one way to take care of Dracula, at least as far as I was concerned. My confidence shaken, I forced myself to stand my ground.

I pulled the cork out of the vial with my teeth and, before I could actually stop to think about what I was doing, I raced directly toward him, splashing the blood in his face. Some of it missed but a few ounces managed to spray his cheek. His face sizzled as smoke wafted up into the air.

Dracula hissed, narrowing his eyes as he reached toward the burning spot on his face. It looked like he had an acid burn, and I realized that Essie was right—witches' blood was an incredible weapon against the ancient vampire. If we could get enough on him, we might be able to put him out of commission for a while. At this point I wasn't convinced anybody could kill him, the energy of his aura was so incredibly strong. If he was like this when he was weak, I dreaded thinking what he'd be like at full strength.

Dracula waved his fingers to my right, and a blinding flash behind me startled me enough into turning around. Max was in his weretiger shape, crouching on the ground, letting out a pitiful yell as he rubbed his face with his paw. I wasn't sure what had happened, but he had obviously shifted quickly enough to rip his clothes off him.

At that moment, Aegis came flying across the room, tackling Dracula and taking him to the ground. They scuffled, rolling on the ground. Dracula might be strong, but Aegis was as well, and it looked as though they were almost evenly matched.

I turned to Sandy, who was kneeling by Max in tiger form, frantic. "How is he?"

"I think he's injured," she said, trying to convince him to let her touch him.

But Max swatted at her, growling deep in his throat, and then he slinked away, low to the ground, trying to hide from her.

"Your pack—the vials. Quick!" I grabbed two more of the vials out of my own pack.

Cautiously approaching the fighting vampires, I was terrified at the display of strength and fury that I was witnessing. Aegis's eyes had turned thoroughly crimson, which meant he was completely caught up in his predator self.

Dracula, too, was fighting fang to fang. This was a fight to the death and only one of them could walk away. I pulled open the stoppers on the two vials, and waited for my chance. As Dracula straddled Aegis, his hands around Aegis's throat, I managed to sidle in at an angle where I could see his face. Before he could look away, I threw the blood directly into his eyes.

Dracula screamed as I threw the other vial on his face as well.

Sandy came running in with hers, but she tripped and fell, the vials slipping out of her hands to land on Aegis. The blood trickled down to Dracula's fingers, and he let go, staggering back, clutching at his eyes.

There were no flames, but it looked like acid was eating away at the flesh. I grabbed up my stake and started pursuit. As I was racing toward him, Dracula whirled, raising his hand.

A wave of energy slammed into me so hard that it knocked me off my feet and I went flying back through the air, crashing against the wall. My stake went skittering across the floor as the room began to spin. I gasped for air, trying to catch my breath.

Inside, I could feel my fire began to grow. I tried to contain it, but it was as if gasoline had just been thrown on my inner flame. As I stood, my only focus and thought was to burn the vampire who had done this to me. Aegis, Sandy, and Max vanished from my thoughts as my sole focus turned to Dracula.

Memories of the village in Romania swept over me, and the passion I had felt as the flames raced down the mountainside returned in full force. I held up my hands, conjuring two balls of fire to flicker in my fingers. Somewhere in the distance, I heard Sandy shouting something, but I couldn't be bothered to listen.

The only thing I wanted was to destroy Dracula in fire and flame, to rid the world of his evil. I stoked the fire, feeding it as it grew stronger. It sprang from a ball of fire in my hand to flames shooting from my fingertips and I held my hands out, aiming at Dracula, and sent the full force of my anger and fury out like a whip of flames in the dim light of the basement.

I caught him in my flames just as he turned into a bat and flew quickly away, wobbling from side to side. He vanished out of sight. In vain I looked for dust, something to tell me that I had killed him, but the next moment, Aegis slapped me hard, bringing me out of my haze.

Sandy was screaming for Max, and I realized that the basement was on fire, blazing so bright and so hot that I couldn't even see the exit. As the manic anger vanished, I realized that we were in danger of burning to death if we couldn't find our way out. If we couldn't escape, it would be my fault, and we would all be dead.

CHAPTER SEVENTEEN

I desperately tried to gather my wits as the flames raged around us. All I could see were the crackling tongues of fire as it licked at the ceiling and walls. They were blocking the trapdoor so we couldn't escape that way. Elementals danced through the flames. Somehow I had summoned them when I had lost control. I shook off my confusion, and looked around for Aegis but couldn't see him. Somewhere, I heard Sandy screaming and I heard the growl of the tiger, roaring in fear.

I stumbled to the left, against Dracula's coffin, and tipped it off the sawhorses. It fell to the ground with a crash and splintered, spilling dirt everywhere. The elementals were dancing around me now as if I were their queen, and I closed my eyes, trying to focus enough to withdraw the flames, to pull them back within me. I held out my hands, persuading the fires to return to my fingers, to summon them back. But there was no putting the genie back in the bottle. They were too hot and too violent for me to retract.

I tried to part them like I had when I first found Bubba, and managed to create a path through the fire. In the corner, I saw Sandy, crouching against Max, trying to stay away from the nearest flames. If she used her wind magic to try and protect herself, it would blow the flames directly onto Aegis and me. Aegis had climbed atop the remains of the workbench, and was looking around frantically for a way out.

"Turn into a bat," I screamed at him. "You can fly out of here."

"I'm not leaving here without you," he said, shaking his head.

"Go get help!" I realized I still had my phone. I dug it out, dialing 911. When the operator came on the line, I gave her the address of the house, that it was on fire, and we were trapped in the basement. And then, once again, I went back to trying to create a path between Sandy and Max, and the door. If I could push back the flames enough for them to get out, they could escape.

The fire raged against me, not wanting to be controlled. I had summoned it in anger, and it was imbued with my feelings. I fought with it, focusing all my energy on wrestling it into submission. Slowly, it began to yield to my will, but it was taking every ounce of my energy to do so and I wasn't sure how long I could keep it up.

"She's trying to create a path for you," Aegis yelled at Sandy. "The moment it appears, get the hell out of here."

I held up my hands, aiming them at the fire, using

them to will it to part as I slowly spread my arms to the side. A tiny opening in the inferno appeared, and then grew as I drove my will forward like a wedge through the flames, through the conflagration.

Sandy and Max were ready, Max's tiger looking terrified. I wondered if he was hurt, but quickly narrowed my attention back to controlling the out-of-control blaze. The next moment, the path widened through to the door, and Sandy and Max went racing through it, managing to get outside before the flames roared back together, trapping me behind them.

"Fly out of here," I yelled at Aegis. "You won't help me if you get burnt to a crisp."

Looking desperate, but with the flames licking at his boots, Aegis turned into a bat and flew toward the door, zigzagging to avoid the sparks. As he disappeared out into the night, I was left alone with fire.

I fell to my knees, clasping my hands. "Great Arianrhod, if I've ever needed you, I need you now. Please, help me. I've tried to be a good priestess, and if it is your will, please help me escape. If not, then lift me up to your side in Caer Sidi, at the center of the Silver Wheel."

As the flames began to gather around me again, I shivered, wondering if this was going to be my end. Would Dracula manage to inadvertently cause my death? I had done everything I could to push back the fire, but now I was drained of energy, and I crouched down on one knee, bowing my head so I wouldn't see the flames as they overtook me. My lungs were clouded with smoke, and I could barely breathe.

"No!"

The voice rang out loud and clear, like an echo ricocheting from cliff to cliff. A terrible scream, like that of a banshee, rolled through the room on a gust of wind and rain. The next moment the flames began to sizzle and hiss as a wave of water rolled into the basement, pouring down the stairs, flooding the room.

It swept around my knees and I jumped up, trying to keep my balance as everywhere the flames let out shrieks of protest as they sizzled and hissed, the water extinguishing them. The room filled to my knees, and then to my waist, the water splashing on my face. A drop landed on my lip and I tasted it—salty with ocean brine.

I looked up at the steps as the smoke began to dissipate. There, standing on the edge of the flood, was Fata Morgana. She was dressed in a long white gown with a blue cape gusting behind her. Shining with an inner light, she held out her hands to me, her hair blowing as bright as my flames.

"Maddy," she called. "I heard you scream for help. I'm here."

It was then that I realize that Sandy and I had not broken the pact. Nothing could. We three had given our word to each other, and it would stand as long as we lived. Forever we were bound, the Witches Wild, and at this moment, nothing in the world could make me as happy as that knowledge.

By the time the fire department got there, there was nothing left of the fire. Delia wisely stood back, giving Sandy, Fata, and me our space. We sat outside in the driving rain, on the stone wall that surrounded the house. I looked up at the sky as the rain pounded on us, streaking down my face. I opened my mouth to catch it on my tongue, the cool water soothing my throat that was raw from screaming and from the smoke. Tears raced down my face, I was so worn out from the events of the night.

Sandy took my hand in hers, and then reached for Fata Morgana's, to complete the circle. We sat there in silence, watching the firefighters rush around. To one side, Aegis stood by Max, who was back in his human form. He was wearing a blanket that one of the firefighters had pulled out of the medic unit. His clothes were inside, now most likely a pile of ashes. While Max was dazed and a little singed, he hadn't been seriously hurt. The confusion had driven him into a dark place, though, and I suspected it would take him some time to recover.

Finally, I looked into Fata's eyes, holding her gaze. "You saved my life."

"You would have saved me, if it had been the other way around." A luminous light filled her eyes. It was the light of the Ocean Mother, the light of the phosphorescence found in the sea and on the shore at midnight. It was the light of sunset on the horizon, over the ocean on a still night.

I nodded. "Always."

"And Dracula?" Sandy asked. "Is he still alive?"

"Yes," I said. "We hurt him, but we didn't kill him. He'll heal up and I imagine he'll be back. But we destroyed his coffin, so he's going to have to find some other place to recuperate. Now that he knows we're on to his weakness, he'll probably be cautious. He's a vengeful and cunning creature, so we'll have to be on our guard."

More and more, it seemed we were having to watch out for enemies. It was beginning to feel a little too much like it had so many years ago, when we had been running across the countryside, slaying vampires and dodging the witch hunters.

"Do you think the Arcānus Nocturni will send someone else after you?" Fata asked.

"I don't know. I don't know what they'll do when they discover we drove Dracula away. I have an odd feeling that he may not return to them. He doesn't want them knowing about his allergy, and he's got an ego to match his legend. Yet we managed to hurt him."

"So you think he may not tell the Arcānus Nocturni what happened?"

"Maybe. I don't expect him to take this lying down, though. He was hit hard by the flames and the blood, and probably won't be at his full power for some time. My guess is that he'll find someplace else to hide and recover, where his kills won't be noticed as easily."

The truth was, I didn't know much of anything. I wasn't sure whether Dracula would be back, or whether he was still hiding on the island, or whether he would leave for good. The only thing I knew was that my fight with the Arcānus Nocturni wasn't over. We had opened a can of worms when we had killed Lucifer.

Delia slowly approached, looking at me to see if it was all right. I nodded her over.

"Well, the basement is thoroughly scorched, and a number of things were destroyed, but the house will be all right. I've called Bjorn and he's on his way over. Are you all right?" She looked at me, and then at Sandy.

I gave her a nod. "Yeah, just exhausted and frightened.

I can usually control the fire but Dracula managed to fan the flames, so to speak, and I lost control. My own element would've killed me if it hadn't been for Fata Morgana."

"I'm all right," Sandy said. "And Max... Well, Max is going to take some time. Dracula forced him into his tiger shape, and that sort of control is humiliating. And then the fire, well, all wild animals fear the fire. I think he's mired in a mixture of embarrassment mingled with an adrenaline rush."

Delia turned to Fata. "I want to thank you for what you did. Maddy and Sandy are extremely important to this community, and they're special to me. Thank you for saving my friends." She held out her hand.

Fata looked at it, almost curiously, and then slowly extended her own, grasping the sheriff's hand and shaking it. "I've forgotten so many customs. There's so much to remember, it confuses me."

"Are you going to be staying in Bedlam?" Delia's question was cautious, and she gave me a nervous glance as she asked it.

Fata Morgana shivered, quietly shrugging. "I don't know. I don't know if I can." She fell silent, and Delia turned and walked away.

When she was gone, Fata looked at us. Her eyes reflected the shifting clouds overhead, and in the dull glow of the streetlight, she looked as alien as I had ever seen her look. She looked lonely, and afraid, and yet so overwhelmingly regal that I almost went down on my knees. She truly was a queen, the queen of her realm, and yet I had the feeling she didn't realize it.

"I can't stay, Maddy. I want to stay, I want to be here

with you and Cassandra. I want my old life back, but even now I feel the pull of the water, the siren song of the ocean. The Ocean Mother calls to me, she misses me. I'm bound by chains stronger than any tangible bonds. Silver, platinum, titanium—all the metals of the world couldn't chain me as much as the ocean has. She owns me, and as much as my heart belongs to you, Maddy, the ocean has laid claim to it." Tears trickled down her face, and I wasn't sure whether they were tears of joy or sorrow. Or perhaps, a mingling of both.

"How long can you stay?"

"Another day perhaps, possibly two. But the pull is getting stronger, and I'll become too dangerous for your town. I can feel myself slipping away again. I don't want to sleep for another hundred years. *Please*, don't let me sleep for another hundred years in the depths."

She began to cry in earnest then, and I wrapped my arms around her and held her as her shoulders quivered. We sat into the night until all the firefighters were gone. I noticed Aegis had vanished too, but shortly he came driving up in my CR-V. He had returned down to Beachcomber Spit and driven it back. Together with Max, they bundled the three of us into the back of the car, and we drove back to the Bewitching Bedlam. All the way there, Fata cried, and Sandy and I stared out the windows, each of us locked within our thoughts.

Auntie Tautau was waiting at our house. An old beater of a station wagon was parked in the driveway. I hadn't realized that any of the Aunties knew how to drive, but apparently they did, although they had lousy tastes in cars. As we clambered out of the CR-V, Fata seemed locked within herself, mute. Auntie Tautau scurried up, Merriweather holding onto the brim of her hat for dear life.

"I'll take her home with me," Auntie Tautau said. "It wouldn't be a good idea to let her sleep here tonight." And with that, she took Fata Morgana's hands, and led her to the station wagon. As they drove out of sight, I let out a shuddering breath.

"I have no clue of what to do about Fata. She's so lonely and she so much wants to be part of our lives again. But it's so dangerous having her around. And I feel absolutely horrible saying that, given she saved my life tonight."

"Let it be for now. Auntie Tautau will know what's best," Aegis said, unlocking the door. He turned to Sandy and Max. "Do you to want to spend the night here, given how late it is?"

Sandy shook her head. "I just want a hot bath, and my own bed. I'll call you tomorrow morning, Maddy. We'll go over to Auntie Tautau's together and talk to her about Fata and what to do." And with that, she and Max made their way back to their car and headed off into the darkness.

It was four A.M., and I was feeling every single moment in my body. The flames had singed me from the inside out, leaving me feeling crisped and dry. Aegis pushed me toward the table, motioning to a chair. "Sit down. I'm going to get you something to eat and drink. You need energy."

"How strong was he? When you are wrestling with

him? Is there anything that we should know?" Fata was very much at the forefront of my mind, but I couldn't forget that there was an ancient vampire out there looking to end my life. And he almost had managed to do so.

Aegis rummaged through the refrigerator. "He's exceptionally strong. If he had been at full strength, I wouldn't have stood a chance of keeping him even partially under control. And whatever magic he has, it's not typical vampire magic. I've never known a vampire who could use his force of will to throw somebody across the room. Pick them up and throw them across the room? Yes. I can do that. But mind power? I don't know what he learned, or who he learned it from, but Dracula has some very powerful magic at hand. We'd better do some research on that before we meet him again."

"So you think he'll be back?" My gut told me he would, that we had just scraped the surface of our entanglements with him.

"Oh, I think he'll be back. He has a personal grudge against us now. All of us. But I don't think it will be for a while. You didn't have the best vantage point when he turned into a bat, but I could see him plain and clear. The blood that you and Sandy poured on him burned him terribly, and it's going to take him time to recuperate. He'll need a lot of blood, and that means a lot of victims. In Bedlam, it would be too easy to track him because we're such a small community. So I have the feeling he's going to hide out in a bigger city. Bellingham, perhaps, or Seattle. But he'll be back. One thing I can tell you about my kind, we hold grudges for a long, long time."

"That gives us some time to prepare. I'll talk to Delia

about how we can keep closer tabs on the vampires that come into the city. Maybe Essie can help us."

"Good idea. She was the one who told us where to find him, after all." Aegis began whipping eggs for an omelet, and ten minutes later a plate of ham and eggs and toast sat in front of me. Aegis fixed himself the same, and after pouring us each a big glass of chocolate milk, sat down at the table with me.

"I need to strengthen the wards around the land. I need to make sure that we get some warning if any other vampires come out here."

"Before you do anything, you need to eat and then get some sleep. The rest can be done tomorrow." Aegis leaned back, shaking his head. "Bedlam is proving to be far more dangerous than I thought it would be when I first came here. But I'll tell you one thing, Maddy. I'm glad I came." He reached out for my hand and I entwined my fingers through his. "I wouldn't have you in my life if I hadn't chosen to stay here. And your love is a priceless treasure."

After we ate, he carried me upstairs because I was so tired that I was getting dizzy again. He drew me a bubble bath, and by the time I was clean, I couldn't even hold my eyes open. He tucked me into bed, sitting by my side and holding my hand. Bubba and Luna jumped up on the bed, curling up against my side. I closed my eyes, and the images of fire and water waging war filled my thoughts. Restlessly, I tried to shove them away. Tried to think of something calming.

"What's wrong, love?"

I opened my eyes, so exhausted that I couldn't sleep. "All I can see when I close my eyes are fire and water, battling. I feel charred and brittle."

Aegis began to sing, old Celtic ballads, and I focused on his voice, following the thread that it wove. The deep rich baritone lulled me, rocking me gently with its notes, until the fire and the water receded, and I fell into a deep and dreamless sleep.

CHAPTER EIGHTEEN

We stood on the edge of the shore, Sandy, Fata Morgana, Auntie Tautau, and I. The waves were rolling in, but the afternoon sky was clear for once, and it felt like the storm that had been battering the islands for days had lifted. Fata was standing barefoot, staring out at the water.

Auntie Tautau looped her arms through mine and Sandy's, and walked us a little ways up the beach. I had awoken to a message to meet her here at four P.M.

Max was standing a little ways up the shoreline, watching us. Jenna stood next to him. Sandy hadn't wanted to leave them at home, and I had the feeling the fire had startled her into realizing how much she loved both of them. I could see it in her face, and her eyes. For so long she had kept her heart protected, not wanting to be hurt again. But the wall was breaking down now, and there wasn't anything she could do to stop it.

When we were out of earshot of Fata, Auntie Tautau

led us over to a driftwood log, where we settled down and stared at the waves crashing against the beach.

"She'll be back, you know," she said. "This isn't an ending, but merely a beginning."

"You know how long it will be this time? And will she be even more dangerous?"

"Fata Morgana is evolving. When you first met her she was the caterpillar. During her long sleep, she was in her chrysalis. And now, she's breaking out of it and discovering her wings. But she doesn't know how to use them yet, and that is her challenge."

Auntie Tautau turned to me. "She's never been like you and Cassandra. All three of you are exceptionally powerful witches, but Fata Morgana was born of two worlds. Yes, she is part witch. But she's also part water elemental, and she has to learn how to balance the two of them if she is to remain sane. And trust me, my definition of sanity for *her* is not the usual definition. She can never be tamed. You could no more tame her than you could tame the Ocean Mother herself. There is a line she can walk, to where she can live in both worlds. But no one can teach her how to do that. We can only help her when she's here, and pray for her when she's not."

"I was praying to Arianrhod when she came to save me last night. I wonder if my goddess sent her to me," I said. At that moment, a flutter of wings startled me, and I looked up as Lanyear swooped down, landing on my shoulder. He looked deep within my eyes, and let out a soft hoot.

"I think you have your answer," Sandy said.

The owl was Arianrhod's totem. She was sending me a

message. She was watching over me, and I had the feeling there was work to be done.

"I think you can safely say Arianrhod woke Fata up from the depths to bring her to shore. There are things for the three of you yet to do, but it will take some time to find the balance of power between you. For all her strength, Fata Morgana is the most fragile. Never assume that because of her strength, she's invulnerable. Tell your friend Jordan to continue his quest, there may be ways to help her adjust when she's on shore. She will never again be able to live completely on land, but yes, Fata will be back. Trust in that."

And with that, Auntie Tautau stood and led us back to Fata's side.

"I have to go now," Fata said. Her tears had dried, and she looked excited. "I can hear her calling, but she's promised I won't have to sleep for long. She says I can return soon." Fata clapped her hands and clasped them, reminding me of a child who had just found out she had been promised a treat.

I reached out and took her hand, uncurling her fingers to place her pentacle in it. "This is yours. I found it the night I almost drowned."

"I haven't seen that in so long." She looked up, gazing into my eyes. "Will you fasten it for me?"

As I draped it around her neck, tears stung my eyes. "Can you ever forgive me for breaking your heart? I never meant to hurt you that way."

Fata cocked her head to the side, then gave me a soft smile. "I'll always love you, Maddy. I can't help it. But I'm willing to let the past be in the past. I think I can see how.

It will take me some time, but I'm learning." She sounded almost perplexed, as though she were putting together a puzzle and hadn't quite found the end piece.

I brought her hands to my lips and kissed them. "Then we'll see you when you return. We'll be here, waiting. We'll see you…in time."

As she slowly withdrew and turned to give Sandy a hug, I tried to hold back my tears. So much water under the bridge, so many years in our past still crowding toward the future. And yet, to have a future we had to let the past go and build on what was now. But the dagger strapped to one of my thighs and the stake strapped to the other told me that wasn't going to be as easy as it sounded.

We stood back, watching as Fata neared the water. As her feet touched the sea foam rolling up on the shore, a wave appeared, heading right toward her. And then in a blur, she was standing atop it, arms outstretched to the side, her head back as she laughed with abandon.

This time, she left in laughter rather than tears, and she left to a clear sky rather than a storm. She rode the waves like she might ride a surfboard, and they carried her out toward the open water. My breath caught in my throat as I watched, and Sandy reached for my hand and we stood there, holding each other, watching Fata leave our lives once again, knowing that, this time, she would return.

"We're watching the birth of a goddess, you know," I said.

"I know," Sandy answered.

And in that instant, the wave vanished, crashing down

to take Fata Morgana beneath the surface. I held myself in check, reminding myself that she couldn't drown, that she was part of the water, part of the ocean that surrounded the world. She was no longer simply the witch I thought she had been, and she never had been.

I realized I was crying and every tear trickled down my cheek felt like it contained a small part of Fata's spirit. She had been right when she told me she was in every drop of water, every lake, every ocean, every stream. She would always be with us, even when she wasn't.

Without another word, Sandy and I turned, and with Auntie Tautau, we walked up the shore to meet Max and Jenna, and then, we headed back to our lives. On one hand, it was as if nothing had ever happened. And on the other hand, everything had changed.

Two nights later, we gathered at Sandy's place. Aegis and Max insisted on making dinner together. Sandy and Jenna and I sat around the table, enjoying our drinks. Sandy and I were drinking tequila sunrises, while Jenna nursed an orange juice.

We had checked in on Ralph and his brother, to find George healing nicely. I warned Ralph to watch him for the next sixty days, and Ralph promised that he would hire a bodyguard to go everywhere with George. It wasn't likely that George would be out of bed before then, he was so weak, but just in case.

"So how are Franny and Henry?" Sandy asked.

It felt so weird to be talking about normal things

again. The past week had been a blur, water-soaked and tear-stained and terrifying.

"This all feels so surreal," I said. I took a deep breath, and let it out slowly. "I confronted Franny, and yes, they are having a romance of sorts. I have no idea how—and I'm not going to ask—but she seems happy, and so does he. I figure it's none of my business to pry unless they want to tell me, and the less I know, the better right now. As for Luna and Bubba's romance, well—it's flourishing quite nicely. They're both so happy, although I caught Luna licking Bubba's belly last night. I'm not sure what that was about, but it made me nervous."

Sandy and Jenna laughed, and I joined them, realizing that even though what I said hadn't exactly been the joke of the year, we needed laughter. We needed a break in the stress. Dracula was out there somewhere, and the waves were stirring again, although this time it was just a typical October windstorm.

I played with the key hanging on the chain around my neck, thinking about love, and how much it could hurt, and how much it could heal. And sometimes, it did both.

Max and Aegis brought dinner over to the table and spread it out. We were having steaks, and mashed potatoes and gravy and a green bean casserole, and there was apple pie for dessert. Hearty fare, and plenty of it.

"I forgot the rolls," Max said. He jumped up and went back to the kitchen, returning with a basket of warm dinner rolls. He handed one to Sandy. "Here, I made this one specially for you."

Sandy blinked. "Since when did you learn to bake?"

"I helped him. So hush up and eat the damned roll," Aegis said with a laugh.

Sandy gave me a look that said *Men*, and shrugged. As she tore open the roll, there was a clink as something fell out of the center onto her plate. I glanced over to see what it was as she picked it up. She was holding a sparkling diamond ring. The gem had to be at least three carats.

Max had been standing next to her chair, and now he slid down onto one knee and took her hand.

"Is this…what I think it is?" Sandy asked.

Max cleared his throat. "I wanted Aegis and Maddy here, because they're family. Cassandra, when Gracie died, I thought I'd be alone forever. I thought I could never love another woman the way I loved her. And then I met you and my world changed. My heart opened up again, and I realized that I never want to be apart from you. I want to marry you, and I want for us to adopt Jenna and to become a family. So, Cassandra Clauson, will you do me the honor of becoming my wife?"

Jenna and I were holding our breaths. Jenna reached for my hand under the table and I clasped it tightly.

Sandy paused for just a moment, and then a smile as bright as the sun spread across her face. "Oh, Max, I thought you'd never ask. I didn't even know I was waiting for a proposal, and now all I can think of is how I've wanted this since we first met. Yes, I will marry you."

He pulled her into his arms, kissing her long and slow. Then, as Aegis, Jenna, and I cheered, Max turned. He reached in his pocket and pulled out a jewelry case. Inside was a simple gold bracelet, with Jenna's name inscribed on it.

"Jenna, will you consent to become our daughter?"

A light flickered in Jenna's eyes, one I hadn't seen since

Derry's death. She sniffled, teary-eyed. "I… I…" Unable to stammer out a reply, she nodded, her face lighting up.

Sandy fastened the bracelet around Jenna's wrist. "We can never replace your mother, but we'll do our best to be good parents. Will you have us?"

And then everyone was crying, even Aegis, as Jenna threw herself into Sandy's arms, weeping.

On our way home, Aegis was quiet. I wondered if something was wrong.

"Are you all right?"

"I'm fine," he said. "I'm just a little overwhelmed by everything that's gone on lately." He paused for a moment as we rounded the bend toward our driveway. As we parked, he added, "You do know how much I love you, don't you?"

I knew right then what was wrong. He was afraid that I wanted a proposal, and he wasn't ready to ask. But he didn't want to lose me, either.

"I love you more than I've loved any man in my life. You're the love of my life." As I said it, it rang true in my heart.

"Even more than Tom?" A sliver of jealousy hung in his words.

And, I thought, a little insecurity.

"Aegis, I love you more than I loved Tom. And I loved Tom with a passion. Aegis, don't worry, you don't have to propose to me. When it's right—if it's right—then yes, I think I'd love a proposal. But it's not time yet, and I'm okay with that. What we have is stronger than any piece of paper." I paused. I still had the ring in my new purse that I had been going to give him at the surprise anniversary dinner. I fumbled for the case and held it out. "Here. I was going to give this to you next week, but I want to give it to you tonight."

He stared at the jewelry box, then slowly opened it. "A claddagh ring." He looked at me.

"You gave me the key to your heart. I give you my heart in your hands." As I slipped it on his finger, I kissed him softly. "I told you, I love you. And I meant it."

He let out a soft sound, but he was smiling. "Maddy, you're the only woman for me. I still feel that we've been around before, together. I don't know how far back, but I knew you the moment I met you."

We talked for a while, then he said, "I meet with the band tomorrow night. We have to discuss what we're going to do now that we're leaving DreamGen. We'll still want to do some touring, but I think we should make it fairly local. We can do live streaming—well, I guess we can't. I won't show up on camera. But we'll manage, that much I know."

"Sing to me, please. I want to hear you sing."

We stayed in the car, listening to the rain pound on the roof, and Aegis began to sing. He sang "Mad Tom of Bedlam," and then "Scarborough Fair," and "The Long Black Veil," and finally, a song that I had never heard before. It was a love song, and sounded both ancient and yet so present that it felt like it had been written for me.

As we finally got out of the car and headed toward the house, lightning split the sky, and thunder rattled behind it. I stopped, staring up as I watched the storm, and I thought I heard Fata Morgana laugh. She was out there, all right, riding the waves, stirring up storms and swimming with the whales and dolphins. I could feel her in every raindrop, I could smell her on the wind that gusted in off the ocean. But most of all, she was in my heart.

Fata had saved my life, and I would do everything I could to help her adapt to her new existence. The next time she returned, Fata and Sandy and I would run out to the shore, Witches Wild once more, and we would dance under the moonlight, and play chicken with the waves in the dark night, and perhaps we would go vampire hunting together when Dracula returned.

Yes, I thought, in some ways, we had to let go of the past. But the truth was, the past was what made us who we were in the present. So we could never truly leave it behind. Because without it, we wouldn't be the people we were. And for all the flaws, all the faults, all the dangers and risks and pain of my life, I loved it. I loved Aegis and Bubba, Fata and Sandy, and I was grateful for everyone who played a hand in creating my world.

And really, how could I ask for more?

CHECK OUT ALL THE FUN ADVENTURES OF THE WILD AND magical residents of the Bewitching Bedlam Series: BEWITCHING BEDLAM, MAUDLIN'S MAYHEM, SIREN'S SONG, CASTING CURSES, and BEDLAM CALLING: A BEWITCHING BEDLAM ANTHOLOGY are all available. Book six—DEMON'S DELIGHT—is coming in November!

Come run with The Wild Hunt. Darker urban fantasy/paranormal romance, the first nine books are out:

THE SILVER STAG, OAK & THORNS, IRON BONES, A SHADOW OF CROWS, THE HALLOWED HUNT, THE SILVER MIST, WITCHING HOUR, WITCHING BONES, and A SACRED MAGIC. Book 10—THE ETERNAL RETURN—is available for preorder now. There will be more to come after that.

Return with me to Whisper Hollow, where spirits walk among the living, and the lake never gives up her dead. AUTUMN THORNS and SHADOW SILENCE return in January, along with a new book—THE PHANTOM QUEEN! Come join the darkly seductive world of Kerris Fellwater, spirit shaman for the small lakeside community of Whisper Hollow.

Meanwhile, I invite you to visit Fury's world. Bound to Hecate, Fury is a minor goddess, taking care of the Abominations who come off the World Tree. Books 1-5 are available now in the Fury Unbound Series : FURY RISING, FURY'S MAGIC, FURY AWAKENED, FURY CALLING, and FURY'S MANTLE.

For a dark, gritty, steamy series, try my world of The Indigo Court , where the long winter has come, and the Vampiric Fae are on the rise. The series is complete with NIGHT MYST, NIGHT VEIL, NIGHT SEEKER, NIGHT VISION, NIGHT'S END, and NIGHT SHIVERS.

If you like cozies with teeth, try my Chintz 'n China paranormal mysteries. The series is complete with: GHOST OF A CHANCE, LEGEND OF THE JADE DRAGON, MURDER UNDER A MYSTIC MOON, A HARVEST OF BONES, ONE HEX OF A WEDDING, and a wrap-up novella: HOLIDAY SPIRITS.

The last Otherworld book—BLOOD BONDS—is available now.

For all of my work, both published and upcoming releases, see the Biography at the end of this book, or check out my website at Galenorn.com and be sure and sign up for my newsletter to receive news about all my new releases.

PLAYLIST

I often write to music, and here's the playlist I used for this book. You might like to know that for the end scene in the book with Fata, I was listening to *Half-Light* by Low with tomandandy, and that Underwater Boys by Shriekback provided a lot of inspiration for Fata Morgana's character.

- **A.J. Roach:** Devil May Dance
- **Al Stewart:** Life in Dark Water
- **The Alan Parsons Project:** Breakdown; Can't Take it With You
- **Alice in Chains:** Man in the Box
- **Amanda Blank:** Make It Take It; Something Bigger, Something Better
- **Android Lust:** Here and Now; Saint Over
- **Arch Leaves:** Nowhere to Go
- **The Asteroids Galaxy Tour:** Hurricane; X; Around the Bend; Out of Frequency
- **AWOLNATION:** Sail

- **Beck:** Loser; Sweet Sunshine; Broken Train; Devils Haircut
- **The Black Angels:** Indigo Meadow; Don't Play With Guns; Always Maybe; Young Men Dead; Phosphene Dream
- **Black Mountain:** Queens Will Play
- **Black Sabbath:** Lady Evil
- **The Bloodhound Gang:** Take the Long Way Home; The Bad Touch
- **Boom! Bap! Pow!:** Suit
- **Broken Bells:** The Ghost Inside
- **Charlie Murphy:** Burning Times
- **Clannad:** I See Red; Newgrange
- **Cobra Verde:** Play With Fire
- **David & Steve Gordon:** Shaman's Drum Dance
- **Donovan:** Sunshine Superman; Season of the Witch
- **Eastern Sun:** Beautiful Being (original edit)
- **Eels:** Souljacker Part 1
- **Elektrisk Gonner:** Uknowhatiwant
- **Eurythmics:** Sweet Dreams (Are Made of This)
- **FC Kahuna:** Hayling
- **The Feeling:** Sewn
- **Fluke:** Absurd
- **Foster The People:** Pumped Up Kicks
- **Gary Numan:** Down in the Park; Cars; Bridge? What Bridge?; My Shadow In Vain; Soul Protection; My World Storm; Dream Killer; Outland; Remember I Was Vapour; Are 'Friends' Electric?; Praying to the Aliens; My Breathing; Telekon; Petals
- **Godsmack:** Voodoo

PLAYLIST

- **The Gospel Whiskey Runners:** Muddy Waters
- **Gotye:** Somebody That I Used To Know
- **Gypsy Soul:** Who?
- **Hedningarna:** Ukkonen; Juopolle Joutunut; Gorrlaus
- **The Hollies:** Long Cool Woman (In a Black Dress)
- **Huldrelokkk:** Kirstin; Huldrehalling
- **In Strict Confidence:** Forbidden Fruit; Snow White; Tiefer
- **Kerstin Blodig & Ian Melrose:** Kråka
- **Jessica Bates:** The Hanging Tree
- **Jethro Tull:** Overhang; Kelpie; Rare and Precious Chain; Something's on the Move; Old Ghosts; Dun Ringill
- **Julian Cope:** Charlotte Anne
- **The Kills:** Future Starts Slow; Nail in My Coffin; DNA; Sour Cherry
- **Leonard Cohen:** You Want It Darker; The Future
- **Lorde:** Yellow Flicker Beat; Royals
- **Low with Tom and Andy:** Half Light
- **M.I.A.:** Bad Girls
- **Marilyn Manson:** Arma-Goddamn-Motherfuckin-Geddon; Personal Jesus; Tainted Love
- **Matt Corby:** Breathe
- **Motherdrum:** Stomp
- **Orgy:** Social Enemies; Blue Monday
- **People in Planes:** Vampire
- **PJ Harvey:** Let England Shake; In the Dark Places; The Colour of the Earth

PLAYLIST

- **R.E.M.:** Drive
- **Rob Zombie:** Mars Needs Women; Never Gonna Stop (The Red, Red Kroovy); Living Dead Girl
- **Saliva:** Ladies and Gentlemen
- **Seether:** Remedy
- **Shriekback:** Running On The Rocks; The Shining Path; Underwaterboys; Shark Walk; Over the Wire; Dust and a Shadow; This Big Hush; Nemesis; Now These Days Are Kong; The King in the Tree
- **Spiral Dance:** Boys of Bedlam; Tarry Trousers
- **Steeleye Span:** Blackleg Miner; Rogues in a Nation; Cam Ye O'er Frae France
- **Sweet Talk Radio:** We All Fall Down
- **Tamaryn:** While You're Sleeping, I'm Dreaming; Violet's in a Pool
- **Tempest:** Raggle Taggle Gypsy; Mad Tom of Bedlam; Queen of Argyll; Nottamun Town; Black Jack Davey
- **Thomas Dolby:** She Blinded Me With Science
- **Tom Petty:** Mary Jane's Last Dance
- **Tuatha Dea:** Kilts And Corsets; Morgan La Fey; Tuatha De Danaan; The Hum and the Shiver; Wisp Of A Thing (Part 1); Long Black Curl
- **The Verve:** Bitter Sweet Symphony
- **Wendy Rule:** Let the Wind Blow; The Circle Song; Elemental Chant
- **Woodland:** Roots; First Melt; Witch's Cross; The Dragon; Morgana Moon; Mermaid
- **Yoko Kanno:** Lithium Flower
- **Zero 7:** In the Waiting Line

BIOGRAPHY

New York Times, Publishers Weekly, and USA Today bestselling author Yasmine Galenorn writes urban fantasy and paranormal romance, and is the author of over sixty books, including the Wild Hunt Series, the Fury Unbound Series, the Bewitching Bedlam Series, the Indigo Court Series, and the Otherworld Series, among others. She's also written nonfiction metaphysical books. She is the 2011 Career Achievement Award Winner in Urban Fantasy, given by RT Magazine.

Yasmine has been in the Craft since 1980, is a shamanic witch and High Priestess. She describes her life as a blend of teacups and tattoos. She lives in Kirkland, WA, with her husband Samwise and their cats. Yasmine can be reached via her website at Galenorn.com.

Indie Releases Currently Available:

The Wild Hunt Series:
　　The Silver Stag

Oak & Thorns
Iron Bones
A Shadow of Crows
The Hallowed Hunt
The Silver Mist
Witching Hour
Witching Bones
A Sacred Magic
The Eternal Return

Whisper Hollow Series:
Autumn Thorns
Shadow Silence
The Phantom Queen

Bewitching Bedlam Series:
Bewitching Bedlam
Maudlin's Mayhem
Siren's Song
Witches Wild
Casting Curses
Demon's Delight
Bedlam Calling: A Bewitching Bedlam Anthology

Fury Unbound Series:
Fury Rising
Fury's Magic
Fury Awakened
Fury Calling
Fury's Mantle

Indigo Court Series:

Night Myst
Night Veil
Night Seeker
Night Vision
Night's End
Night Shivers
Indigo Court Books, 1-3: Night Myst, Night Veil, Night Seeker (Boxed Set)
Indigo Court Books, 4-6: Night Vision, Night's End, Night Shivers (Boxed Set)

Otherworld Series:
Moon Shimmers
Harvest Song
Blood Bonds
Otherworld Tales: Volume 1
Otherworld Tales: Volume 2
For the rest of the Otherworld Series, see website at Galenorn.com.

Chintz 'n China Series:
Ghost of a Chance
Legend of the Jade Dragon
Murder Under a Mystic Moon
A Harvest of Bones
One Hex of a Wedding
Holiday Spirits
Chintz 'n China Books, 1 – 3: Ghost of a Chance, Legend of the Jade Dragon, Murder Under A Mystic Moon
Chintz 'n China Books, 4-6: A Harvest of Bones, One Hex of a Wedding, Holiday Spirits

Bath and Body Series (originally under the name India Ink):
Scent to Her Grave
A Blush With Death
Glossed and Found

Misc. Short Stories/Anthologies:
Once Upon a Kiss (short story: Princess Charming)
Once Upon a Curse (short story: Bones)

Magickal Nonfiction:
Embracing the Moon
Tarot Journeys

Printed in Great Britain
by Amazon